JESUS' SILENT YEARS

VOLUME 1

T0161026

Parable

VANCE SHEPPERSON

Parable (Jesus' Silent Years, volume 2)
Copyright © 2021 by Vance Shepperson

ISBN's:
978-1-952025-56-3 (softcover)
978-1-7344471-3-2 (e-book)
978-1-7344471-3-2 (audiobook)

Published by Carpenter's Son, Nashville, TN

Publisher's Note

This is a work of fiction. Names, characters, places, and incidents either are the product of the author's imagination or are used fictitiously, and any resemblance to actual persons, living or dead, events, or locales is entirely coincidental.

Unless indicated otherwise, all Scripture quotations are taken from THE MESSAGE. Copyright © by Eugene H. Peterson 1993, 1994, 1995, 1996, 2000, 2001, 2002. Used by permission of NavPress Publishing Group.

Scripture quotations marked NIV are taken from the Holy Bible, New International Version®, NIV® Copyright ©1973, 1978, 1984, 2011 by Biblica, Inc.® Used by permission.

Scripture quotations marked NLT are taken from the Holy Bible, New Living Translation, copyright © 1996, 2004, 2007 by Tyndale House Foundation. Used by permission of Tyndale House Publishers, Inc., Carol Stream, Illinois 60188, USA. All rights reserved.

Scripture quotations marked CJB are taken from the Complete Jewish Bible (CJB) Copyright © 1998 by David H. Stern. All rights reserved.

Printed in the United States of America.
Cover and interior illustrations by Dorine Deen

To my encourager and life companion, Bethyl Joy.

There are so many other things Jesus did. If they were all written down, each of them, one by one, I can't imagine a world big enough to hold such a library.

John 21:25

AUTHOR'S NOTE

Sacred writings tell us very little of Jesus' life. This series of four books, entitled Jesus' Silent Years, is a work of historical fiction— most often more fiction than history. I worked at telling the truth by making up lies. Jesus' thoughts, words, and feelings are not intended as "holy writ" by any means.

All teens and young adults go through the same tasks: leaving home, managing puberty, hormones, shaping their own identity, forming friends, finding a vocation and life partner—or lack of one. Jesus was no exception. Each book walks alongside Jesus as he ages, in four- or five-year chunks of time, from age thirteen to thirty.

Think two thousand years ago, Middle Eastern culture, an enemy-occupied country, and a growing Son of Man. Embedded in these stories is a training manual for how to live a wise life, regardless of your faith ... or lack of it.

LIST OF MAJOR CHARACTERS

Augustus, also known as Tavius to family, Roman emperor, and sometimes called First Citizen or Caesar Augustus

Claudia, daughter to Tribune Gaius and Livena, granddaughter of Caesar Augustus

Claudius, twin brother to Claudia

Crispus, Samaritan terrorist, demon-harassed all-around bad guy

Deborah, Jesus baby sister, the youngest sibling

El Abba, God the Father in Hebrew Scriptures

Eliazar, Jesus' uncle, married to Abigail, Joe's younger brother, also a carpenter

Esther, Rav Moshe's wife

Gaius, Roman tribune, father of the twins, Claudius and Claudia, husband to Livena

Giorgos, Greek physician, father of Luke and Sophia

Gomaria, sister to Leah, wife of Laz, name changed to Slow by Jesus

Ioanna, Greek wife to Giorgos, mother of Luke and Sophia

James, Jesus next youngest brother, three years younger

John, also called John the Baptist, Jesus' second cousin

Jesus, also called: Jesus bar Joseph, Messiah, Jesus of Nazareth, Jeez (by a few)

Jude, Jesus middle brother, after James, before Justus

Justus, Jesus' youngest brother

Laz, called Lazarus, Jesus' best friend, husband of Gomaria

Leah, daughter of Achan, sister to Gomaria, or Go; wife to Rabbus

Livena, wife to Tribune Gaius, illegitimate daughter of Caesar Augustus

Livia, wife to Caesar Augustus, also known as Augusta

Maltesa, known also as Maltie, husband to Rastus, rich merchantess in Jericho

Mary, wife to Ehud, daughter of Hez and Beta, sister to Martha and Laz

Mary, Jesus' mother, daughter of Eli, a scribe

Martha, wife to Mordi, daughter of Hez and Beta, sister to Mary and Laz

Miriam, Jesus younger sister

Moshe, called Rav, Jesus teacher from age eight to twenty-eight

Rastus, murder-thief, married to Maltesa, half-brother to Zacchaeus

Sophia, daughter of Greek physician Giorgos and sister to Luke

Tiberius, adopted son of Augustus, birth son of Augusta (or Livia), Roman emperor

Zacchaeus, tax collector in Jericho, husband to Esmeralda, half-brother to Rastus

CONTENTS

1

JESUS

Deborah's eyes popped open. She didn't even know she'd been dead for three days. She lay naked in the warm mud, sinking into it up to her chin. A leech had fastened onto her ear. I picked it off, careful to get the suckers out of her skin.

Did she remember Crispus tying her in a bundle on the end of his fishing pole, hoping to catch my attention?

Did she remember him dropping her off a cliff?

Did she remember dying?

Thank you, Father, for all your selected not-rememberings. You keep an ark around my memory when it threatens to flood me.

What I did remember was this. I wanted to go home with Debbie, be done with this stinking planet and its people. Maybe try another world, another galaxy. I was done with these Jews, this Messiah stuff. Finished, pure and simple.

A vine had snarled around my ankle. I had face-planted in the mud. I'd left my face there in the mud a long time, tempted to inhale the mud and be done with this place, be dead with Debbie. But then, in that no-hope place, a conscious breath raised my head out of the muck. Father and Windy, His Spirit, were in front of me. Father had crawled through the mud to me, on all fours, and had said words in that mucky place for all of time—words for her, me, and all who dared to believe in the resurrection from the dead, *Rise!*

I returned from that memory to this moment. Father and Windy were no longer visible. My baby sister smiled at me from the mud, teeth so white and bright I could have read the Torah by their light. She said, "Jesus, happy, happy!"

I picked up her two-year-old body. The mud burped its release. I said, "Deborah, Father was happy, happy to give you back." She babbled happy noises and held tight to my neck. I washed her in the creek, put her dress back on.

I felt the presence of evil. Hangry shadows lurked and, as usual, weirded me out. Weeping willow trees pointed twisty fingers. I could feel him. I stopped, scanned the forest. And there Lucifer sat, lounging in silk pantaloons under a huisache thorn bush. He rested on a plush, red-velvet cushion. No horns. No red tail. No pitchfork. Ordinary face. Maybe an angel of light, but with an attitude and a six-pack. His chest and stomach muscles rippled in the morning mix of light and shadow.

He looked up from what he was doing and sipped a steaming drink with some whipped cream on the top. He put his drink down and continued braiding thorn branches in a circle, holding them this way and that in the slippy shade to better see his work. He was familiar to me from days gone by, days when we were friends. Now mischief was his mission—many spikes in that handiwork, but only one point.

He called me over, "Like me to pour you a Trinidad Scorpion? My barista skills are outta this world, if I do say so. Guaranteed to blow the back 'a yer throat right out yer butt."

He gave me his most fetching smile and offered me his drink. Tipped his head slightly toward the sun, "Do you think this is my best side, bro? I have so many of them."

A tiny flame escaped his eyes. He blinked; it disappeared. He reached up for Debbie on my shoulders. "Come to Uncle Luce, little one. As it is written, suffer the little ones to come to me." In the process of reaching, Lucifer spilled his drink, as if by accident. The viscous liquid ran all over his thorny handiwork.

I pulled Deborah off my shoulders and held her close to my heart. She'd begun to cry, sensing the presence of evil, perhaps remembering whatever had happened in that cave. I shushed her with a soft lullaby, my face inches from hers.

I softly sang, "Jesus loves you, this you know, for I'm here to tell you so. Little one, to me belong. You are weak, but I am strong. Yes, yes, I love you. Yes, yes, I …."

Lucifer interrupted. He jibed, "Well, well now, ain't that precious? A regular crooner. But no drinkie-poo with your ol' bro, Luce, from back in the day—or should I say, before days began? I'll whip up a couple, *Toots Sweet*." I declined.

He tsked, "My, my, *my*. Where's the walk in all this 'love your enemy' talk?"

I turned to leave. He drawled, "Somehow, your ol' buddy Luce ain't feelin' the luuuv, Jeez. Not even an itsy-bitsy, coochie-coo from precious Debbie?" I walked away three, maybe four steps. Swooshing sound. Searing pain. His woven crown of thorns, drenched in drink, had landed on my head and dug in deep, like it was trying to root itself. He must have looped it high. Stung like hell, little bleeds all around my head. Debbie looked up and saw the blood. Her eyes grew wide, and her whimper grew into a wail.

Lucifer laughed. "Just getting a hat-size check for your Jerusalem finale. Perfecto! A little souvie from Luce. Preview of coming attractions, King of the Jews."

I faced away from him and bowed to Father, who'd appeared from behind an olive tree. When I bowed my knee, lowering my head, the thorny crown fell to the ground between Father's feet and Lucifer.

Father spoke directly to Satan. "Son's done with you, for now. His character is mine, exactly. You're free to go. *Now*."

Satan took a long swill of his Scorpion, picked up the thorny crown, and took a squint at me, shading his eyes against Father's glow behind me. "I'll hat-check this for you, Junior, at Antonia Fortress. Just wanted to take your measure. See ya 'round *my* patch!"

He vanished in a swirling dust-devil. Lucifer was hell's master gardener, grafting seedlings of honest doubt into snarls of choke-vine. *Who do you think you are, bastard child? Mama's little man, making "the Virrrgin" happy? Give it up, or drift into Coo-coo-ville with her. Or maybe graduate into a full-fledged messianic narcissist, living on the adoration of strangers. Such a special one, you are!*

The voice droned on and on, too often. I wouldn't catch that old Goat till he was out the gate, disappearing over the hill, chewing on my peace of mind. This very human life I loved and hated required my full attention.

I was eighteen, a man and no longer a boy, but others' doubt, especially someone as clever as Lucifer, sometimes undid me. My sense of *Me-as-Messiah* still came undone like a handful of dropped quicksilver.

I limped through the warm forest muck and moss. Rain played peek-a-boo with the early morning sun. New bamboo shoots, the color of ripe celery, sprouted from the rich earth. A patch of golden light cut through the soupy haze. Last night's rain dripped off oak leaves with faint pops and pings on gnarled roots.

We rounded the bend of a limestone overhang, and there in the wood hollow was my family. The camp, so full of life— Ma draping damp towels over a clothesline by her tent, Rav smoking his pipe by the fire and scrolling thru his precious copy of the Torah, Justus having fun ordering Jude around. I guess he'd discovered his inner emperor.

John, my cousin, was by himself, shuckling Scriptures. His head bobbed up and down under his prayer shawl. *Like you were juggling his head, Father. Ah, John, a prophet that you will use so well, Father.*

Miriam, my six-year-old sister, was the first to see us. "Ma, Jesus has come back—*and* he's got Deborah! Oh, Ma!"

She jammed to a stop when she saw a snake wrapped around my leg. "Jesus, don't move! A snake's on your leg, about to bite you!" I hushed her fears and knelt in front of her. "It's okay, sweetheart. This skin's a wrapper for my wounded heel."

We bounced along into the family throng. Everyone had piled out of tents, joyful, hugging, and dancing us around. Somewhere in the melee, the viper skin flicked off, and my heel began bleeding once again.

Deborah yelped, "Jesus, foot red, like head!"

Ma rushed to get some linen wrappings and dittany to bind my bleeds. While she was rooting around in her tent, John picked up the skin, turning it this way and that.

He said, "Think I might take that off you? I could use it as a border around my hyena loincloth. And, cousin, you *do* know the prophecy, right?"[1]

"Yes, I remember, John—a serpent wounds the heel of God's anointed. And I crush that serpent's head."

I held my breath, waited for blowback—my first divinity claim with my own family. Rav's face had a look of calm. John nodded soberly. Ma beamed.

James, my next youngest brother, stood on the outside of the family circle. His smile was tight. His jaw worked, like a muscle he hadn't yet learned to unclench. Tight lips, working jaw, raised eyebrows shouted louder than any words, You are Mr. Special, aren't you, brother?

His rip tide of unbelief swept me out to sea. *Had I popped that prophecy out too early, not fully baked?*

Windy breezed Father's reply to me. *Son, it was time. Most won't believe till later, and some, not at all. For now, walk with me. I'm enough.*

2
WINDY

The next morning Jesus' sprawling family ate breakfast together around the open fire. Mary looked at her oldest son sitting beside her. Jesus was playing rock-paper-scissors with six-year-old Miriam—laughing so hard, those two. She smiled, at a remove, with their play. When Jesus took a play break to scoop hummus from a bowl, her hand was also in the bowl. Each caught the other's eye; each felt the contrary pulls, the joining and the tearing.

Mary would often look up, and Jesus' body would be mirroring hers—momentous, effortless. She got the impression, like now, time and again, that he was feeling with her, thinking with her, acting with her, half-step ahead of her. His head-hopping, heart-swapping sensitivities alarmed and comforted her. She wanted to be seen by those brown and gold-flecked eyes, yes; those eyes so like hers—but that much, that often, that deeply? Such a tearing in this truing! Stay close, but not that close; grow up, but do you have to go? She'd always known he didn't belong to her, but still….

Jesus too chafed within his gifting, like a schoolboy in an itchy wool sweater. Father coached him. *You asked for this assignment in heaven, Son. Now make room in there for more than you. Make room for doubt while keeping the faith. Hold your mother's feelings lightly while you harbor your own. Know the difference. Escape smallness.*

He made it plain to Jesus. *No one here feels safe. Satan trails you at every turn, deploys his cleverest demons, reframes worst as best, evil as good, dark as light. Each of your family members has bred-in-bone knowledge that they, like your abba or Deborah, could be victims of opportunity.*

I prompted Mary. It was time. She called everyone from play and food for dessert. Dream-food, for this family, was an essential food group. Their family circle was bigger now than when Joe started the ritual in Egypt, but the ritual was the same, preserving their connection to themselves and Us.

Anyone who'd harvested a dream from Me during the night could speak. The dreamer would stand and say the dream like it was happening in the moment. Then the dreamer would share thoughts and feelings about the dream. Only then could others comment, and then only if the dreamer had heart and headspace to hear from another.

Today only Mary and Jesus found my living stories dancing in their dream-nets. These particular parables rippled into the whole family and branded them like a hot iron.

Mary went first. She stood, widened her feet, bent her knees, and stuck out her belly like she was about to give birth. She brought her knees together and bound her knees with strips of cloth. She put on a pained face and acted out an ancient torture— Assyrian soldiers binding together the legs of captured Jewish women during childbirth. Tension sizzled around their circle. People considered what this dream might mean for them, brows furrowing. *Didn't sound good.*

Jesus waited till everyone had their say about his ma's dream. He then shared his dream. "A dragon coils in a circle. His tail is stuck in his mouth, razored teeth stripping meat off the bone. He slithers toward a boy baby lying on its back inside a clear, protective bubble. The baby juggles three Hebrew letters, רְבַד, with hands and feet.[2] These glowing, golden letters floated, stable in the midst of instability. The dragon keeps eating his own tail while he wraps around the baby's bubble. When I wake up, I don't know if he will penetrate the bubble and eat the baby or not."

Jesus, like his mother, acted out his dream— tumbling Deborah over him with hands and feet. She shrieked with glee. Once Jesus had put Deborah down, she flopped on her back, wiggled her feet over her head. "Jesus, dream me?" He said nothing to this one who had been his worst nightmare. Now he hugged her close, with the grip of all eternity.

Mary took charge of all that she could. "We all need to leave for the Caesarea. Let's digest soul food with our feet as we walk. Breathe and walk your way into these dreams, children—with Spirit's discernment and love's eyes and ears. All else is mist."

A day or so later, Jesus' family stood on a sandy bluff above the seaport. I picked up handfuls of golden sand and aqua sea, swirled them in rooster tails, and did joyful backflips. My pilgrims zig-zagged from the bluff to Sebastos Harbor along a narrow trail, people and mules picking their way single file, down trail.

Jesus felt my joy as he walked alongside Mary. Then he would look at his mother, time and again, and his joy melded with concern. The demands of house and children without her husband had thinned her delicate frame. She seemed so slight. He wondered how she even displaced air.

Jesus' concern broadened and deepened when he stopped and surveyed Caesarea. Herod's designer port raised the hackles on his neck. Warrens of alleyways seemed like locking sets of puzzle doors. Red roofs caught the fire of morning sun. Even the anchored ships seemed full of moment and mischief, ready to catch a spare spark and self-immolate.

Roman soldiers swaggered down the streets in pairs, casual power on display. Locals, Jews and Arab alike, dropped their gaze whenever Rome passed by. They could be hauled in for questioning at any time for any reason. Some returned alive from their interrogations while others didn't. Hope for freedom had been put up against a wall and executed. Serenity had been exiled for the foreseeable future.

Caesar had promised to protect Son's family. Jesus' interpretation of this promise varied, depending on his mood. For the most part, the meaning was moot, an enigma wrapped in a conundrum. Jesus waffled, thought about turning back. He inquired after Father.

I wove Father's voice into Son's heart. *You complained about your Rome assignment. Can I remind you of an earlier entrant in the Nineveh Marathon? Father put his name forward, as you recall, but Jonah refused more traditional travel plans. Ah well, a good reminder not to blow off Mission Control.*

3

CLAUDIA

My twin barged into the cabin mother and I had been assigned on board the ship, the captain's tiny room with only one bed. I sat alone on the bed in my underwear, applying make-up, getting ready for Jesus' arrival. Claud leaned against the wall, playing with his sword. He turned, locked the door, and raised his eyebrow.

I said, "Claud, 'No! Not now. Not ever. Never. I'm done with you. Do you hear me?'"

"You've only started saying that since Jesus came along. He's messed up our good thing, *my* good thing. One last time, sister, before I go bust his chops." His voice whined, "Besides, we're going to be locked up in this box for over a week! I need an outlet!"

"I'm not an inlet for your outlet, idiot. If you can't stick someone with your sword, you break out in hives. Face it. You've got issues."

He put on his frumpy face and threw himself out into the narrow passageway. What a relief! I looked out the porthole and watched him head for shore, sword banging against his leg. My father's favorite brothel was a block off the harbor. Both he and Claud knew everyone there. When I thought about how we'd used each other, I felt filthy. But Jesus' kindness overwhelmed my dirtiness. Jesus loved me with his eyes, asked good questions, felt what I couldn't, went where I wouldn't.

I wandered to the stern of the boat and sat on the balustrade, gazing at the whitecaps and fish jumping, spinning in the sun. I lifted my eyes to the bluffs above Caesarea. Ha! There! Zigzagging down a far trail, a ragged flock of people. Looked to me like Jesus in the lead, limping, leaning on a staff. I'd better go and check this out.

Jesus, John, Claud, and I were in the same stage of life—all wrenching ourselves away from parents, managing hormones, and scissoring adult selves from our bolts of swaddling. That's how we were alike. Other than that, present weirdness won—Claud *thought* he was a god. Jesus *was* a god. I was a god-groupie. John was weird.

When I'd met Jesus, we were both thirteen. I lived as a royal among the world's elite. My life was literature and theatre. Antonio, our tutor, once told my father, "Claudia digests the classics like forest fires eats hay. Tell her something once, and she owns it." He'd said that five years ago, and I still snacked on it.

But my smarts paled in comparison to whatever Jesus had going on. He did 'serious,' inside of jokes. He told weird stories that ended up asking embedded questions, one inside another. He banged opposites together, didn't wreck either one. He made friendship more than an algebra test that no one could pass. On top of all that, he had a hotline to heaven with regular info dumps from 'Father.' A little spooky, but I cleared room in my heart to store his stuff.

All this pissed off Claud. "He makes me feel like army ants are crawling around under my skin. Believe me, sister, if he even pisses me off slightly, I'm going to whip my sword out and drop-kick his head into the harbor." Ah yes, I was so glad Claud was otherwise occupied right now. I raced down the gangplank and made a beeline for the Jews.

When I met them along the road, I threw my arms around Jesus and he didn't even flinch. He introduced me to his whole traveling family, including the Rav. Zoo Boy ignored me, with a razor's edge of judgment leaking from his eyes.

I edged towards Jesus' mother, curious about this peasant woman who'd helped spawn the God-man. I rattled on about my own mother. This might be the only time I could speak without Mother hovering over a conversation. "Tell me how to deal with my mother, please. I cannot *stand* her."

I glanced at Mary. She didn't advise. Her face held a bovine placidity. Didn't even raise a 'holier-than-thou' eyebrow like John and his kind from the lunatic fringe.

I gulped and raced on, "My mother resulted from one of grandpa's affairs. He had a bunch of them. Anyway, she was raised in a villa by nannies, on the other side of Rome, after Grandma banished the courtesan. Mother ended up wrapped in silk, draped in jewels, and acting like a ragged hole in another set of panties. I'm not kidding."

Mary laughed at my description, but it was a good laughter, kind and honest, with no knives in it for either my mother or me.

I kept talking, "Take her compliment, for example, when I walked into the breakfast parlor this morning. She patted Claud's hand and left it there. 'Pass the bacon, dear boy.' I was expecting Claud to jump in her lap, but he didn't. She glanced at me and commented to father, 'Well, she's *almost* pretty today.' She balanced her two hands like scales, side to side. 'Not quite, but passing.' Father was reading a news posting. He didn't hear her or see me.

"I walked out, folding up mother inside me like a stack of poopy nappies. The queen sow could eat her precious boy piglet like bacon, but I was outta there. I oink-oinked over my shoulder and left to wait for you to get here."

Mary didn't interrupt my gabbling. She kept breastfeeding Deborah, serene as Latona, our Roman goddess of maternity.

I said, "Now I know where Jesus learned to listen. Do you think I could take my mother back to the warehouse and trade her in for you?" Mary's expression didn't eat me up. Instead, I felt fed. I hoped this full feeling would last, but then we turned a corner. Mother stood on the pier, foot-tapping out her displeasure when she saw me coming.

I headed toward Father, next to mother. Both of them faced different directions—his face was out to sea; hers, out to lunch. A dream came to mind as I approached them. They were at different ends of the same ship, captaining the ship in different directions. The ship split in pieces, ocean waves flooding in at the midline. Both parents slid toward each other from opposite prows. Their arms still stretched out, each pointing in opposite directions. At the last moment, they gave up their need for control and reached for each other. They both drowned, almost touching. They couldn't swim—but for that matter, neither could I.

An icky feeling suddenly swamped me. I bound the dream, icky feelings, and drumbeat of danger down low in my guts, almost like I was about to give birth to something. I locked it down real tight and climbed aboard the ship.

4

WINDY

Three armor-plated warships bobbed at the quays, waiting for the next high tide. Each quinquereme was state of the art—one hundred ton, iron-plated, ninety oarsmen on each of five floors. These war galleys had but one purpose on the voyage: guarding the emperor's ship, *Ouroboros*. Her stern proudly displayed the infinity symbol Caesar Augustus had chosen for his vessel—the snake eating its tail.

This double-hulled mother ship was lashed together with four hemp cables, each two inches in diameter, all strung horizontally, every twenty feet. They shrank when wet, binding the ship's wooden, mortice and tenon joints even more tightly.

The night before, Tribune Gaius had supervised the loading of all that tax gold into *Ouroboros'* belly. A local man, Crispus by name, was foreman in charge of hoisting the two pallets onto the ship. He'd snatched a soft shackle knot into place when no one was looking—not the standard, stevedore hitch-knot. When the two covered pallets hung above center bay's bare floorboards, he slipped the knot. The pallets tumbled twenty feet or so. When they hit the wooden hull, the inner hull cracked, and gold bars spilled across the bay.

Tribune Gaius, cursing, got on his knees and scrutinized the floorboards, lantern at eye level. No damage to the outer hull. He ordered a master carpenter, "Get this fixed. Be quick about it."

Crispus said, "Lord Tribune, could I aid the master carpenter, sir, free of charge, to make up for my grievous error?" Before Gaius could answer, a voice called in the night, "Urgent business for the Tribune—new cargo order from Rome!"

The tribune shrugged and left to see about the business. Once he'd gone, the two pirates were quick as loosed mercury. They pried up the cracked inner hull here and there. Crispus' velvet tipped iron hammer silently spaced four metal-tipped wedges into the starboard outer hull's joints, right at mid-ship. Wet spots appeared, but he threw sawdust all around, covering them. Then the carpenter securely nailed inner over outer hull.

Gaius returned and stomped around the center bay. Examined the repair. Peered at the work product, not the workmen. He shouted, "Pour on the grain!" Huge scoops of Israeli grain for Rome's warehouses flowed over and around the golden metal.

The hatch doors didn't quite close in the middle— too much 'muchiness'. Four men sat on the doors, bouncing around, smashing grain down, filling all the space. Iron bars finally squeaked through metal rings. Keyed clasps locked—everything, tighter than a tick. Nothing would get in or out of that opening, for sure.

The next day a hundred or so paying passengers crawled over each other on the main deck, haggling for space, playing, and flirting. Their hot, sweaty fug rose in waves off the deck. Tribune Gaius shoved past a tumble of barking dogs on the wharf and into this scrum of stink on deck. Jesus and his family trundled along behind him. They slugged toward center mast, where a Greek family of five had nestled since boarding in Alexandria.

Gaius ordered them to move. The father, a physician, protested, "We've slept here since we left Alexandria. We paid extra. My wife is nursing our newborn. She needs a stable…"

Gaius interrupted, spoke with clipped diction and raised volume like he was talking to an idiot. "Your. Space. Gone." The physician trudged his family back toward the only open spot on the deck, the open stern, where ocean spray curled over the gunnels when the ship was under full sail.

Rome's 'might-is-right' approach didn't sit well with Jesus. Once Gaius had gone, he chatted with Father, his ma, and Rav Moshe. The older and younger men invited Greeks to join Jews. Now, like sardines in a can, they crammed together between center mast and the locked hatch doors.

Ioanna, the wife, cried—overwhelmed with gratitude. Tears still flowing, she busied herself, re-fastening her husband's money belt all around him with leather cords. Giorgos sighed with satisfaction. He'd made a lot of money in Egypt doing his doctoring. Now his family could return home to Greece and live comfortably.

Luke, an eleven-year-old, was exactly Jude's age. He was a noticing sort of boy. He'd observe people's actions and scribble his thoughts in a journal, developing all those skills he'd need for later writing tasks.

Sofia, a year older than Luke, was a lovely piece of work. Her finely crafted eyelids were weighted with long, silky lashes. She batted her sapphire eyes at Jesus' next younger brother. James, a very sober Talmudic scholar, experienced a sudden vision of flying off with her, far from public spaces, Torah scrolls flapping behind him in the wind.

I smiled at Father and He at me. *Ah, young love, so much fun!*

Tribune Gaius was oblivious to kindness. That had never been his North star, as much as duty, honor, and discipline. That particular trinity guided him.

The tide was high. Time to say good-bye, and be quick about it. He good-bye'd in an orderly fashion, marching from one family member to the next in stiff, little goose-steps. Pecked his wife on the cheek. Avoided her eyes. Kissed Claudia on the cheek too, looking her in the eyes briefly, as much as he could manage. Held both her shoulders. His embrace for Claud was a fist-slam against his armored chest, which Claud reciprocated. Finally, he shook hands formally with the tutor, Antonio. Marched down the gangplank, back stiff as a Roman cross, and headed for the brothel.

Once her husband had gone, Livena hauled Claudia into the captain's cabin, where she had ordered her space to be "prettied up." The eighteen-year-old practically swooned when she re-entered the cabin. An overpowering smell of talc and hydrangeas slammed her nose. She thought, *this will be the longest year I'll ever spend in one week. How do I get away from mother and be alone with Jesus?*

She promptly fled the cabin and watched one of the quinqueremes tow *Ouroboros* out of the harbor, rowers rhythmically stroking "dead-slow" at the coxswain's call. The mother ship plowed heavily after the quinqueremes, wallowing in the swells at the mouth of the harbor. I allowed it to scrape over razor-sharp barnacles. A worn *hypozomata* cable sheared. Then I scooched the ship loose, sliding her into deeper waters.

One tenon loosed from its mortice in the outer hull. The iron-tipped wedge was a great asset, allowing seawater to seep into the separation. Tiny tears grew, from snivel to trickle, as the vessel picked up speed. Seawater found passage from outer through inner hull. Dry grain began to swell. I wove Mary and Claudia's dreams together two stories directly below Jesus' family.

Dreams became physical, in the normal way of life, visible coming out of the invisible.[3] These two dreams grew a grain baby, swelling ever so slowly into a monster.

5

LEAH

I looked at husband. Rabbus had captained himself into the traces of his plow behind Goodness, our plowing mule. Rabbus' sharp bit waved soil on either side of the plowshare prow, exposing rocks or old stumps. I walked behind him, basketing the stumbling stones and dropping barley seeds into the furrow at regular intervals. At the end of each row, I dumped my stony load. We slowly sailed into a crescent of land, forming field and boundary with stones and seeds. I figured boundaries were walls with doors or altars in 'em. Walls said, 'no.' Boundaries had room for a 'yes.'

Rabbus had names for all the ridges, creeks, and coves—and anything else worth naming. The places, names, and people had been quietly wound together for so long there was no way to unwind them. This ground sucked in sound and let little escape, including husband. He was silent as sunlight reflecting off the point of his plow.

My Samaritan husband was only eight years old that night when the killers came to call. He'd hidden in a bale of hay while the Jews slit his father's throat, raped and killed his mother, set the house, barn, and fields on fire. Scorched earth meanness, pure and simple, visited him at every turn on this farm. He'd stopped plowing just a week ago, looked at me out of those green, washed-out eyes, the color of the pond water on his property. "The smells in this field grab my throat. Fingers start squeezing, don't let go."

Samaritans had a saying—*When fathers fall, their heads land on the sons' shoulders.* My husband had taken careful "father notes." He toted these learnings in an invisible box that took after its invisible owner. Rabbus could make his face into a starless night, quick as a wink. That face would vanish from memory 'fore he'd finished calling your name.

His heart was also on disappearing terms with his mind. He'd fall into thoughts and disappear. One night, not long ago, he sat, fallen into a thought hole. I was washin' up. I dropped a plate. It shattered. Before I knew it, he'd spun around, throwing knife in hand, ready to let loose. I begged him, "Please, husband, don't kill me."

He stepped back from the edge of all his fear and coughed up some daylight. He busted out crying, "Wife, please, don't leave me, please."

My plate wasn't the only thing in this house that had shattered.

A reedy voice called out, "Hey there, Rabbus!"

We turned to see Ben with Liza. These elders sat on the buckboard seat of their creaky cart. Buzz, their burro, muzzled his feedbag. I guess they'd been watching us for some time. They were the kind who'd learned to sit small, so young folks like us could feel tall.

I ran to Liza for a hug. She was a bent-over woman with a tack-sharp mind. Her memory made up for Ben's holy mind, a block of cheese where the rats had been chewing. His straight back, her strong memory, had simmered them into a fifty-year stew that fed anyone they met.

We invited them, as usual, to stay the night. We needed parents. They needed children. We'd adopted each other.

That night, 'round the cooking fire, Liza said, matter-of-fact, "I heard something interesting from your old friend, Crispus. 'Member the last time you saw him?"

Rabbus nodded wryly. "'Course. The time we tried to kill each other, and he got your goat?"

"That would be the time," Liza agreed. "Crispus was always odd. After Romans killed his family, he got wound up real tight—since then he's always been a-lookin' for a fight to throw himself into."

I felt a quiver ripple under my ribs, like an itch I couldn't scratch. I wondered afresh what I'd gotten myself into—marrying a Samaritan murderer-thief not so different than Crispus. A man who'd lived isolated on a farm soaked in blood.

I took a deep breath. *He's not Crispus. God has his hand on my husband, and on me.* I loved saying the word *husband*. I savored it like a bitty glob of honey, hanging sweet 'n golden every time it left my lips. Yes, my beautiful warrior-husband, who chose a very ordinary-looking girl like me to marry.

Liza continued, "Crispus, he done broke bad. Took up with a bunch of crooks. Long time now, them pirates been lootin' 'n killin'. He back 'n forth's from here to a hidden bay north of Sidon."

Rabbus replied, "Been there. Pirate's Cove, good size village now."

Liza nodded. "Yep, 'zactly. Anyway, he hurried in yesterday—shopping for supplies.

"Told me, 'Treasure ship's leaving Caesarea for Rome, real soon. Got tax gold on board. Yep, we're gonna get back *our* gold.' Mr. Full-on Snarky, he wuz."

I stirred the spiced lamb 'n lentil stewpot from my place next to the fire. Ladled some into each bowl, one by one. Rabbus passed around a hot loaf of bread fresh out of our oven there in the yard. I blew on my spoonful of stew, rubbed my low back with my left hand. I soothed a new ache, one I'd not known before.

"Husband," I said, "I fear for Jesus and his family. They're on that ship."

Rabbus said something I'd not heard from him before, "I'm not worried about Jesus. I worry about us. A chunk of the ol devil's right here on our patch, and he means us no good. Jesus and us, all in the same army, far as I can figure—all fighting the same war on more'n one front."

I said, "There's a war? I thought the Romans had won."

"War's a-happenin' all around, all the time. Fight to the death. Jesus' body is somewhere else now. Reckon he spread his Spirit 'round for his friends he left behind. Might not have much book-learnin', but I 'spect that man can shepherd even a lone wolf like me."

Liza raised her eyebrows and tilted forward, "Who's Jesus? H'aint heard-a him."

I told 'em our stories 'bout Jesus and us, times we'd had together. Baptizing lepers who'd lost their spots on their way home. Glowing vases, like the one we poured our wine from. Ben's ears perked up. His eyes got sudden wet, two bluebells peering out through a pitcher of water.

He slid a little bit closer to me. "You really think he's the Blessed One, Leah?"

Both Rabbus and I nodded solemnly. Rabbus shared how he had almost killed him. How Jesus fed him bread, even as his side was bleeding from Rabbus' blade.

We, the younger, reeled in the older, packing light back into two old stars that teetered on edge. Family does this for each other.

6

SLOW

El Roi and Lydia owned and managed Rahab's Rehab here in Jericho—synagogue, workshops, inn, retail outlet, and brothel—all under one roof. Many sex workers came to Rahab's when first arriving in Jericho. El Roi said to us when we'd arrived a year or so ago, "When you come to Rahab's, everyone gets a choice: hotel and retail are behind you, synagogue is right, workshops for tailoring and pottery are left, and sex is straight ahead."

All my me's were still dubious. Shame intoned, "what looks too good to be true usually isn't. Don't trust. Stay armored. She passed out these orders to the others, and Fragile followed her like a new puppy. I wouldn't even know when Cutter was around till I looked down and my arm was bleeding, or another eyelash went missing. Harlot roamed the rooms along the back wall, listened to the sounds, and practiced her passion moans. Escape floated in and out, like a bad memory.

One of our newest whores was a beautiful, blind blonde. Cyrena stood alone in the courtyard when she first arrived, shifting from one foot to the other. She looked for all the world like a quivering, restless question mark, sniffing the air.

I got El Roi from behind the potter's wheel. We slid our sandals slow through the gravel, announcing our presence. I touched her shoulder. "Cyrena, this is El Roi. El Roi, Cyrena, an ex-working girl from Shechem. I think she'd do great in pottery."

Roy looked around for our blind, ex-rapist pottery-instructor, Cy. We'd both seen him disappear into his bedroom a few minutes before, after having worked the night shift. Now his door was still open. I saw him, circling in front of his pallet like a dog, cozying loneliness to himself like a second skin.

Roy shouted, "Hey, Cy, we're over by the front gate with a new student for you."

Cy got up and shuffled across the courtyard, counting steps between his door and the gate.

Leah made the introductions. "Cyn, meet our new friend, Cyrena."

Cynico corrected Leah, "They call me Cy now, not Cyn."

Leah sighed. "Suits the man you're working into, Cy. Less is more, huh?"

He flapped his hands, pushing the air down like he was driving away a clutch of pigeons. "Less is less, but I'm startin' to accept who I ain't."

Cyrena's milky eyes searched the space where Cy stood. She said, in a voice sweet and plain as butter-cake, "I'm blind, far as eyes go, but I hear colors."

She turned to Cy, sun full on her face. "Your voice looks like reddish-brown rust, in need of scraping."

She turned to me. "Your voice looks like pale lemon streaked with blood. Hear you, see that."

Cy scraped out a wheeze in response, scratched his shaggy, reddish-brown beard.

She kept talking. "About ten years ago, my mind got fuzzy like my eyes. Heard strange voices. Pushed this way and that by weirdness. Cut myself a lot."

She pulled back the sleeves of her singlet, both arms a mass of scars. I pulled my sleeve longer, covering my own forearms. She reached to where Cy's voice had come from. I put his hands on her arm. She ran his fingers up and down her arm.

"In those days, I scarfed, barfed, and raged a lot—always a powder keg, waitin' to explode. Warehouse for demons. Now, since that guy, Jesus, came through the city gates, the one with the pure gold voice, my mind's clear."

Cy asked, "How'd you know that Jesus guy?"

"I didn't," she replied. "The demons did. They know lots more than me, like him being the real deal. But now I need people, not demons, to get rid of all that blue lonely."

Cy said, "Same guy put me right too, more or less. Mainly less."

Roy said, "Nice memory of Jesus, Cyrena. You might rub off on Cy, who sometimes forgets to remember what a mess he was. Remember, Cy, the root of the word 'truth' means *not to forget*."

Cy said, "I'll try to forget you said that." He nodded toward where Cyrena's voice had come from. "Okay for her to share Corn's room, next to mine? Empty bed in there."

Roy got a thumbs-up from his wife, Lydia. "Maybe you can find Corn and introduce 'em, before she moves her stuff in."

"She's weeding the garden back of the workshop. Come along, Cyrena."

She put her arm on his, and the blind led the blind.

Soon as they left, I did too. I went to the workshop, slid into the potter's seat, and looked at the retail shop's order sheet. Today, as usual, I brought a fistful of my own crush from the dump. I sifted it into the mud. I wanted the pain to squish through my fingers into my work.

With every pot, or vase, or bedpan, God trickled through my fingers more than my thoughts. He did what he could, and I would. He did, and He did, slow-like. My body kneaded this work, but un-crushing us was complicated. Cutter liked chopping and grinding down others' discards. Fragile was drawn to beautiful porcelains that broke easy. Harlot imagined shaping naked women out of mud but mainly slept on the job, sharing a bed with Escape.

In spite of them, and sometimes with them, I worked the crush, worked the crush, till a few god-bits glittered in my mud. Shame took on a new name, No Blame, time to time.

Today's lesson with Roy was on 'glazes.' He taught me how to make every shade of glaze pigment from pink to crimson to deeper, darker violets. Roy taught by example, showing and then watching me, his hands over mine, adding or subtracting out color to get exactly the right shade.

After a while, he said, "I've got synagogue business. I'll be back later and see what you create." When he'd gone, my mind glazed over. Fact was, being a wife spun me around like the wheel spun the clay. Got me dizzy. I fingered my wedding memories and watched them fade when I thought about sex with Laz. I coiled and recoiled like a child, panicky, when Laz started slathering all over me. Escape got gone, and Fragile broke into pieces.

I said to myself, *get over yourself, girl. Slow. Down. You're eighteen already. Soon you'll be like those Moab girlfriends who'd grown udders after the third kid. They'd turned into flopping sacks, shaped like squash with nipples.*

Cornelia and Esmeralda, my two African friends, walked into the workshop while these thoughts worked me over. Cornelia stopped, put her hand on my shoulder, raised an eyebrow.

Tears streaked my cheeks. Glaze dripped on the floor. "I was bein' a crybaby … in another world, Corn. My me-pot's fractured."

Esmeralda asked, "What you be thinking-on, Slo?"

I told 'em what I be thinking-on.

Esmeralda knelt next to the wheel. Eyes leaked like mine. "What you say, gurlfren, dat be happening *all* de time when Zac doin' me. I tighten up de bones, send de mind a-travelin. This be normal for us trafficked womens."

"It might be normal, but it's not right, Es. What's the meaning in it?"

Esmeralda said, "You be turnin' into more Jew-gurl, I tink, not Moab haf-n-haf. Jew alway be askin', 'what de meanin' of dis; what de meanin' of dat?'"

She pulled a long face, a pouting camel. "Here be Jericho, darlin'. I preachin' myself *all* de time: don't ask *meanin'*. Be happy, I say t' my *fine* self. *Buy* something."

Corn took a different tack. She prayed, "Lordie Lord, men maka de vex wid' we women. And *You* maka de men. You be Man yo' own fine self, and vex us proper, meaning no disrespect, your Bigness. Now we be-a askin' dat you change dem vexy-sexy slime sultans we be forced by your Bigness, yo' *Holy* Bigness, to screw wid. Maybe take some whack outta dey stack, huh, Abi? Make path in de bush safe. Amen!"

I caught a little of her words, and a lot of their love. A ping, down low, buzzed my gut. Bubbling kindness trickled through my Jericho dust-bake.

7

JESUS

My family settled in with the Greeks. We all circled the ship's mast and made a shelter between mast and hatch. The Rav talked Torah with Giorgos, the two mothers discussed breastfeeding, and James leaned over the gunnels, laughing at some private joke with Sophia. James was entranced. Was it her spontaneity, great body, or aquamarine eyes that animated him? I didn't know, but I sure did wish Abba was alive to see James having his first good flirt.

After a cold supper, each of us took turns making our evening toilet. It was my night to dump the waste from our slop bucket over the side. When I came back from ship's stern, everyone else was bedded down in a cluster, cheek by jowl. Ioanna made sure that her daughter was between her and Giorgos, safe from a certain Jewish fourteen-year-old.

The next morning, ten-to-twelve-foot swells rolled under the ship sideways, from open sea toward the coast, about a dozen miles east of us. I took a tortilla egg wrap and mug of cold tea to John, back in the spray zone, where he'd slept alone. When I found him, he was soaked to the skin, and his mouth looked like Father had nailed an upside-down horseshoe to his face. He refused his wrap, so I chowed it down on top of mine.

Between bites, I looked over at him and said, "The human smile has never been so thoroughly defeated as right now in your face."

He rolled his eyes. The green pallor of his skin suggested he might throw up any second. I began to feel how he looked. Queasy clouds, the color of week-old mold, looked like they might blow their load. John and I tried gazing at the unmoving coastline. Tried deep breaths and a steady gaze. Tried to man-up and swallow our seasick. Prayed for the sea to calm. Finally, neither of us couldn't hold it. What went down came up. My tortilla wraps looked like they were shot from a cannon.

Emptied of comfort and food, we slumped over the weathered balustrade and looked at the coastline. *Ouroboros* continued its northern heading, not yet ready to turn west toward Cyprus. This stretch of coastline, north of Sidon, was full of bays and coves with natural harbors. One harbor, northeast of us, seemed really busy. A number of sails billowed.

John sighed, wind whipping through his wild hair and wispy beard. "Getting danger vibes, Jeez. Have any idea why fishing boats are heading out at dawn? Maybe they're not fishers of fish but fishing for something else?" We stared at these triangular patches of white sail angling toward us the way a cow stares at a new gate in an old fence.

I turned to look at the 100-ton quinqueremes behind, left, and right of us—a perfect Roman trifecta. I should have felt safe, but I didn't. The coxswain's cadenced call increased in volume and tempo. Our heading changed, a few degrees further west.

I queried, *we're safe, aren't we, Windy?*

She murmured, *You're always safe in my arms, Son. Hold tight now.*

Waves slapped the hull underneath. Wind snapped the canvas above. Plumes of white spray flew back and hit us in the face. I complained to John, "I miss Abba. I can't protect and provide like he did."

John felt his dagger's blade, thumb testing its edge. "I'm different than you, Jeez. I'm an angry guy. I like fighting, uh … for the Kingdom of Heaven, of course."

I said, "Father's better with violence than me. I'm a realist. Take angels, for example. Father has hundreds of thousands of angels to protect us from danger." Holding forth on the fine points of realism distracted me from the yuks.

John bumped my arm and motioned to our right. "Speaking of danger, Jeez, here she comes …"

8

CLAUDIA

Jesus' face looked a little green when he turned around. He leaned on the bulkhead and picked me out of the crowd just as my eyes locked on the back of his head. Synchrony like this always gets me going.

I'd chosen a peasant smock over my usual glad rags to make nice with the *hoi polloi*. I still wore Grandpa's gift, my diamond and emerald belt under the smock. I turned my ruby ring in, so only the band showed. I tipped my shoulders and slid this way and that through the throng of commoners who snoozed, played dice, or hung their heads over the side, retching.

"Hey, you two!" I said. "You're stuck together, as usual, like honey and bread. But from the color of your faces, let's make that lettuce and spinach."

They groaned and stifled a heave.

"I'm bored. Antonio is droning on about celestial navigation. Claud is still sitting there, but I got it, *already*. Besides, I got the rumbly tum thing going on too—and you're not helping." I paused, waggled my eyebrows, looked at Jesus. "Still the sea for me, God-man?"

I kept trotting out inanities. Jesus seemed glad to see me, in spite of my smart mouth. I faced into the wind and readjusted my headscarf. "Antonio was showing us a sextant and ragging on about the Polar star. But who cares? That's the captain's job. I was busy plotting out a play the whole time, with me as the lead star, of course. That's the only kind of star that interests me."

I ignored John. Turned my eyes upon Jesus. "What are *you* doing?"

Jesus said, "We're talking about Father's protective arm. He stretches around all kinds of stars, protecting those who trust in him."

I arched my back and pointed with my right arm to the closest warship—all those long oars stroking in and out of the water, all those men with swords doing some kind of drill on deck. "I trust no gods except those. They're paid to keep harm's way and my way two separate ways. Makes me downright worshipful."

I beamed at Jesus, showing him my best side. "But, in the remote possibility of a Roman flub up, I'm sticking close to you, God-man. Got *all* my bets covered that way."

Someone screamed my name. I twisted my head. Antonio stood on the quartermaster's deck, waving for me. He could wait. I swiveled my neck, turned my eyes back on Jesus.

At the same time, Jesus faced me. "I always like to smell milk before I drink it. See if it passes the sniff test. Religion's no different."

I arched an eyebrow, questioning.

He said, "Here's the sniff test: does my faith help me love God and people? Your pointy weapons pass the sniff test?"

I grinned. "So, here's the test before the test—does power trump love? Tribune Pop and Emperor Granddaddy blow *power* perfume my way. You blow the other one. One nostril gets each one, and they tangle in my head."

Jesus fixed me in his gaze. *He* passed my sniff test, for sure. His power and love wrapped me in a calm I couldn't find anywhere else.

John ruined our moment. "I count about twenty of them. Pirates. All of those galleys surrounding your three warships right now... stinks of power. Emperor Grandpa going to blow his nose on you now?"

I did a full circle turn, horrified with what I saw. A bunch of small, fast boats was closing with us. Nasty looking swordsmen and archers looked decidedly unfriendly. I looked from ships to sky, the color of burnt beefsteak. Layers of clouds, shaped like wolves, raced toward us. Far above them, thunderheads nimbused. None of these cared a whit if I lived or died.

The captain bull-horned a general alarm, "Get down NOW, undercover!" His silver muttonchops and white beard bapped up and down behind his megaphone. He'd make a great stage actor in Rome. *This is all a play, isn't it?* That thought had not finished zinging through my head when a zillion flaming bolts slammed into the deck. A mother holding a small child, immediately to my right—they were both speared to the planks with one bolt right through their middles.

Screams filled my ears. Stench of vomit and tang of blood blew up both nostrils. Another bolt buried itself into the bulkhead between Jesus and me. A few inches this way or that, and either Jesus or me would have been dead. *Maybe I wasn't going to be the star in this play.*

Another round of arrows arced high in the sky. Some of them lodged in our sails, setting them ablaze. Others randomly slammed into people or things. *An image of a grinning skull floated in front of my eyes, blowing flames out of red holes in her face where her nostrils should have been.*

Jesus yelled in my ear, "Get inside quick, Claudia." Then he bent over and ran back to his family, gathering Miriam, Deborah, and his ma under the tent between the cargo hold doors. I desperately wanted his arms around me, but his mother and sisters already filled those arms.

Sails and masts burned merrily. John stood at the waist-high starboard bow surveying the scene, face serene, unperturbed. He acted like a curator examining art in a museum.

I ran up the ladder into the captain's quarters. Two arrows thudded into the ladder beneath my feet. I slammed shut the door. Thick wooden walls protected me from any more danger. Let Grandpa's rough men deal with this. We'd be on our way once again soon. I was quite sure of it. Rome would win. Wouldn't we?

I leaned against the closed passageway door. Claud yanked open the door of his stateroom that he shared with Antonio. He fumbled with his sword, barely glancing at me. He used both hands, finally succeeded in yanking sword from scabbard, held it high in his right hand. His spear leaned upright in a corner. He grabbed it with his left hand and banged its butt on the floor, "Ha-yaa!"

I swooned, "My hero!" My warrior twin, vanquisher and perpetrator of evil, gave me a rakish grin with a double spear-pump. "Yeah, lover-girl, now we're talking! I'm gonna kill me some bad guys!"

He ran out the door into a flaming bolt that fastened his right shoulder to the bulkhead. His sword clattered to the deck. From my vantage point, behind the cracked door, he looked like a sow bug stuck to Antonio's corkboard.

Claud looked confused. Then he looked down and saw the source of his pain. What *was* this new appendage? Why was it growing out *his* shoulder? The fiery pitch set his tunic ablaze. His wiggle to free himself from the fire grew into a frantic struggle. He couldn't escape. Claud's shield slipped off his left shoulder into his hand. He dropped his spear and raised the shield in time to collect another bolt. This one would have secured his skull to the ship. The force of this blow flattened his back against the wall. His shield smoked. Fire traveled upwards from the bolt in the gathering wind, crackling, crisping his neck, bubbling his chin skin.

I actually *felt* something as I watch my brother burn. Was this what they called terror?

Claud wailed. His feathery caterpillar moustache crawled up and down his lip with each face scrunch, each howl. He stomped his feet and screamed in a high-pitched yowl, "Ow! This isn't right! I'm the emperor's grandson. I kill bad guys, and the navy protects *me*." All the ship's sailors were getting to battle stations or dodging for cover. No one gave a rat's ass about this spoiled, rich kid.

Then, out of nowhere, a rough, gravelly voice. "Oh, shut up, Claud! Hold still."

John stripped off his clothing, threw his wet camel skin on Claud's fire. He cut the wooden bolt between Claud's back and the bulkhead with his hatchet and yanked out the arrow, all in a couple of fluid motions. He swept brother dearest up over his shoulder and into the passageway, dumped him at my feet. He stood there naked for a moment, eyeing me before he reclaimed his camel skin. He threw it on, retreated back into harm's way, down the ladder, and joined Jesus' crew.

Claud was a smoking mess. Mother found him splayed in the tiny hallway like a puddle of vomit. She promptly collapsed beside him, squawking and sputtering. Antonio pushed past me and helped them into the captain's salon. He sat Claud down and smeared ointment over Claud's neck and slitted right eye, the one colored vermilion and gathering black. I scrutinized the deck out of the forward porthole. Tried, without luck, to see Jesus in this mess.

Mother announced, with a regal sense of surety, "Those pirates have learned I'm the emperor's daughter. I'm worth *so* much money. Not to worry, precious boy. My father will pay their ransom." She racked her shoulders back and assumed imperial mode, one who could bend Fate to her will.

"Antonio," she commanded, "bolt the door shut and push furniture in front of it. Secure our room." Antonio dutifully did what he was told. Together he and I shoved a heavy desk in front of it. Now no one could get in or out.

9
WINDY

John stood outside Jesus' flapping canvas, silhouetted in the glowering sky. Surveyed the situation before he ducked inside and sat on his haunches by the tent flap.

Deborah slipped her arm tight around his leg and hugged him with artless, desperate affection. Son held onto Mary and Miriam as well as the psalmist's words reminding him of Our protection.[4] Luke and Jude peeked under the tent cover, then popped their heads back inside, each looking wide-eyed with open mouths at the other's shocked face.

Jude broke out of his shock long enough to motion Son over to him. "Jesus, since Abba fell from the fortress wall, I'm so scared of falling."

Jesus felt his fear, hugged him close. "Jude, angels hover over us. We're held inside Windy's breath."

James overheard his comments, mimed sticking his finger down his throat. *Who's pirated away big brother's sanity now?* He crawled over to Sophia inside the crowded space and held onto what warmth he could find. Mary felt his unbelief squeeze by her. She briefly removed her face from the deck's floorboards.

She said, "If Abba were here, he'd say, '*Yahweh* is over all, blessed be His name.' Maybe this means life or death for us. We don't know, do we? We're driftwood cut loose in a wild sea. But one thing I *do* know—two seconds after we hit heaven, we'll wonder why we clung so hard to our little life here."

James and Sophia crawled over to Mary and Ioanna. The two mothers were scooched tight together on next-door knees. The teens put their arms around their mothers' shoulders. What James couldn't take from Jesus, he took from her.

And John? He planted his feet by the starboard bow, leaned over the railing, and calmly issued battle reports like he was reciting Torah to particularly slow students:

"Two pirate ships, sinking in flames....

"Soldiers from Roman warship now boarding another galley.

"Two other warships ramming pirate ships, smashing them to splinters but, now, there's trouble. One can't pull free. Fire everywhere.

"Hm. Four pirate ships, boarding the first of Rome's warships."

John stood like a desert rock, immovable. "Two other pirate ships now throwing grappling hooks over *our* gunnels, right beside me. Getting ready to board us. Hmm. Better do what Father's saying to me."

Sound of chopping. Jesus peeked out the tent flap. John was cutting the grappling ropes with his hatchet. Men yelled, splashing into the sea. John walked down the deck, chopping and whistling, arrows flying 'round his head.

John's greatest gift always had been sheer obedience to revelation. He taught this by deed more than word—chop-chopping doubt with dogged determination. He refused education beyond his level of obedience. He said to Jesus once, *When I know the right and don't do it, God will judge me for that. Better not learn too much. Preach repentance. That's enough.*

Rome's soldiers joined John's rope whacking. Some dumped pots of pitch over the side on pirates' heads. Others twanged arrows from taut bows down into pirates' bodies. The remaining pirates from this boarding party were crushed when a random wave slammed their galley into *Ouroboros*.

A dozen or so pirates from yet another galley mounted the deck on the other side of the mother ship. One pirate, enormous as a nightmare, slashed a swath through sailors with his sword. He was the point of the prow, others behind him, all moving steadily toward the central cargo doors.

Jesus positioned himself between the lead pirate and his family. He had no intelligent speech, no fancy prayers. Instead, he arrowed a simple, two-word prayer, "Father, help."

The prayer had barely left his lips when another galley, piloted by a wild-eyed man, rammed *Ouroboros*, knocking everyone, friend and foe, to the deck. The galley sank its metal battering ram into our side, mid-ship, beneath the waterline. Crunching, tearing sounds, grinding metal on wood.

Now a crack, like a clap of lightning. Ripping sounds rippled from a center that could not hold. The snake's tail vomited out her mouth. *Ouroboros* unzipped horizontally, one tenon after another popping out of its mortice, pressurized grain exploding from its womb. Gold, under grain, screamed, "Let go of me!"

A pirate's prick had popped *Ouroboros* wide open. The bottom of this mother ship willingly opened to the sea. She dropped her load of golden babies to the ocean floor far below, watched them tumble into the darkening blue, sighed with relief, and the sure knowledge she would soon join them.

The ship's superstructure became more and more a tippy, tilting planet—either end inching higher, trembling, trying to absorb what had happened to her middle. Anything and anyone in between both ends of the ship slid toward the middle—down, down, into the greedy sea.

Ouroboros also listed to starboard. Pirates had energetically used their grappling hooks to pull this burning house sideways to them, and them to the gold. They succeeded. That part of the ship's superstructure collapsed on them. They became their own unintended consequence as the weight of Rome's newly divided house squashed them like an overripe papaya.

All aboard the ship—living, dead, and the soon to be dead—tumbled into the maelstrom. All mere humans, adrift under the heaven's vast canopy, were promptly right-sized.

And what of Jesus' family? Hatch doors. Everlasting doors lifted up their heads. [5] Two sections of six-by-eight-foot planks, solidly connected by crossbeams, blew off their hinges. Restraining bars and locks blew sky-high, leaving the hatch doors askew, but with handles still attached, conveniently.

Rav spotted these excellent ex-doors, now rafts, lying beside him.

He shouted, "Grab the crossbeam doors, family—we're going down!"

Everyone at ship center had the least distance to slide, so they hit water before anyone else. Jesus held Deborah in his left arm. Miriam clung to Jesus' back with both arms and legs as he grabbed a door handle with his right hand. Mary and Luke, Jude's new friend, held onto the other door handle.

They all tumbled into the heaving sea. When Jesus popped up from under the water, his head swiveled left and right, drinking in people's struggles like a whirlpool sucks in waves. Mother and sisters, along with Luke, held tight to the raft. Giorgos, the Greek physician, had missed the hatch door exodus. Jesus yelled for him to jump and join them. Giorgos teetered on the ship's canting deck, arms windmilling, eyes wild. He fell awkwardly, hit water sideways, vanished.

James and Sophia clung to the other cargo hatch door along with Ioanna and her baby. A screaming body in flashing armor streaked into the sea a foot away from them. The impartial sea sucked Rome's sailor out of sight.

James yelled to his new girlfriend, "Kick hard with me. Get away from that ship!"

Rav held the other handle on this cargo door with his right hand. Esther held his left hand. Rav checked his waist. The oilcloth-wrapped Torah satchel he'd bound to his side had slipped higher in the melee. Now it rested closer to his heart, even closer than his wife.

A man and woman from another family group desperately grabbed for the other side of Jesus' raft. A giant wave passed over both rafts. When it had passed, so had they.

Jesus looked for the rest of his group. Jude, Justus, and John were missing. Son dropped inside his heart and asked, "What next, Father?"

John popped up from below the surface, about ten yards away. He kicked hard for the raft, pushing seawater behind him with his right hand, dragging two twisted tunics with his left hand. Justus and Jude were still attached to their tunics and John's ham fist. John and Jesus, from above and below, hoisted the unconscious brothers up and onto the raft. John also clambered aboard.

John bled from head and arms—slashed by something wicked sharp. He yelled in Jesus' ear, "Jude and Justus both got whacked on the head, same metal box that cut me. Knocked 'em clean out. Likely dying, both of 'em."

After John finished his medical advisory, he pulled Miriam and Mary further toward the tiny raft's center. He took Deborah out of Jesus' arms and gave her to Mary. Mary tucked her daughters inside her arms. She bent her head against the storm and held to her prayers like poured concrete to a rock foundation.

10

CLAUDIA

When the ship suddenly listed, we'd all plummeted against the cabin wall. Mother was groggy from a whack on the head. I'd landed on her stomach. Claud slumped to our right in the corner, right arm cinched tight to his chest. He alternately sniveled and snarled curses from his blistered lips and a face that now looked like a scarred frog.

Mother got conscious. Wall canted an inch higher. She shrieked, "Come here, my precious. Let me hold you."

She wasn't talking to me.

"Oh, shut up for once, Mother," Claud said. "Life isn't cream and roses. It's a nightmare before death gobbles us. I can't do nothing, and it's a false step to stand still. All I want is to take some of those bastards with me on my way to the bottom."

He straightened his helmet. Red feather cock stood straight up. He got his sword in his left hand and used it to leverage himself to his feet. The desk blocked his exit.

I screamed, "Antonio, help me push the desk sideways! This safe room's our tomb if we don't get out!"

Timbers quivered around us, hesitated. Then they groaned again, shivered, and closed their eyes for whatever would come next. The ship shifted a degree steeper. This tiny shift slid desk from door. I pulled. The door flopped open.

Claud saw his opening. He didn't look or think. Instead, he crashed out onto our viewing balcony—a cut above, placed there for us elites to survey the commoners.

The balcony had sheared off. Thin air swallowed him whole. The last I saw of Claud was his sword arm, pointing straight up. He dropped, his banshee war cry following him. Leather shield, iron sword, breastplate, greaves, and plumed metal helmet all ensured that he was well-weighted, secure as Rome itself.

11

JESUS

The ship swayed and creaked, towering five stories over me. An armored body in a bright red uniform and raised sword ran out of the captain's quarters onto their missing promenade. Claud screamed 'till he hit water, maybe twenty yards to my right.

Father, try to save him?

A scroll of water sloshed in my eyes, filled my mouth, and sent me into a fit of choking. I couldn't read that scroll, but I didn't need to. By the time I'd recovered, Claud was well on his way, plummeting toward Augustus' gold.

Flash of auburn hair, fear-etched face, peering out the open door of the captain's quarters. I stood, and John held my feet in place. The raft rolled as I waved both arms over my head. "Claudia, jump! Jump to me!"

She saw me. Shook her head, sobbing. Disappeared inside. I remembered her laughing, months previous. "Nope, Jesus. Can't swim a stroke. Too busy studying."

She poked her head back out the door.

"Jump!" I yelled again. "Trust me, Claudia... trust me! I'll get you!"

I thought, *trust me or die.*

A third time, I mouthed the words, "Jump!" I pointed to the boiling sea next to me. She closed her eyes and put her hands over her face, disappeared once again, inside the cabin.

12

CLAUDIA

I went back inside grandpa's dying ship. Mother's eyes were like saucers, staring at the empty space where her son once stood.

What is this push and pull you have on me, mother? You never stopped pushing me once you'd delivered me. I've run toward you and away from you, back and forth. You bob along, all the while, out of touch. Maybe sex with Claud was my way to get your love. After all, you loved *him*. But he's gone now, and you're undone. It's time, mother. Life started with you pushing me out. Now I'll push you out.

I ripped off jewelry, shoes, and diamond belt, threw them out the door. They were all too heavy for me. Two seconds later, I stood on a burning mast that had only now fallen into our doorway. I dragged mother behind me and then pushed her out in front of me. She didn't look at me at all, but at the waters below, searching for Claud.

Antonio peered over our shoulders, horrified at what was unfolding before his eyes. I stepped in front of mother, into the burning on the crossbeam. Flames licked up my cotton smock.

The high end of the ship was slipping now, heading down. Jesus, my still point, bobbed about in the terrifying sea. I shoved mother into the void, four stories up. Then I, I became a leap of faith, head flung back, arms flying overhead, tumbling into thin air.

13

WINDY

Antonio, carrying his wooden treasure chest of valuables, was airborne a split-second behind Claudia and Livena. He yelled, "Neptune, help us all!" The three of them fell forty feet or so, tiny lightning bolts.

Livena pushed away from Claudia in mid-fall before hitting the water feet first, a split second ahead of Antonio. They bobbed back up. The two of them latched onto Antonio's treasure trunk. They each hung onto a handle and looked dazed at the sheer, dumb luck of being alive. Antonio confused Us with Neptune in his prayer of thanks, but Father and I knew what he mean and accepted his gratitude.

Claudia fell alone. She pancaked hard with a resounding splat. Jesus leapt off the raft and stroked hard to where she'd hit. He gulped air once, twice, thrice; jackknifed over, and kicked for the bottom. *Ouroboros* sped by him less than twenty feet away, drawing him down faster in its wake. The captain's face, framed in a porthole, eyes bright with terror, zipped by him.

There! The tangle of drifting auburn hair, body spread-eagled, a few yards below. Son saw in a glance her downward course, caught in the draft of that massive ship.

He kicked harder, grabbed her loose tunic with his left hand. Reversed course and stroked for the surface, right hand pushing water down. Legs kicked up. Body moved down. The ship's titanic force suctioned them deeper, further down in the blackening sea. Jesus' lungs burned. Vision spotted around the edges, his head locked in a vice, his ears screaming with pain.

He didn't stop kicking, kicking, kicking. Prayer housed his desperation. *Help, Windy! Help, Father! The plan is I get crucified, right? Help me get there! Now would be good.*

On the edge of his blacking out, I gave him another breath from within. Father assisted with a push from below. Son looked up and saw tiny bubbles above, green waves foaming. He broke water's surface, gasped sweet air. Waves choked him on the first inhale. He racked out a cough, then inhaled a pure breath of air, not water.

Son did a quick 360-degree look around. John, on the tossing raft, maybe ten yards away, looked Jesus' direction, hand over eyes.

Son screamed, "John!" His cousin paid him no mind.

I instructed Son, *avoid distractions, pull Claudia closer, flip her over on her back, cradle her chin in the crook of your left arm, and side-stroke toward the raft.*

John jumped in and swam past Jesus and Claudia, not stopping to help them. Son was puzzled 'til he saw John join Livena and Antonio bobbing around on top of a wooden chest. He grabbed Antonio's right hand, turned, and towed the two Romans toward their raft.

Jesus reached the raft with Claudia before John did. Rav helped pull unconscious Claudia on board. Jesus stayed in the drink, cheek by jowl, helping Claudia's mother. He wondered, *Why is her mouth so crusted, even when she's soaked?*

I suggested, *Meanness? Spite has puckered her soul and her lips.*

Once Livena was onboard, Son yelled my words through his mouth, "Antonio! Let go of your treasure! It'll be the death of you. Come join us on the raft." The tutor sighed, let go, and crawled on board.

Mary remained steadfast on her knees, forehead touching the wildly canting raft, bent arms surrounding Deborah and Miriam, both her fists grabbing the door handle. She looked up and mouthed, "Thank-you, Husband." In that moment, a beam of sun crowned her with radiance. The moment passed, and the sun hid her face once again behind an iron dome of mammatus clouds. Mary's head dropped back down. Her lips kept moving, anchoring hope heavenward.

Son turned Claudia on her back, pushed her head sideways to his left, swabbed vomit out her mouth with a hooked finger, guided by My touch. He straight-armed Claudia's chest down, my Hand pressing the back of his.

Nothing. Again, my force within directed his touch. Jesus stiff-armed Claudia's chest straight down with both hands. He tipped her head back, straightening her neck, put his mouth on hers, and blew my breath down her lungs. Nothing, no breath, no consciousness. Son asked, *Windy, is she gone for good?*

I put his face down sideways, two inches from her nose. I wanted Son to see more clearly Who was in control of this event. He pushed again, listened, looked, tilted her chin up to meet his mouth again, gave her a second kiss, blowing deep into her throat. A gut geyser of stomach acid and ocean water spewed from her mouth onto Jesus' face.

Claudia's eyes flipped wide open as if surprised to see his face dripping vomit. She first gazed into his eyes, then turned on her side and threw up whatever else was in the bottom of her stomach.

She turned to him, struggling to shape a thought. "I fell for you. No one else."

Captain Crispus of the pirate flotilla watched a number of his galleys go down, all hands aboard. He cursed his bad luck. Crispus yelled for his coxswain to call dead slow, hoping they'd row into a patch of clarity. All they did was row away from wherever they were, hoping for better luck in the fog.

Today couldn't get much worse, he thought.

It did. He stroked their galley right under the prow of the remaining quinquereme. The Roman warship, moving at quarter speed, crunched the pirate galley with its forty crew members into matchsticks and red pulp. Kept moving, didn't look back.

A shiver of sharks made short work of these men. Only one or two survived. One of these glared at all creatures great and small, eyes rolling wide and wild. He bashed the remaining pirate (his best friend) in the head. Fed him to a hammerhead shark. After all, he reasoned, there's only room for one on this half-burned plank. He laid back and drifted through wisps of fume, mixed with fog and a grizzle of shower.

Only one warship was seaworthy. *Ignis Aurum Probat*—Fire Tests Gold— searched for the faithless mother ship that had gone without a good-bye.

The coxswain called quarter-speed cadence. The ship circled, visibility less than twenty yards in dense fog and high seas.

What saved the Messiah? Babies. Deborah began wailing in a loud cry at the top of her little lungs and didn't stop. Alexis caught her distress and began wailing from the other raft. Out of the mouth of babes came forth salvation. *Father and I love making the weak strong.*

The captain on the warship tilted his head sideways and peered his ears toward what sounded like a seagull cawing. My wind whipped the sound out of his ears. He waited. The crying-cawing came again. "Quarter turn, starboard," he yelled, "then dead-slow." The massive, flat-hulled ship was practically on top of the two rafts before a lookout saw them. The wake of the near-miss flipped both rafts over. Everyone, desperate for life, stayed connected to a hand, handle, or chunk of wood.

Survivors were hauled aboard in netting, beginning with children and women. Jude was last to be rescued, except for his big brother. The younger brother had caught the net with two fingers of his left hand and the toes of his right foot. A rogue wave pitched up from the black bottom of the sea, silhouetting a tiger shark in its curl. Jude looked over his right shoulder, saw the monster on top of him. He freaked, lost his nerve when the wave hit, and let go.

Jesus, right behind him, grabbed his waist and held on. Together they waited till the wave broke over the ship and washed back into the sea. Jude shivered and held tight to the one who proved able to keep him from falling. Years later, when Jude penned his short epistle, this was the moment that would stay fresh in his memory, the raft he would hold onto when he was sinking. [6]

The limping *Ignis Aurum Probat* was tested by fog, not fire, for a day and a night. It lay in the doldrums, adrift with no clear direction in sight. The other half of Seneca's truism about fire testing gold was revealed— *Miseria Fortes Viros.* "Adversity tests strong men."

14

RASTUS

I was sick and tired of bein' sick 'n tired. Jesus done saved me. But I wish he'd never run me down with his kind of goodness. I missed cracking heads open. Missed leading my gang. Missed cutting a throat now and again. After all, Zac needed my muscle to gouge taxes out of them scheming Sadducee tight.

He'd looked over his righteous shoulder on the way to synagogue one day. "Rastus, you're getting soft. Your life of crime needs you. So do I."

That was the same day pops looked at me and shook his head. "No more parties for you, prodigal. You just keep screwing up, time and again. You've run my patience and your inheritance flat out, boy."

I'd roved Judea with my gang for over twenty years with a few comings-back home when I was down and out. Once my feet wuz on the ground, off I'd go again.

This ragged, downhill slide lasted 'til I ran sideways into this Jesus guy. Purloined-vase caper broke bad. He stuck us with a bad case of leprosy. Really bad. Edge of dying bad. I figured we should take that vase back. Maybe magic redemption on the other side of magic disease. Who knew?

Us lepers showed up at Leah and Rabbus' place. Jesus, this guy who done us in, was there. He did his magic rigmarole and flipped the switch. I'm sure it were him who done it. Leah was his yakkin' hole, sayin' we had to do good stuff and fold our hands jus' so.

Right. Me, do good? Anyway, Jesus' said we needed good talk an' walk to ditch that friggin' disease. So, 'course we signed up, bein' cuz he wuz the only game in town.

Jesus, this guy's a slippery sort, slidin' through this whole story 'bout bad guys like me. Probably never figger how he does stuff. Leper's spots long gone, 'long with him. He left me without my gang of 20 years—what a bum.

Maltesa-the-merchantess, my betrothed, wanted my new life to circle 'round her. Wanted me for her moon. She plum' outta luck. No sir, ain't mooning over her.

She says, "Rastus, you're a case of arrested development." Ha! What'd she know? I'd never been arrested. In addition to bein' full-on ignorant, when the Big Dog made her, he gave her a razor for a tongue. Ok, but I'm off track. Maltie ain't all bad. She's rich. And, top 'a that, she's the only daughter of a rich Jew daddy and even richer granddaddy. Plus, she's grateful to find a man that'll have all four hundred pounds of her.

I headed toward Rahab's. Wanted to see if our wedding wine jars wuz finished an' maybe score a whore on the back wall, like my bro, Zac. We both wuz cut from pop's same cloth. But Zac greased 'em who pleased 'im with flattery. Those who didn't, I greased in back alleys. Together, we killed it.

I popped through Rahab's front gate, looked around, and saw a super fox right off the bat. This babe carried a case full of fat, glazed wine vases that chattered as she walked.

Fox headed for the side street shop. I slouched along after her, this one with honey-blond hair above *that ba-ba-boom* figure. Her sparkly eyes matched her blue hair ribbons, 'xactly. Fox's one cheekbone was a bit lower and angly-like than the other. Hoped to dear god she was a newbie workin' the back wall.

About then, a tallish Heebie, by the looks of his Jew-nose, came hustling out of the synagogue and called out, "Slow, come quick, darling; I got news."

Well, crap.

Jew-Nose said, "Slow, a traveler just checked in from Caesarea. He said he'd sailed from Greece, seen a pitched battle between three Roman warships, a merchant ship, and a whole fleet of pirate galleys."

He continued on, "Lots of fire and boats sinking, high seas. I think Jesus and his family were on that merchant ship."

Fox's voice broke. "Laz, tell Leah. She'll know what to do. She's a true seer, like Jesus—got the gift straight from him."

I butted in, "Hey there. Been listenin' ta yur yakking. Name's Rastus. Jesus healed me and my gang of the Spots. My wedding's this Saturday. I came… for your jugs." I eyed Fox's front.

Fox rolled her eyes and flat-toned: "You certainly didn't waste your only chance to make a good first impression." Ha! Same time, her idjiat husband stared at me, open-mouthed.

I said, "Jesus changed my skin, not my habits. Those ol' leopard spots still just under the surface." My right hand worried the flap of loose skin on my left hand's middle finger, the one that ain't grown back.

I said, "Fun life of crime's appealing, 'specially if Maltie don't work out."

Laz said, "Planning your divorce before your wedding? Leprosy might be in the old leopard's future, just like in his past."

I made a face.

He shrugged. "Just saying."

"Ya think? I'll make sure ta hang out with you *a lot*, Laz."

Laz grinned. "Jesus heals, but you have to do work too, change your habits. You pray. His Spirit will help."

"Might as well take a push broom and try sweeping dirt off the desert. By the by, I heard your news. My opinion? If ya wanted to keep yur ships safe, leave 'em in a harbor, or stick 'em in a museum up 'n Jerusalem. Know what I mean?"

Fox said, "Not only good marriage material but the soul of empathy too."

"Ha! Only a *few* of m' better points. Anyway, I know 'xactly where Rabbus and Leah live, and I need to get out of town. I'll pass your news along."

Fox said, "What a guy. Marriage certificate in one hand and divorce papers taped to your hind leg as a back-up. For now, take some gifts to my sister. Come back in an hour. I'll have the stuff ready."

I spun on my heel to leave and ran into a brick wall. Looked up and saw my betrothed, the one with enough thick, black braids to crowd half-dozen normal heads.

Crap-eating grin hit m' face, "Oh, Maltie, jus' coming your way."

Elephant ears flopped off the sides of her head, an' a real cold smile pasted itself on her lips. "Indeed, you rascal. I was listening around the corner."

"We wuz talkin' 'bout important stuff, like some deliveries I gotta do. Back in a few days, *Lovie*."

Maltesa dragged her squinty eyes over my frame, licked her lips, and said to Fox, "He'll be such fun to house-break, Slow. Got me a wild one, I did."

Her face softened. A rare moment. She kept looking at Slow. "You're a new bride, aren't you? Come see my wedding gown! I need some expert advice and maybe a little tailoring. The one Lydia made for me has shrunk."

She popped a sweet in her mouth and licked the leavings from her fingers. Marched out the front door, dragging Fox behind her. Headed toward alterations. She went one way. I went the other.

15

JESUS

The robe of darkness slipped off Night's shoulders, and she went to bed. Artist Sun pinked the flat sea, throwing his rays like a net in search of land. I stood, leaning against the bulkhead, admiring Windy's handiwork.

The ship's captain barked orders. *Ignis Aurum Probat* headed west toward Rome.

I huddled on deck center with my family and the Greeks. We were telling our stories about the disaster. Ioanna told the story, "We were all sliding helter-skelter toward ship's middle when it broke wide open. Grain exploded. All that gold blew Giorgos off-kilter. One moment he was there, the next, gone!"

Ioanna sobbed. "I'd tied our gold to him. He was heavy with it."

I watched Luke, the ten-year-old son who sat on his mother's left side, writing stuff down. Jude sat silently by her right side.

"What do you remember, Luke?" I asked.

"Everything's a blur. If I'd been braver, thrown him my tunic to hold onto, done something, anything."

I studied Luke, chapter and verse. I remembered saying words like that after my abba died. *Survivors, time-out-of-mind, sharpening the "if-only" razor and slicing themselves up.*

I prophesied, under Windy's tutelage, "One day you'll be a physician too, like your father."

Luke startled, looked at me steadily, taking my measure. Jude clasped a hand over his shoulder and squeezed.

At this moment, Remus, the ship's captain, approached our little group. Livena, Antonio, and Claudia followed him. "We have you Jews to thank for saving the emperor's daughter and granddaughter."

"Our God, Yahweh, saved them," Moshe said. "We were only his instruments."

Remus replied, "Neptune, Jupiter, Yahweh—I can't keep up with all these gods. Your arms pulled them out of the sea." He added, "We could use someone to help with the wounded. Our ship's physician was killed in the battle."

Ioanna piped up. "Sir, I'm a trained nurse. My husband was a physician. His skill rubbed off on me and our children. We could help."

"Certainly," Remus said. "Are you disembarking in Athens before we head across to Malta and then north to Rome?"

Ioanna looked unsure. "We *were* going home to Thessaloniki. But I'm not sure now." She broke down crying.

Livena stepped in front of the captain. "The least expression of gratitude Rome can provide is to give you and your children a place to live, a nursing job, education for your children."

Luke spoke up. "Ma, do you think I could go to school and become a physician like Jesus said?"

Livena pressed further. "My son was lost. Your husband was lost. Both were brave men. Let me assume responsibility for your son's education. No reason why he couldn't become anything he wants." She seemed happy to have another son spring full-blown from the same disaster that had cost her Claud.

Livena continued, "We could begin lessons today. You'll be quite busy, won't you, Antonio?" And with that, she cast her eye on tutor and studentry—James, Justus, Jude, Luke, Sophia, and Miriam. She didn't look at Claudia.

I said, "Perhaps Rav Moshe could assist. He can instruct from love's lesson book, our Torah. Its author teaches treasure isn't metal in boxes, belts, or cargo holds."

I looked at my brother and mother. "Real treasure is inside conscious people holding faith like cloud wisp."

I stopped and glanced at Claudia. "Even unconscious people, drifting in deep currents."

Antonio gazed at me solemnly.

"Hold onto people, tutor. Let metal go. Holding on, letting go, knowing when to do which—that's a good chunk of wisdom from our Jewish traditions."

Antonio shifted his eyes down to the deck. Remus scratched his head. "Well, there you have it. I guess things are settled. Madame, could you begin your nursing duties now? Several sailors are on the edge of death."

The group broke up. Claudia came over to me. We walked to the ship's stern, past all those oars beating water below us. These men's efforts, and what wind our ragged sail could hold, moved us toward whatever our future might hold.

I leaned out over the stern, looking at where we'd been. Claudia, a step behind me, was dressed in a damp cotton shift that clung to her frame. No jewels or makeup. The sun silhouetted her from where I stood. Seaspray whipped through the air and soaked us both, leaving a thousand drops of spray, beaded like tiny diamonds on her dress and hair.

Claudia wiped the spray off her face with her sleeve, stared at a wing of seagulls flying by. She stepped to my side and leaned on the balustrade with me. I remembered the feel of her skin on mine, her lips on mine, on the raft, two days ago.

She reached out and took my hand in hers. "Your love, Jesus, is scary costly, scary deep. What do I know of love's accountings, compared to you? What do I know?"

She picked at a splinter on the railing with her other hand. "I'm deep enough to love this splinter or that flock of seagulls on the wing."

Two dolphins surfaced, spinning streaks of silver, disappeared. "Yeah, I can love those as well, flickers of life streaking along some surface, bits that come and go.

"But you, *you* let a mother ship drag you to the ocean's bottom, saying 'yes' to me and 'no' to yourself. Coming down deep for me."

She said, after some time, "What in the *world* made you say 'yes' to me?"

I gazed out to sea, trying to get my mind off her body. I shoved down a wailing wanting, a moaning need. My longing or hers? Satan tempting me? Probably all that. In this moment, I didn't know and didn't care.

I looked at her, my brown gazing into her blue. Sweet, pure desire sang between us, mingling hope, longing, relief, like the whole prayers of the world chanting in unison. A quivering sort of heat flushed through me, mounting a high note in every cell of my body. I held that high, felt its fingers hold me. Urgency poked up and smeared a glop of forgetfulness over any shred of clear thought.

Claudia tipped her chin softly up. Her lips found mine. A silky cascade of sensation swept through me, a tide pulling me out to sea. I teetered, twisted in that current, felt one with the swell that passed beneath the ship. Then a warm wind blew, and that blow traveled through me. Formed a single word, a complete sentence. A command. Formed it inside me, to me. NO.

I pulled back from some brink, pulled away from her body, and said, "Wow! What was that?"

She laid her head on my chest, smiled, and did finger twirls in my beard.

"I forgot what you asked."

"I did too."

"Oh, oh yeah. 'What did I feel when I said 'yes' to you and 'no' to me?' Intense desperation, then, and now. Desperation drove me, dove me, deeper.

"Windy breathed me; Father moved me. Both of them breathed 'yes' to you. He, We, said 'yes' to you then… and now…. And a 'no' to me."

16

CLAUDIA

Jesus said 'yes' to me. That interrupted my recovery from our kiss, but not really. I wanted him. But really, I wanted much more. Not just sex, though there was that. The 'more' was that this man contained me, completed me.

His outside face was malleable, mirroring the hidden face I couldn't or wouldn't see inside me. He did this in a blink of real-time. How did he do that? I don't know, but he routinely pulled chaos out of my guts, messed with it, and gave me back myself, clear.

Memories focused unbidden. I remembered Claud stepping into space, screaming as he fell. I remembered the burning mast, a crossbeam, landing in our doorway, inviting me to step into the fire. I remembered flames licking at my feet, catching my singlet on fire. I remembered pushing mother into the sea. I remembered a scorched thought, hot from the altar, *I'm falling for Jesus.*

These confused memories crystallized. A perfect, lucid moment. My eyes presently focused on Jesus. This man was indeed a present given by the gods.

Present waited 'til I'd unwrapped my thoughts. He waited, polite-like, for me to catch up. Didn't snatch me bald-headed with quickness, like I might have done to him. Now, only now, could I risk the wreckage of another's point of view.

I asked, "How did you feel, doing what you did, even though it might have killed you?"

Jesus said, "I watched you hold onto your mother, pull her with you into thin air. That was a leap of faith if ever I saw one. Your faith triggered mine. We worked with Windy and Father, a team."

Jesus' voice faltered, "And then I saw your mother push away from you in mid-air. You fell alone. I followed your fall, all the way to impact, that whacking *splat*. Like watching Abba fall. I felt his fall, felt yours."

Jesus wept. My own eyes started to burn with some kind of wet. What was this? Water of a new life I'd not yet known? [7] Water that came from him seeing my fall? Him seeing how long I'd been falling, all alone?

He said, "I remembered you couldn't swim. I inhaled deep three times; then I kicked down into the sea looking for you. *Ouroboros* zipped by, heading for the bottom. The captain stared out his porthole, absolutely terrified."

He paused. "Then I saw you, blurred image in the water, maybe ten feet below me. The ship was pulling you after it and me closer to you."

He was silent and weeping, weeping, and shaking. I put my hand on his arm. Tenderness owned the air blowing between us and within us. He laid his hand on top of mine. "I wanted you to *live*. I kicked down for you. Grabbed your tunic. Swam up, pulling you behind me. My lungs burned. My ears screamed. I swam up. Mother-ship's suction, stronger, pulled us down. My vision got full of spots."

Talking through his weeping, "I needed Father. You needed me. Father pushed up from below, and Windy pulled up from above, lent me her breath. Waves broke over us. We popped up into the free air. It was that simple, that hard."

My frozen core warmed, cracked, calved. Salty tears ran down not only his face but mine as well. I not only was alive—I *felt* alive. Before I'd met this man, I was a ghost of a lie haunting a hollow house at midnight. Hadn't yet arrived. God-man saw me becoming, even when dawn was far off.

He hugged me close. That kiss I had given, he returned, turned me upside down, saved me from drowning in an ocean of loneliness. All my loneliness and love came together, lifted me into a wild abandon of loving and being loved. My face slid into his chest. I wrapped his beard in my fingers. Trembled, shook, held on. The sea rolled under us.

17

LEAH

Husband and I worked his father's fields. He wore only a loincloth, leaned into the traces, eyes set on the new place we were building above his parent's ruins. Goodness, our plowing mule, was sick. Rabbus was feeling poorly too, but he pulled our plow. He said, "Mule's a lot better creature 'n me. She ain't no thievin' murderer. Let 'er rest next to Mercy." Mercy was with foal from Goodness, a creature that one day we'd call Kindness.

I followed him, picking up the rocks he unearthed, dropping in seed—like husband had done in bed last night. In both fields, he was quiet, his plow moving the ground beneath him. I moved with husband, our bodies bunching, then relaxing, in the morning sun.

Rabbus showed humble and invisible without words—still skills. I was a good student. For instance, today we ate our breakfast of fried fast-bread and half a turnip each. I was feeling like that turnip, pale and shriveled. I sat still, chewing and remembering the time in Moab when famine came before breakfast and stayed a year.

I must have been ten or so. My job back then was to scrape up all the neighbor's horse, pig, and cow droppings and make 'em into pies. Throw 'em on our south-facing stucco wall to dry—fuel to heat water. If pa brought home something we could put in that pot, we could both drink and eat—a plus.

My sad musta been catching. Rabbus held my face against his face. Dropped word stones into the air. "Not a clod on this farm that don't make me want to scream. Can't forgive my memory for that." Felt like he was straining to remember as near to nothing as he could, and failing at it. His tears rolled down my face, crowding my tears, clogging my nose, hanging on my lips. I held his hand; he held mine. We each reached over with our other hand. Finger-swiped my tears off his lips; his, off mine.

He said, "You've told me you hate your brown hair and eyes. Wanted eyes and hair like your sister, sky blue 'n blond. But how can I plant new crops in thin air and sun? Your eyes earth me. Make me want to dig deeper, claim ground. Now you're here, and I don't have to feel like a not-person not-livin' in a place that's not mine."

He hugged me, shy-like. "Trouble. That was the only thing Romans or Jews let me own. But now I got you. And our baby, on the way." We got up and kept working. End of each row, I dropped my basket of rocks, and Rabbus would work with me to dry-mortar those stones into boundary markers.

I said, "Rabbus, remember God's just-in-time walls in Shechem— angel walls? I talk to God about our walls here. I say, 'God, give me only walls I need. The rest will be too heavy. They'll keep me from your people, and them from me, when we need each other.'" I ran my finger over the drywall. Saw glimmers of angels dancing on 'em. I strapped my basket back on, slipped the strap around my forehead.

We'd started a fresh row when I heard a noise and looked up. Rastus was walking his horse toward us with eight ex-lepers trailing behind him on foot. Rabbus and I walked over.

Husband said, "Jesus told you guys to go home. Why are you here again?"

Rastus said, "I was on my way here alone. And then, surprise—these men popped out of cracks in them hills."

The shortest and darkest of the bunch, an Edomite named Esau, looked like God had cut him straight from a dwarf blackwood tree. He stood as tall as his backbone and legs would take him, maybe five feet off the ground. Even so, his tunic was too short in the sleeves. His hands hung out like a batch of twigs—flopping around, nervous twigs.

Esau said, "Once I got home, no one remembered me. I got lonely. Nothing to do that I liked doing—killin', robbin', stealin'. So, I went back to the only place I knew. Found my mates there. That's it."

Rabbus looked at me. I looked back, prodding with my nodding. *Pick up these living stones, my love. Make a bridge, not a wall.*

"Leah and I have a big piece of land," he said. "Short of help. Maybe you could settle here, turn a new leaf." The men's eyes lit up. Their feet scuffed a bit like they were getting a feel for the ground beneath them.

Rabbus continued, "Rahab's handles women. We'll do men. Get together now and again for a dance or two. Maybe marry all you guys off. What d'ya say?"

Heads nodded, faces full of doubt mixed with hope. I studied around the circle while my right hand rubbed my tummy. Movement in there, like Rabbus moving toward destiny's call. I wasn't showing yet. He was. Men probably need more than nine months if they're going to push out something useful. But here we stood, with Rabbus' child being delivered while we were laboring unawares.

Rastus turned away as if he'd suddenly remembered why he'd come. "Oh yeah, I'm supposed to tell you that Jesus probably croaked. Pirates 'n Romans. Bunch of 'em sank. Forgot."

I crumpled to the ground. Felt like wild horses had trampled me. Baby flopped around inside me. Rabbus quietly said, "If she loses our baby, Rastus, I'll choke the livin' tar outta you with my bare—"

I interrupted. "Settle down, Rabbus. He didn't do bad on purpose. He's mainly sleepwalking, bumping into stuff."

Rastus flashed a confused look at me. "Wrong about that, little lady—I sleep fine. But I'll ask around if you want."

"I think Jesus is okay, now that I think about it. I had a vision of him as a peace ship, throwing off rainbows of light's sufferings, all shattered into bits."

Men stood there, scratching their heads at this snatch of weirdness. I said, "My vision didn't include him dying, just suffering. Rastus, go. The rest of you, stay. We need your help."

I wasn't sure how we'd feed all these mouths. Harvest wasn't for a long time yet. If they weren't good at hunting, I'd have to practice starving again.

Rastus turned to go. "Oh yeah, one more thing. Your sister sent presents, Leah. Food, by the smell of it." He dropped a bag on the ground, slung his leg over his horse, and cantered down the hill toward Jericho.

18

JESUS

The *Ignis Aurum Probat* rounded the last wriggle of Italian coastline. The Tiber River, up ahead, made a grand, roiling entrance to the Mediterranean. Our exhausted rowers picked up energy with the hope of home so close. They heaved in their oarlocks toward the Port of Ostia.

Once we'd docked, I took my first conscious breath of Italy. Smells smacked me. Odors sang a chorus in my nose. Crates of fresh flowers and barrels of spices threw their song to the wind. Curry, cumin, ground garlic, mint, lavender, and all manner of incense tangled together, each swirling around in the moist heat. The sweat and stink of people and animals, each played in my nosy, noisy orchestra.

Jasmine perfume wafted all-around an African woman waiting on the pier. She stood, shifting one foot to the other, eyes wide open, cheeks vermillion over ebony. She examined us one by one, real serious, as we walked the gangplank down to the pier. Her face looked like someone who'd been abandoned but was the last to realize it.

"That mommy sad?" Deborah asked me, holding onto my ears while sitting on my shoulders. I nodded. The sad woman wore happy clothes like she'd wrapped herself up as a present for someone in jungle greens and oranges. Heavy, looped gold earrings stretched her earlobes down to her shoulders, and a macaw perched on her shoulder. Salmon-colored neck feathers merged with a cobalt blue chest and tapered along his back into violets and oranges. His tiny legs looked bouncy, spring-loaded.

I whispered to Debbie, "Look at that gorgeous bird!"

The macaw, a perfect mimic, shrilled back to me, "Gorgeous bird! Gorgeous bird!" I looked up in time to see my baby sister's mouth open in a perfect 'oh.'

The African woman touched Deborah's cheek as she went her lonely way. Windy spoke into my inner ear, *Gorgeous Son, leave that woman to me. She's not your concern.*

I instantly messaged Windy, *Thanks.*

She replied, *Vital life lesson, Son. No before yes. Sort what's best. Leave the rest, including better and good.*

I looked down the riverbank. Dozens of piers hosted more ocean-going vessels than I could count. Longshoremen hoisted amphorae of oil, grain, and exotic goods on their backs from many cities. As far as my eye could see, workmen poled a steady flow of galleys twenty miles upstream to the capital city.

Remus directed us into an open galley. Guards surrounded Livena, Antonio, and Claudia as they boarded yet another, much more luxurious galley with covered cabins. Claudia waved at me before her mother pushed her down into a darker space.

We all headed toward the largest city in the world, houses more densely packed the closer we got to Rome's city center. Some apartments were six stories tall. Finally, round yet another bend, the City of Seven Hills lay drenched in sunlight. Remus' grin was broad as the Tiber, "*Voilà, bella Roma!*"

Antonio had taught us of Rome and its ruler on board the ship for the last few days. Rome was supposedly founded by the wolf-suckled Romulus and Remus over seven hundred fifty years ago. Only the most enterprising survived and thrived. Lesser souls were pushed into the provinces. Untaxed Roman citizens got free money and food hand-outs from the emperor on a quarterly basis, beautiful fountains that delighted the eyes, and clean streets patrolled by brigades of paid civil servants. Rome even had a goddess of excrement, Cloacina. The Cloaca Maximus piped a million people's pee and poop out to sea—all courtesy of Caesar Augustus' riches and rule.

Rome wore its history like a patchwork quilt, with triumph and tragedy joined together in slapdash stitchery. Bones of saints and sinners were catacombed with the bones of those lions who'd eaten them. Above all, Rome was religious, a froth of gods and temples of all shapes. But above all these gods floated the one who provided for you, spread jam on your morning toast, put pork sausage on your table. *Hail, Caesar Augustus!*

19

CLAUDIA

A week or so after our arrival in Rome, we all rode the grief train and ate Claud's dust. Professional wailers led the charade parade. This cutting edge of Rome's royal threnody spewed a lather of incredible grief. Grandpa and Grandma rode the first carriage, mother and her half-sisters, Julia and Agrippina, were in the second. My male cousins—Caligula, Posthumus, and Gemellus—rode in the third. I rode in the fourth carriage between Rome's two official Vestal Virgins. I lifted my chin high, looked at my public looking at me. My outfit was the only form-fitting dress in the funeral shop. Me, the princess of sexy grief.

A Claud memory blindsided me. He and I had talked about death one night when we were about twelve. He'd snuck into my bedroom, into my bed, as usual. Afterwards, dark, quiet. Antonio had schooled us on Epicurus that day in class. Before he left for his own bed, Claud said, "Epicurus got it right. Pleasure *is* the highest virtue. But I'll see his pleasure, and raise him pain—give others pain, take their pleasure."

He'd laughed. "When I'm gone, I'm gone. One and done. Don't feel anything about me. I didn't even exist."

Got it, Claud. Unfortunately, I do have feelings these days. Jesus infected me with that choice disease. For example, your absence feels like a blue-washed fresco stabbed with crimson. *Okay, now I'm done with feeling. Done, I tell you. That feeling stuff wears a body out.*

A long line of speakers stood to praise Claud. *Blah, blah, blah.* Gemellus and Caligula were silent. Grandpa kept catching his head like it was too heavy for his neck. Then he'd jerk it up, just before his chin hit his chest.

Posthumus was the last speaker. Postie was short with a muscular, thick neck and oblong, thrusting head. His face looked like a pug who'd lost one too many dogfights. He was his mother's monkey-on-a-leash, hopping around on-stage, grinding her organ. He even summoned up a tear or two. Looked suitably aggrieved. Ha. Maybe grandpa would give him a reprieve and allow him off his solitary island, other than for funerals. Postie had been in the exile slammer, off and on, for the last couple of years, like his mother before him, on another island, for sexual indiscretions.

Postie was Julia's single remaining piece in the game of thrones and she was grandpa's single legitimate birth daughter. Her other sons, heirs to the throne, had croaked. Postie was her leavings. He stood up and squirted out obscure words, lies she'd written for him. Like an octopus squirts ink, her words from his mouth clouded her presence. But everyone knew she played ventriloquist through her dummy and hid her glee back of his drivel.

He finally wound down. And then, a surprise. One of the Vestal Virgins, Bathenia, whispered, "Want to come over to *Atrium* after the funeral, Claudia? We can get to know each other. I'm fascinated by boys, and I hear you're a great teacher. Please?"

I looked at her, poop-sniffer on alert. We'd only risked empty chatter to this point, superficial conversation that kept each other at arm's length. Now I probed her face for signs of subtext agendas. She seemed as sincere as a virgin could be, but I wasn't a crackerjack judge of virgins. Desire usually billowed off me like steam.

I felt some pity for her and her virgin buddy, Warthenia, but not a lot. Their lives were absolute graveyards of buried hopes. Their very best hope for getting laid was to wait another twenty-five or thirty years, keep Rome's eternal flames burning—then petition for release from their vows, find husbands, and live out their years. It had been done before. But for now, they were two suppressed teenage girls, coopted by the state, with no hope in sight. I smiled blankly at her, noodled on her invite.

20

SLOW

Rastus and Maltesa's wedding was really happening! He'd stood her up a couple of times, running off into the hills for months between promised wedding dates. He'd drag back when he ran out of money or pride. Now, a couple of years later, he'd gotten word that his pops was about to croak. So, he sucked it up, made nice with his abba and Maltie. There they both stood, under the chuppah, at long last.

Laz and I slouched at couch, half-way down the wedding table from bride and groom. He winked at me. "Slow, my love, you're the most beautiful woman in this room—for that matter, the town, the country, the world …"

We hadn't had Shabbat sex last a week, since I'd been on my period. He was frustrated.

"My slow hands will make you feel double-good, baby." *Double-wink.*

Harlot winked back at him. But inside, I slipped into a cracked part-self, Fragile. Shame intoned, "Didn't I tell you? The other shoe will drop if you don't perform. All those whores are waiting to take him away from you at the drop of their panties."

I thought about her warning while Cutter bit my fingernails and pulled out an eyelash. Escape was nowhere to be seen. Come to think of it, maybe that's why I felt numb.

Meanwhile, at the front of the room, Maltesa looked victorious, and Rastus, desperate—an islet adrift off her continental shelf. All his murderous thugs looked almost respectable if you squinted at them sideways and thought about other things.

Maltesa's father and grandfather had pried open their purses for this wedding. Grandfather nodded at the maestro. *Get that band going.*

Rastus' and Zac's father, Mordecai, looked dubious at best. The story was well known around town. Mordecai had waited at the top of the hill outside of town the first few times Rastus had run away. Welcomed him home, killed the fatted calf, the whole routine. But Rastus kept being a screw-up. Zac was the responsible one, the shining light, even if he was a despicable tax collector in cahoots with Rome.

Each kid was a mess. Zac, the younger, successful son, smelled like an armpit that had smoked a cigar. Poke any hole, and greed gushed out. Esmeralda, Zac's new-bought Nubian wife, couldn't be bothered to pretend interest. She practically clawed at the door, eager to spend his money.

All in all, a festive Jewish family.

Leah, reclining next to me, looked happy, dreaming her baby into life. Put my hand on her tummy and felt the kid kicking. All those stretch marks coming her way! My body had maxed out with men's use and my cuts. I'd not told Laz my 'morning-after' tea secret. I routinely whacked any tiny tot before the sucker could latch on and claw my guts. A kid would be nothing more than a brick welded into a metal tunic I'd have to wear for years.

Esmerelda and I were of the same mind—no need for romper room weasels to suck our boobs, steal our lives away. Leah said she'd pray for my fear to go away. Okay, Sis. But miracles were for other people, not me. I was still a moody Jewish optimist, sure that today would be better than tomorrow.

I looked at Cynico and Cyrena, now established as common-law partners—Rahab's Double-Cy. Cy had settled down out of his morose, bluesy blahs since Cyrena had come. Who'd have thought such a loser would boil down into a decent human being?

El Roi finished tying the knot. Everyone clapped. The couple crunched the cloth-wrapped wine glass beneath their feet. Uh, make that, her foot.

Jesus told me at my own wedding, "you know why we Jews do this glass smashing thing?" I'd shrugged. He continued, half-serious, "Every celebration contains sadness. Husband's gain in father's loss. Israel partied, and Moses smashed stone tablets. The temple was obliterated after years of peace. When the good times roll, we know they're probably rolling into a grave around the next corner."

He'd winked at me. "Progressive thinkers, us."

My mind arrived back in the room in time to hear Roy introduce Rastus and Maltie for the first time as a married couple. I clapped twice, the back of three fingers tapping lightly on a sweaty palm.

Rastus' eyes were twitching. He was probably wondering if he could ditch Maltie for a hunting trip with his twelve closest buddies. And what was this? Leah had sidled up next to the happy new couple. Time to eavesdrop.

Leah rubbed her tummy and bubbled, "Rastus and Maltie—such a beautiful, rich beginning!"

Maltie, new husband tucked under her arm, waddled into the fray. "You're so right! It was rich! The crystal wine glasses were specially imported from Venice. The blue tablecloth? Linen from Alexandria—the most expensive, cobalt-blue pigment! We were *so* pleased, weren't we, dear?"

She looked down at her diminutive husband, big as a wheeze. Rastus' chin and the front of his wedding garment were festooned with a paste of fish eggs and pink champagne that had missed his mouth. He looked bewildered as if wondering how his jot got downsized to a tittle.

He opened his mouth to speak, but Maltie plowed on, trampling unborn initiative. "And, oh yes, that thick, luxuriant carpet from the Orient? Let's see, if I remember rightly, it cost about five thousand! Worth every shekel, right, dear?" Rastus nodded submissively, not sure of his footing, even on such rich carpet.

Leah commented, "God will use each of you, I'm sure, to humble the other. Both of you, in your own ways, have been very successful. But you've crossed a new threshold." Rastus looked dubious; Maltie, bemused.

Leah mustered on, "Your lives will get more fruitful—but also more difficult."

Maltie started to launch. Leah interrupted, "You will both pass through fire in this new marriage. When that happens, hold your silence, each other, and your resolve. If you don't endure, your marriage will dither into fight or flight. Instead, let truth mix with kindness, and you'll flourish."

Windy must have been at work. *Leah* didn't know any of that stuff. Guess that's how it goes with oracles.

Rastus asked, "Does this mean I can't get time away from Maltie or I'll come down with leprosy again?"

Maltesa cut in, wedding quick. She pointed a pudgy, pink-painted forefinger down at his face. "That's exactly what she meant, peckerwood. No more running off into the hills." She motioned with a wave of her hand, "No more playing rascals and robbers with that bunch of hang-dog dispicabilea."

Rastus ignored her helpful influence. "As I was saying, Leah, what's the cost of a little distance? Leprosy?"

Leah smiled. "You two! Look at you go on."

She turned sideways to Rabbus. "I noticed something, probably the same thing you saw, Rabbus. Maltie may have had her finger in Rastus' face, but she was holding his other hand. That's what I mean." She grabbed Rabbus' hand and made push-pull motions. "Rabbus and I push and pull all the time, but each of us knows our hold is stronger than our hit."

Rastus tried a third time, exasperated, "And leprosy? I don't want that again, even if I hold onto Maltie. Answer the dadgum question!"

"Rastus, remember Jesus' words, not mine. He said to act honorably, live honestly. Don't vow one thing and do another. And, for you, Maltie, the vow to respect your husband will challenge you."

Maltie's desire for a cowed husband was a pulsating thing. Put me in mind of some great, horned beast panting in a summer mudhole. She turned away, towing foiled desire behind her like an oxcart. She paced a few steps, heaved a sigh. She rooted herself in Jericho red dust, her alternate honeymoon destination to Mount Sinai. Leah picked up on Rastus' doubt. "My words only carry freight when Jesus' Spirit gives them weight. Pray, Rastus. Ask God to show you, then obey whatever He says."

"I've prayed, Leah. Heard nothing. Zip. Nada. Nothing but wolves howling at night. Or maybe that wuz Maltie snoring, next room over."

He smiled, looked at his bride. "Just kidding, dear."

He continued speaking, "Your God talks in ways people like me can't hear. God speaks to *you*, his mouth to your ear. So, when you get some drool from the Big Dog, bark it over, huh?"

Leah kept the conversation going while I entertained doubt. I imagined Maltie tonight, their wedding night, insisting she be on top. She'd squash

Rastus flat. Just like that, it'd all be over. Mercy, Leah's mule, could haul his body out a side door. I'd leave Escape behind to keep it open it for him.

That was when I heard a voice, a woman's voice that interrupted my fantasy life. The voice said, *Jesus is dancing in a den with a prowling lion. The lion has a golden crown. Pray for him.* I recovered from my shock enough to say, *God, keep Jesus alive wherever he is. Please, God. Do this, for Jesus' sake.*

21

JESUS

Augustus sat on his throne, beneath his favorite tapestry, a roaring lion poised on his hind legs, ready to strike. He commanded, "Seer, on pain of death, tell me, "Why did my ship sink? Perhaps Neptune sent a storm to sink her because of *you* since *you* pagans worship the wrong gods."

I said, Father, help!

Father looked through my eyes at the man before me, the man who had fashioned himself into god. Augustus' golden crown set on hair the color of ash and smoke.

Windy mingled with Father. They floated an inner vision that distracted me from the outer lion—Lucifer's thorny crown, on my head. Together They whispered, *Augustus is the King of Gold, gold that perishes. You're the King of Thorns, who will show him the path of enduring humility. Notice this ex-infant tyrant, who now sits on a different kind of highchair, the one who uses intimidation as his own pacifier.*

The King of Gold waited unhappily on the King of Thorns. He sat stiffly, restless, on edge. His throne, overlaid with gold filigree, was studded with rubies and diamonds that his fingers polished like worry beads. He appeared to be enjoying a case of invincible melancholy.

Augustus' servants had stripped me of my own clothes and given me a plain, worn, wool toga with a cloth belt and no shoes. My toga chafed as if I was wrapped in iron wool, not plain wool. My toes were twinging blue from standing on his cold marble.

Windy got my attention, tuning my ears to His voice more than the fear Augustus was pushing my way. Windy commented, *Augustus' heart is clogging. His brain's getting fuzzy. His hand tremors worsen, day to day. This man, so hollowed by pride, will not endure for long, and he's terrified of death.*

I whispered back. *He's not the only one.*

Augustus spoke. "Your lips are moving, seer, but I can't hear you. Speak up. Tell me why my ship exploded."

I dragged myself back into his presence. "I have no knowledge of such things. I was in the middle of the ship one moment. The next, I was in the sea, clinging to cargo doors, fighting for my life."

"You saved my granddaughter."

"As Yahweh willed, Emperor."

"But you let my grandson drown."

"He was heavily weighted with armor and sank like a rock. Claudia had thrown off your emerald and diamond belt, ruby ring, anything that weighed her down." I looked pointedly at the diamonds and rubies on his fingers, the emerald encrusted tiara, woven with gold filigree, the golden breastplate he wore.

Augustus' eyes followed mine. He pressed his attack. "Death took six hundred Romans and a few worthless pirates that day. Why not you?"

"As God willed. Father dangles all of us on a bight of rope over a vast sea."

Factotum, standing behind Augustus' left side, scribbled away.

Augustus said, "You expound poetic. I need practical. Pierce the mystery of my mortality." His voice softened. "Tell me more of what you saw in Sepphoris—the time and manner of my death."

I pushed out Father's words with Windy's breath. "Excellency, that vision hastens and pants toward that day. Father will not be rushed. You, First Citizen, will soon stand face-to-face before my Father in a higher court than this. All you've done and left undone will be weighed in His scales."

I looked to my left. A bolt of sun slanted into the throne room. A softer sheen of brilliant viridian flowed through the sun and hid back of an ashlar. I knew in a flash that Claudia hid behind that marble column. Excitement, wrapped in shadow, thrummed within me.

Augustus' words, layered in ice, called me back. "These threats of your Father's judgment in a higher court than Rome are your truth, seer? What if I present you with truth that includes your execution on a cross?"

"Your judgment in this empire is final, sire. I know this to be true, even as your granddaughter knows truth within her. Don't you, Claudia?"

Claudia, called out, flounced into the open. She sat on the arm of her grandpa's throne and grazed a flirt my way. Her brassy self was on display today, hiding her affection for me.

She said, "Gramps, he's always going on about truth. It's like trying to pick goose down out of honey. His words, slippery eels drenched in oil."

Augustus leaned over to Claudia and whispered, "What's this guy's name again?" Claudia rolled her eyes as she spoke my name in his ear.

Augustus said, "Of course. Jesus of Nazareth, you said I'd die in Nola, in less than three years. That was two years ago."

He looked next to him at the water clock, a marble sculpture of the Goddess Justitia, blinded. Her scales of justice dripped one second to the next. "Time's dripping, seer. Birth a date for my death."

Claudia slouched on an alpaca fur that stretched over the arm of her grandfather's throne. She hugged her emerald chiffon robe around her and shivered.

A seductive voice, fear-laden— *You're a peasant from the provinces. This is the Emperor. Be realistic. See you through their eyes.*

I resisted this voice and grabbed inside for Father. His reply came from my mouth, exhaled in a focused Wind. "Is it not true that 'to give birth,' in Italian, means to 'give to the Light?' The dim hour of our death rests in the blazing light of Father's presence."

"I don't need bright light, seer. I need candlelight. Wave a lit candle over my tombstone. Show me the day, the year. All I see now is the sheen of a blank tombstone."

"I could claim to dig the wax off your stone, but how sincere would that be when only Father knows the date? [8]

"What Father *has* given me to say is this, 'Give up the killing delusion that you are a god in control of life and death.' There's only one God in the entire universe—and you're not Him. You can relax."

The Emperor's face raged rutilant. Pride's ham fists clutched him. A lion's roar broke against his teeth. "You and your impudence can go to Hades, seer!"

All four of us in the room felt the force of his outburst. How could we not? The throne room felt like a balloon that Windy puffed up to the popping point. Augustus' crown slipped down over his nose. He let it settle there for a moment before he righted it, glaring at me all the while. The marble floor felt like it was crisping into light ash. I imagined the lion on the wall jumping out of the tapestry, snapping me up in his razored teeth.

Windy wisped across the space between the throne and me, flowed over Claudia's robe, ruffling it with his passage. He poked a pinky finger inside the emperor's chest, touched his heart ever so lightly. I felt His breeze, smelled a heavenly fragrance like honeysuckle. A mote danced in a patch of light on Augustus' golden breastplate. He grasped his chest suddenly. His fingertips trembled, dancing a jitterbug at the end of his wrists.

"That heart attack just now was a warning, Emperor, sent by Father's Spirit. The weight of a god delusion crushes even the bravest heart into cinders."

Augustus, slumped to one side, grasping his chest, panted. He pointed a stiff finger at me, pushing out his anger even in this extremity. "Power trumps truth. I could flay you alive and hammer you to a cross."

My knees shivered in this sure knowledge of my future death. My skin goose- bumped. Windy flash-forwarded my vision—*Claudia, in the wings of a nearby palace, dreaming her dreams. Me carrying a cross, on a raw back, toward a skull.*

I edged toward collapse. In this micro-moment, Father flowed through Windy into my voice. "If you order my death, so be it, sire. That might even be my Father's *crowning* achievement. He has each of your life's heartbeats, and mine, cataloged. When Father says we're done, our ticket's punched. We'll all stand face-to-face with Him."

The emperor glared at me, one hand over his heart and the other waving dismissively. "Enough of this pain. I'll call you back another day when I feel like taking another beating. Go."

22

SLOW

I left the wedding hall with Leah, Laz, and Rabbus. Heaved a sigh of relief. "Something really strange happened back there. I saw Jesus' face in a vision. His head was tangled with thorns. He fought a lion. I asked God to protect him. Waited maybe ten, fifteen minutes. Tension flowed out of my body. Weird, huh?"

Leah looked sideways at me. "I'm not the only prophetess in this family. God rests his Spirit wherever and on whoever he wants. Your prayer may have saved him from a lion, for all we know."

We all entered Rahab's courtyard and found a prowling lion there, of a different sort. Tribune Gaius stood in his chariot, squinty-eyed, nostrils flaring, talking with our blind couple. Warhorses circled them, along with armored soldiers.

Laz's hand developed a sudden, jerky tremble. Here we stood, cheek by jowl, with the highest officer of the occupation army. Even scarier, Gaius was speaking with his previous foreman. Cynico could blow the whistle, tell his old boss how we Jews had ass-reamed and blinded him. We'd all be crucified.

Gaius spotted Laz, dark-ringed eyes glaring. "I know you! Come here, Jew."

Laz moved forward and stood beneath Gaius' whip. He said, "Tribune, we meet again! Jesus and I helped secure your home's foundation in Sepphoris. How might I help you here?"

I stood directly behind Rabbus. His throwing knife dropped down into his hand. Leah grabbed his arm, took a half-step in front of him.

Gaius said, "Pirates ambushed our flotilla of ships. I'm looking for a man called Crispus."

Laz shook his head, "Don't think I know that man, Tribune."

Rabbus inhaled sharply. Gaius noticed. "Speak—yes, you, the one hiding behind that woman."

Rabbus said, "I went to school with a kid named Crispus in Samaria. Long time ago. Common name."

"We're headed there tomorrow. A guy with a wandering eye?"

"Matter of fact, his right eye did go for solitary hikes."

Leah broke the tension. "Tribune, do you have a word about your family's safety—and Jesus?"

Gaius' face fell. A tiny crack in his granite features. "My son died, wife and daughter lived. Jesus lived."

Cyrena turned and shuffled off with Cy toward their bedroom. Gaius silently watched him walk. It was the kind of silence that had a cat-of-nine-tails in it.

He shouted, "You! Blind guy! Don't I know you from somewhere? I'm sure I do. Come here!"

Cy paused, turned toward his old master. Gravelly voice, "No. I don't know you."

I exhaled. I'd been holding my breath and didn't know it. I did a gut scan and found, to my surprise, that I was holding Escape in one hand and Fragile in the other, gently.

Gaius dismissively waved his hand.

Laz saw the dismissal. "You're free to go, Cy."

A quickening wind ruffled Cy's long beard. He stepped into the threshold of his room, one foot in his room, one foot in the courtyard, half-turned to Gaius and his old life. Cyrena tugged. His fingers saw her love, and he moved inside, laying down blind rage.

Gaius got down from his chariot and commanded Laz with an imperious tone. "Prepare rooms for my officers. Foot soldiers will camp in your courtyard. If you have other guests, send them away. We head to Samaria in the morning."

Once dismissed, some soldiers headed for the back door with a red lantern over it. Others rambled toward Bloody's Bar, down the block.

I stood outside Rahab's gate, watched from the shadows. Gaius walked alone, hunched over, to another tavern a few blocks away. I followed him, slipping down the side of the street, veiled. He looked like a haunted man who'd changed into a hunting man—a man who wanted to get seriously drunk.

23

WINDY

Jesus passed two years peacefully in Rome. He worked as a journeyman in the palace carpentry shop. The emperor didn't risk another cardiac event. Instead, he settled for weekly reports from supervisors on the seer's activities.

Meanwhile, Claudia studied theatre arts and Greek classics at the palace academy. She hung out with Jesus on weekends with their friends when he wasn't busy teaching and arguing with the other men at the synagogue.

On this particular Sunday morning, they met at a bridge over the Tiber. Their elbows touched on the rail. The brown Tiber rippled beneath them in the soft morning light—slanting shafts shot through with ash from a nearby fire.

Claudia said, "I've blown off Rome's Eternal Flame, but she keeps lighting matches to warm herself. Wants to see me. Could you come along?"

Jesus turned his head sideways to study her. He ignored her question, changed subjects. "I've been thinking about something else. Remember our one fiery meeting with your grandpa in his throne room? The time he had a heart attack?"

"All I remember is we two ganged up on you, and you managed to beat the crap out of both of us. You've got an unfair advantage, being God and all."

Jesus didn't blow her off. "You love your grandpa, and he loves you."

"You do know Grandpa sees you as a hedge bet in the god games."

"And, uh, am I your hedge bet too?"

She huffed out a dramatic sigh. "I trusted you with my life out there in the Med, didn't I?"

Jesus flickered a smile her way. "When you were on fire, and a ship was sinking beneath you. But I'm talking about something else—how your grandpa's heart attack hit *your* heart."

Claudia stood stock still, caught in a tangle of sun and shadow. "There *was* a moment that day when a strange wind whirled a smell of jasmine up my nose. That what you meant?"

"Yes, plus Windy put his finger in your grandpa's chest and gave him a severe mercy, a wake-up call."

"You been doing drugs? My actor friends can get all kinds of stuff."

"There you go playing peek-a-boo again—'Now you see me; now you don't.' You let my love in, then you race away, joking."

Claudia smiled coyly, "I can take in only so much god at one time. Then I close up shop. Calculated neglect. Works every time to reel in the men I want."

"Treat your true feelings to Neglect, and Fear gets thrown in with the deal, rent-free."

Claudia's eye twitched. "I wouldn't know about that."

"You're wiser than that."

"Really? I'm not wise. Besides, wisdom's just smartness with all the poo pounded out of it. I'd rather be smart any day than wise. Never met a smart person I didn't like."

"Smart people know how to make the rules they think will keep them safe. Wise people know what to do when the rules go missing."

Claudia said, "That's smart. And, by the way, is there a Jew rule against Roman women asking Jewish men out on a date?"

Jesus stared at her, not at all smart in the "dating game."

She didn't wait for a reply. "We've always done group stuff together with friends. But tomorrow, I'd like you to come with me to see a play. Reprocessed oldie but goodie, *Psyche*. It's on at the Forum, and the actors are all the rage in Rome these days."

"You and me, alone-together, at a play?"

Claudia blustered on. "Your whole family's invited, of course. I'm an understudy at the academy for Psyche, the protagonist. The actress with that role is my teacher."

"There's room for my whole family?"

"The top-center section is kept open for Jupiter and his bunch. Also, Grandpa and his family when he attends."

"I'll check with my family. Now tell me about these Vestal Virgins."

"Both are daughters of senators, groomed to be Keepers of the Light from babyhood. Virgin Bathenia wants wise counsel. Obviously, she confused me with someone else. That's why I'm inviting you."

Jesus took this in. "Let me check with Ma, since we're in the neighborhood." They passed a carpenter's shop next door to his apartment. The owner was a shaggy-looking mongrel of a man cutting a timber over two sawhorses. A smack of children circled his heels, play-fighting. Jesus picked up one of his little girls and kissed her. She'd escaped the fight for his hug.

Jesus, laughing, put the child down. The couple climbed the stairs to his family's apartment on the sixth floor. This was Claudia's first visit to Jesus' home. Mary sat by her dinner table, darning socks.

Jesus said, "let me show you something I made at my friend's shop downstairs."

He whipped off the tablecloth and smoothed his hand over the polished surface. "Made the table, after hours, with James. This gives us exiles a taste of home while we're pitched up here on the shores of Italy."

The two of them spread the tablecloth back over the table. The pattern in the cotton caught Claudia's eye. She bent over to look at it more carefully. A brass-colored serpent had been carefully cross-stitched into it. The serpent spiraled around a green tree that pointed up into a bright blue sky. She figured it was part of their Jew religion. This family put their tin plates on this cloth, spilled food and wine on it. Maybe showed their kind of faith—an everyday thing that held food, could be used, spilled on.

Claudia turned from the tablecloth to a scene that tightened her gut. Jesus had taken a knee in front of his mother and was giving her a kiss on the cheek. Her face lit up with pure joy. Jesus beamed back at her. *She'd like a piece of that, thanks very much.*

Jesus said, "Ma, is it okay if I go with Claudia down the street to meet with the Vestal Virgins? And is it okay if we go as a family to a play at the Forum tomorrow night?"

Mary didn't argue on either count. "Sure, sounds like fun."

Mary came over and gave Claudia a soft kiss on the cheek. Claudia's "mommy-bone," close to her heart, pinged. She hugged long, let go slow.

The couple walked down the steps and stood under an overhang. A stripe of orange light sliced across Claudia's body. Jesus saw an eye and a part of her mouth painted in that light, but her heart was shaded.

"Jesus, you're a grown man, almost twenty years old. Why are you still asking your mother for permission to go down the block?"

"Only kindness. If I were her, an alien widow with six children in a strange apartment, strange country, wouldn't I want to be treated like that?"

Claudia thought, *Huh. Why don't I think like that?*

Jesus said, "You opened your heart to my mother back there, didn't you?"

Claudia squeezed the hand she held, looked straight ahead. Jesus didn't press for more than what she could give. She walked the edge of tolerable frustration, let him another step deeper into her heart wound.

Once the two young people had gone, Mary went to the window with her cup of tea. She watched them walk into the pulsating, pagan world of Rome. It was as it should be, but it still hurt to see him go. Children do this all the time, trading parents for peers.

She prayed, *Heaven Husband, I don't need a sinking ship to provide an emergency. Jesus walking away from me, down the block with this pretty girl. That's crisis enough. Help me cope.*

She looked down and saw she'd crumbled a dried violet in her hand while she wasn't aware. It hadn't even made a sound while being crushed, but she could smell its fragrance.

Father, you're afoot, speaking healing through Jesus to Claudia, from Claudia to her grandfather, from her grandfather to the world. You and our Son are busy making all things new.

I gave her a hug. She took in comfort for her necessary pain.

24

CLAUDIA

Jesus and I headed the last half block to the House of the Vestals. It was noonish now. Maybe we could turn this into a lunch date. Virgins could be a sideshow.

I asked him, "Do you like hanging out with me?"

We stood at the corner of the House of Vestals, under a weeping willow that made confetti of the light. Jesus' eyes, wild honey on olive heartwood, reflected light my way. I gave him the best bashful smile a brash girl like me could ever hope to muster.

I knew my answer even before he spoke. *This was a fool's folly, seeking specialness with a man I should never have loved.* He would give me holy god-words, something that included me in his affections, along with the whole world.

He didn't crush me with the whole world. Instead, he smiled shyly at me, no covering for his heart, no words. He whispered his fingers over to my cheek. I thought, *all he has to do is brush my face and my ears roar, like when gladiators are loosed at the Coliseum.*

We stood at the House of Vestals' front door and knocked. An older warden opened the door. She wore a white habit, full-length black scapular, and engraved vigilance. She looked Jesus up and down gravely. I read her thoughts for her, just to save her the trouble. Yep, one of the *other* kind. Male. Watch out, ye nuns of Rome!

I asked for Bathenia. Eternal Vigilance herself fingered three knots on the rope around her waist—one each for poverty, chastity, and obedience. Her fingers seemed stuck on the middle one, white-knuckled.

"Miss Bathenia will appear shortly."

We waited. I was wary of sudden sightings. But the dimly lit foyer was cold, empty of spirit sightings as if its ghosts were making appearances elsewhere in the empire, or at work on more pressing concerns. Worry Warden finally came along with the Virgins. She ushered us into a shrunken blizzard-scape, white as a year of Januarys in the Alps.

This drawing room featured four carved chairs with rigid backs, painted snow white, spaced precisely in a square. Each corner of the square room held statuaries of virgins on pedestals. Each pedestal, as well as the marble table, rested on sheepskin rugs of pristine white. A vase of freshly cut white lilies sparkled in a splash of pure, white sun through cut-glass window panes.

Wilhelmina the Warden lurked. I thought, this woman probably wears a chastity belt with a rusted padlock that creaks when she squats to pee.

Bathenia eyed her warden and said, "We're going to show our guests the gardens, Wilhelmina. You watch over us through the windows, please?"

"As you say, Miss Bathenia."

We four made our way to the garden. The air was redolent with the fragrance of white gardenias and snow jasmine. We strolled. I took in Warthenia, the other virgin, from the corner of my eye. She was a striking ash-blonde with a straight nose, high forehead, big breasts, and eyes the color of desert sand in the first light of day. Your basic nightmare.

She favored Jesus with a smile that flickered with a flirt. Ducked her eyes back down—like they'd been discovered playing hooky and needed to be retrieved for a good spanking. I'd personally never heard her speak or even heard of her speaking. I was hopeful. Maybe she'd been de-tongued by a stray icicle blowing through the nunnery.

Jesus wandered off by himself, probably having a heart to heart with the Wind, his Father, angels, or demons. For now, mere people had zero chance of sighting him.

Bathenia bubbled. Words torrented through her lips, waterfalled off her chin. I'd only known her from a distance before father dragged me on his two-year field trip to the maggoty ends of the earth. And now, I was her best friend forever?

Her close-set eyes reminded me of a ferret—blazing, black lumps of coal in danger of spontaneous combustion. She was flat-chested with invisible hips that cradled a potbelly. Her raven hair was the color of two in the morning. Sandaled feet poked out from under her white gown, bony twigs dancing on the end of sycamore saplings. She was all angles and energy, like the Goddess of Anxiety tap-dancing through a holocaust.

She fired-breathed, "Claudia, can you keep a secret?"

She didn't know enough to be afraid of me. I could always tell you both the news *and* gossip—what people had done and how much they'd enjoyed it. "Bathenia, I find secret-keeping onerous. Confidences pour through me like water through a cholera victim."

Bathenia continued her fire-whispering anyway. "I think I might be pregnant, dearest Claudia. Who can fix this for me?"

What now? This would be bad for Rome, losing half its eternal light. How much was half of eternal light, anyhow? Perpetual, spooky twilight?

I gave her what I could, the appearance of listening. I focused on a mole between her eyes. Was that a tiny hair starting to grow out of it? Then I scrunched up my best Sofia-the-Goddess-of-Wisdom face. My earnest effort to fool Bathenia. It wouldn't take much.

Jesus came around a corner. He'd strung together three garlands of gardenias and smelled like a flower shop. He bowed with an elaborate flourish, hung the garlands over our heads. Impossible goodwill, irresistible, beamed out of him. I arranged my lei fetchingly. "Jesus, how do I look?"

He nodded pleasantly, holding his hands out to either side, including all of us. This was not the whole world, but I was already picking through my ruins, rebuilding on the run.

I gestured to him and said to Bathenia, "He'll know better than me what to do."

Warthenia-the-Smitten emitted words: "Trust him, Bath."

Three whole words. Maybe the first three of her life.

Jesus turned to Bathenia. Presence flowed from him, defined him. Didn't *act* wise—was wise, without speaking a word.

Bathenia spewed sideways, so Wilhelmina couldn't read her lips. "We were appointed to bring our symbolic light to the Forum's new theatre on re-opening night for *Psyche*. You were still in Palestine. That was two months and four days ago."

I nodded, impatient. *Get to the point, will you? I hadn't passed any course on patience. Hadn't signed up, even when it was offered.*

Bathenia continued, "Afterwards, we went backstage with our white candles to congratulate the actors, and the rest of the cast occupied Willie and War, singing the play's sad songs for them all over again. Their own special performance."

Bathenia's brow fretted into a knot. "Cupid led me to a dark corner of the backstage. He said, on one knee, 'Vestal, I treasure your flame. You warm me. In fact, you make me all hot.'"

She examined our faces. I disguised my disgust at Cupid's duplicity. Looked at Jesus, and tried to reshape my face into kindness, like his. A mirror would have clearly revealed what a howling disaster *that* was.

Bathenia kept vomiting words, "I have to tell you, he looked pretty hot to me too. I felt a swoon coming on. Anyway, he took me to another backstage room where they kept all the stage props. We closed and locked the door. Quick as a wink my clothes fell off. His did too. He got me against a wall."

She stage-whispered, "We walled."

Bathenia frowned. "And one more thing. I'd put my fire down, you know, while we were walling. The drapes ignited. We burned down the stage's backside. I was *so* embarrassed. My fire leaked."

I looked to Jesus. Bath was giving virginity a bad rep with our local Israeli. Surprisingly, he didn't look offended at all. He asked, "What will happen now?"

Warthenia spoke again. "Buried alive. They'll give her enough food for two or three days and brick her into a crypt—maybe Romeo too, if Bathenia fingers him and they believe her. That's Roman law."

She looked right at Jesus, not at me. "*You* have to do something to save us all."

Jesus' eyes leaked something, maybe sadness. Like he had seen people self-ignite since time out of mind. He looked at Bathenia. "You get to choose your life. What choices do you see here and now?"

Bath started whimpering, suddenly helpless. Warthenia gazed into Jesus' eyes, her eyes sparkling, beseeching. A fresh glow of heavenly pink lit up her cheeks like she'd been dropped off Mount Olympus solely to spread streams of glory out her butt. I looked around. No available lever that I could see to drop her into a snake pit.

Jesus asked me, "Do you think you could intercede for Bathenia with your grandfather? He listens to you."

Bath got on her knees, fingers steepled, clinging to my dress. *How mortifying. Get up, virgin imposter.*

I said, "Best option I can see is a quiet abortion, soon as possible. I can source what you need—birthwort and pennyroyal. Make a tea, drink it. Body'll push the kid out."

Bathenia nodded. "Get me the stuff, quick. Now."

We all looked to Jesus. His lips moved quietly.

God-man is having a chummy little conversation with unseen Beings.

I cleared my throat and poked him with my elbow. "Uh, not meaning to be rude, *but there are actual people out here that might want your attention!*"

Unoffendability leaked from his pores and mixed with a cocktail of moral unfussiness. All would be restored to its place. He turned to Bathenia. "Do you really want my opinion?"

She nodded furiously, impetuously. Her miracle-seeking eyes searched, sucking up any shreds of life-support on the Italian peninsula.

Jesus said, "Bathenia, perhaps we could figure a way together how not to let your fire leak in the future. Let's tell each other truth, kindly. Weave our way into a whole cloth."

Bathenia started to breathe again; her shoulders slipped down to where most humans keep them.

She asked, "What next? Kill the kid?"

Jesus replied, "Live out truth born from our discussion. Don't abort your God-instilled sense of right and wrong." He added, almost as an afterthought, "Whatever you choose to do with this living child, you will always carry that choice. Pray. Become like me. *My* yoke is easy. *My* burden is light."

Bathenia—practicing persistence—asked for a third time, "What should I do?"

Jesus said, "If I were you, I'd pray and fast for three days. Then I'd ask for an appointment with Augustus. Go with me if you like. Be straight up, speak truth. If you're pardoned, you live. If you perish, you perish.[9] Regardless, God will stand with you and work it for good."

She agreed, shakily. We four talked, heads together in the gathering dusk of the garden. We hammered out some kind of friendship from a parfait of layered deception, goodwill, and a mild topping of envy.

25

LEAH

Rabbus and I traveled all night. We had to warn Ben and Liza. I rode on Mercy. Rabbus steadied me. The road beat on me from beneath, and our baby beat on me from within. We arrived just as Crispus was mounting his horse. His evil eye, under a bloody bandana, wandered over us. His left arm dangled, blood oozing from a bandage wrapped around his hand.

Rabbus said, "Looks like you ran sideways into a meat grinder, Crisp."

"Ship sunk from under me. Lucky we'd learned how to swim in Blowfly Lake when we were what, 'bout five?"

Husband nodded.

"Took me five days to wash ashore."

"Well, 'nother close call's coming up the hill right now, Mr. Pirate. Roman cavalry."

"Liza told ya 'bout my crew, did she? She never forgets nothing. Tell yer secrets to Ben—his memory's a sieve."

Rabbus said, "Live long enough, ours will be too. For now, the cave where we hung out as kids, near Eagle's Wings, might be a good place to hang for a few days. Romans are scouring the countryside, looking for pirates. But anybody'll do."

Crispus said. "You figure I'll be safe in *our* cave?"

Husband nodded, "No foreigner will find you there."

A cloud of dust rose out of the south. Crispus' wandering eye held still, dark as a well into nowhere, not even picking up a glint of light. That eye needed signposting, so others wouldn't trip and get lost in there.

Rabbus said, "I've got Rastus' old crowd building houses on the side of my barley fields. Take 'em with you, 'else they'll get hammered. And, Crisp, remember the trap doors."

Crispus blew north on his horse, bleeding arm flapping behind him like he was riding some black chariot at a sharp angle down into hell.

We entered the store, warning Liza of things to come. Ben wandered in from an outhouse visit, a clutch of three speckled eggs in his right hand. Hennery was between here and the toilet. He sniffed his left hand, wrinkled his nose. Looked at his right hand and whooped at a new discovery there, nesting in his fingers.

We were edging Ben out the back door when Tribune Gaius stomped through the front door. Some men followed him while others watered their horses at the village well out front.

Gaius glared at Rabbus. "How'd you beat us up here? A hawk strap you to his wings?"

"When you're a farmer, crops don't wait for you, Tribune. My plantings are young in the field. Sun's scorching. If I didn't walk through the night with my pregnant wife on our mule, barley crop might die. I was askin' Ben 'n Liza here for help. Maybe your men could help too."

Gaius snorted. "Maybe help tack you up on a stick."

He ordered his goons, "Interrogate Smart-Mouth here. Pry open his yap."

I fell at his feet. "Please, Tribune, husband's a good man. I need him, same as Claudia needs a husband."

Gaius flinched at the sound of his daughter's name but paid no mind to my plea. His men dragged Rabbus to the well, stripped his clothes off. Found his throwing knife strapped to his arm—proof of lawlessness.

Gaius weighed his knife. "Get him talking. If he doesn't, use his knife to work on his tongue, or his lady's, if his doesn't start flapping."

Two soldiers lashed husband's hands to one hitching post, feet to another. Stretched him out, face-down, naked. The floggers, one on either side, stepped back on their hind legs, wound up, and cracked their whips down. Skin and muscle peeled away from Rabbus' ribs. The floggers were exact, laying down cross-hatched diagonals.

Time crawled. I burned. Blood spattered. Husband's life flowed into the dirt beneath him while his secrets stayed buried inside him, like a tin box shoved down deep and rusted shut. I wailed—for me, Rabbus, our baby. Liza howled with me. Ben looked puzzled.

Gaius kicked Rabbus after he'd passed out. I saw it, like I was looking through clear mucus. Gaius' right foot reached back and crept forward in slow motion. Husband's body lifted up slow, a foot off the ground, in inches, then flopped down slow, splashing his blood all 'round. My ears had stopped working. I crawled inside a womb where the only beating I could hear was my own heart.

Gaius' face purpled, neck bulged, mouth opened as he leaned over Rabbus. I heard nothing. Me, the one with good ears. Nothing. Soldiers dragged Ben toward the hitchin' posts. His turn for a whuppin'.

His mouth was moving. Suddenly, I could hear again. Ben said, "Why you beating Rabbus? He's the good 'un. Why not Crispus? He's the bad 'un. He left here a few minutes ago."

Gaius stopped yelling at Rabbus, mid-scream. He shook his head, disbelieving his ears. "What did you say, old man?"

"Only what's obvious. Rabbus, good. Crispus, bad. Why you beat the good 'un, not the bad 'un?"

"Where'd he go? Tell me now, and I won't burn your store down."

"You'd do that? It's got stuff in it. Stuff I need. We gotta eat, you know."

"Shut up. Tell me where he is."

"How can I tell you, if I shut up?"

Snow-headed Liza broke in before Gaius strangled her husband. Both were wrinkled sacks of skin, rheumy eyes, composted goodness. Her humpback rose higher than her head. She stood between him and Ben, looking sideways up at the giant soldier who towered over her. She said artlessly, in a prophetic voice, "Young feller, you *do* see beatin' and slicin' folks up will come back on ya? But yur eyes can't see with all that smoke in 'em, bein' as yur heart's burnin' down."

Gaius looked shaken, momentarily. Grabbed her hair with a thick, muscled arm, lifted her off the ground. "Look at me, hag! Where'd this Crispus go? Tell me, and I'll let you and your idiot husband live."

Liza yelled, "Ow! That hurts. Let me go. I'll tell ya."

Gaius dropped her in the dirt. She landed sideways, her leg bent at an awkward angle beneath her. Pain passed through her face. Dust settled. She stood on her one good leg, arm around my shoulder. I dusted off the burlap sack with two armholes she called a dress.

Gaius ordered, "Speak up, woman. You're mumbling." She murmured shreds of dignity over herself and her husband, the same way a mouse chitters when a hawk's shadow is circling overhead. "Crisp came for supplies. Got what he wanted. Headed north, place called Pirate's Cove. 'Bout ten mile north of Sidon. Bunch of 'em got boats there."

"Why didn't you speak before?" Gaius asked.

"You didn't ask *me* nothin'."

"You knew what I wanted. And you watched that piece of crap splatter your front yard. Why didn't you speak?"

"You done stuck fear 'n me. Stripped me to the studs. Couldn't talk. Both Rabbus and Crispus running around here, like it was yesterday. Now they're grown. But like Ben said, one's gone good—the other, bad."

Here was the stumper. Gaius believed her. Maybe it was her honesty. Or Ben's inability to lie. Or my nodding friendship with Claudia. All of that, or none of it.

Tribune mounted his chariot. "Everyone, let's go! We're on the right trail. No time to lose." They all wheeled away in a roiling cloud of red Samaritan dust.

I kneeled over my husband. His backside looked like a butcher's shop. Liza and I put a folded towel under him and then washed his back, butt, and legs. He lay face-down, unconscious. We massaged balm into the raw meat of his body, sat him up between us. Tendered him round and round with strips of linen soaked in wound wart.

Rabbus climbed up through mental haze. "Where'd they go?"

I said, in Liza's hearing, "Liza told 'em Crispus was headed north toward Sidon. They galloped toward our farm, my love."

Ben came 'round. "Those men were mean. They beat you bad, Rabbus. An' you be the good 'un."

Rabbus smiled thin through a moan. "Ben, God skinned me 'n I deserved it."

Ben stood speechless, scratching his head. Not the boy he knew. Rabbus spoke of a God I didn't know. Jesus' Father forgave and forgot, 'cause of Jesus, somehow. Gaius worshipped angry gods of different stripes, gods of terror. He'd become like the gods he worshipped. I whispered prayers into the wind for husband and one for Gaius.

26

CRISPUS

I spurred my nag toward Rabbus' homestead, cuttin' through plowed, red fields, dust flying behind me like the world were catchin' fire. Sun hung low, drippin' red, on the rag. Looked at my hand. Nutin' there but drippin' red. It were a red day.

I remembered the first red splashed on me. Rome balanced little sister up there on the ramparts. Sun hitting her blond hair like licks of fire. I scrabbled for her. Our fingers almost reached. Then the soldiers tossed her over the wall. Bunch of guys at the bottom caught her on their spear tips. Half-dozen holes in her spouted red.

Rome laughed. They taught us pagans a lesson. Burned ma alive. Bent pa over, skewered him with a pike pole from ass to neck. Took him a few days to die, sitting on his pike 'n me chained to his leg, face to face. I beat the ground with my head, eye going wonky red when a bitty stick flew up and stuck in it. Eye's stayed red, still wonky.

Red fire, red sister, red stake poking outta pa, red Roman uniforms. Like the Good Book says, Isaiah and 53, I were a man of sorrows soaked in grief. [10] Man can only take so much of that 'fore wailing red turned to rage red, *don't cha know?*

I rounded a bend, and there wuz Rabbus' bunch, hammering sticks into pathetic shacks. Dwarf Esau knew me 'fore Sebastos fell to the Romans. They clipped his pa too.

He yelled, "Hey, Crisp! Where ya been?"

I screamed at 'em all, "Gotta move, now! Romans coming. Gonna crucify *all* of us. We can stop it if we act now!"

I lit their eyes on fire. Their "Jesus-pie-in-the-sky-by-and-by" were tossed seed, hain't yet rooted. Only thing grew in this ground were rocks 'n killin'. They rounded up their huntin' stuff. We melted into the woods.

Hustled past where those guys had buried them ear necklaces, dug 'em up real quick, put 'em on. Half of us hid on each side of the narrow pass, high up. Almost like we was the ones on Sebaste's ramparts, us looking down on Rome now. *Ha! Tables turned, wops. I wuz all ears 'n Satan filled 'em both, spun me up.*

The road below us were pitted as hell's gates. Gaius' horses had to slow down, men had to slow down, chariots had to slow down. Perfect slow-down for a show-down, right before sun-down.

Rabbus' pa were an engineer type. He made these front and backdoor traps long time back. Piled boulders high on the pass tops, either side, tangled 'em all up with brush. Timbers levered boulders, real delicate like. Dominoes ready to fall. Quick jump 'n thump'd roll these rocks—enough to bury the pass, 'n whatever wuz in it.

Ground shook. Hoofbeats, creak of chariots comin' on, clackity-clack, bumpity-clunk, comin' on. Hundred or so. Roman-red thumpin' fast as they could to Squash Central. *All them bodies, not travelin' much longer with their souls. Might miss each other, the one simmerin' in hell and the other ground into dust.*

Familiar voice, real *ed-u-cated-like*. "Quick now! Whoever nails Crispus' ass gets a bonus! Ai-yaaa!"

The crowd of mothers' sons trotted double-time, hell-bent for leather, coming on, coming on, slowing down now. Red road risin' real purdy ta meet 'em. All of 'em tucked inside the pass now, fore and aft.

I raised my arm. Esau jumped his tree trunk tip-lever. I wuz ready to jump too, smack on. *But, hold on, now, hold on!* Wounded squirrel down there, trapped 'neath the beam. I stooped over, let that poor little feller go. Prince's own precious creature.

He scurried away. I jumped the tip-beam. Boulders rained down, gathering speed, crushing anything down there, soundin' sweet. Heads splittin' like rotten melons, like ol' *Ouroboros* splittin' in two. Crackity-split! Men and horses a-screamin'. Bones shatterin' like twigs. Snap, crackle, pop—skull-crack dead, most of 'em.

Dust cleared. Clambered down. Lookin' for live 'uns. Loved cuttin' them throats. Long, slow slices, ear to ear—that wuz fun. Addin' the nearly departed to the dearly departed, *don't ya know?*

Ah yahh! Here's a live 'un! Almost all covered over. Tipped chariot saved him from getting whack-ass smushed. Man's legs and guts was crushed, but he needed some tender, lovin' care from me. Left eye, still open; right eye, slammed shut. Looked a'feard. Well, should be. *This ain't the charity brigade, wop.*

I climbed down over rocks, bent down, sliced right below his left ear, pushed in the blade with a twist. But, hold on! I recognized 'im, I did! Dropped the wanderin' eye razz-ma-tazz. Tribune Gaius 'n me wuz having us a meet-up. *Woo-hoo, baba-loo!*

His one eye beggin', but cat got 'is tongue.

Told him, "Well, boy-howdy! Here's yur stupid, eye-rollin' wench operator with the slippery-shackle. At yo' service, Tribbie, sir!"

A tear dripped out of his one good eye. He looked straight up at the sky, face muscles a-twitching.

"Heard ya offerin' a bonus fer me, jus' a minute ago. Well, guess what? *I be yo' bonus!*"

I pushed the knife in a little deeper, leaned into his face, and gave him my best smile. Ah, true ain't it? Ya never know how much badness be packed in a man till you watch him smile. Badness slopped clean over 'im.

Tribbie squinched that one eye shut.

I teased 'im a tad. Cut around the bulgin', pulsin' blue tube in his neck. Didn't wanta make it spurt—nooo, no, *not yet.* Cut a little muscle here an' there instead, all around it, probin' an' a pushin'. Practicin' for my next career as a neck surgeon, *don't cha know?*

He screamed. *Yeah, baby, let 'er rip. Let me hear yo' best song!*

I said, "Probably don't know wuz me who offed your boy on that big ol' ship. He'd come out to kill him some bad 'uns. Well, surprise, surprise! Wuz me who shot a bolt smack into his chest. Squealed like a littl' girl, sissified—just like his pa right now. My fire cooked his face. So much fun seein' his skin peel off and get all … Crisp!"

Trib hardly breathed.

"Watched him jump out on his hi 'n mighty big-boy porch. Oops, sucker'd gone missing! Screamed till he hit—glug, glug, glug. Like father, like son. Neither one a youse looking' 'fore you leaped."

His one good eye popped open, glaring at me.

I scooped it out with my blade. "Whoops, got a wandering eye, do ya? Well, well, well! Must be an idjiat." I popped his eye in my mouth, chomped down with my eye-teeth. Might even improve my seein'. Leaned over close. Right next ta his good ear, so he could hear me chomp, squish, swall'er. Yep, fearsome hungry.

In between chewing, I said, "An' it were me who tapped little wedges in the hull of that big ol' ship—wedges Stupid-You didn't see. Split that whole ship in two, two itty-bitty wedges."

He was shaking, snot running out his nose.

I said, "Tribune, know what comes next? I'm gonna help clear yur mind—saw your head off, scoop them bitty blobs of brain outta ya, boil 'em up in a viper's stew, and eat'em fur din-din. Use your skull for a beer stein. Like Tribune at Sebastos did with *my* pa's head, after he pushed him, ass down, real slow on a pointy stake."

Trib said, "you'll pay with your life. Rome *will* have her vengeance."

"Yup, yup, yup. Vengeance being had all right. All ready now, ready, *reallly*? Count of three. Here it cums—one, two, three."

I worked with 'im real gentle like, cuttin' nice 'n slow, right through gristle and neck bone. He rattled out his last breath too soon, crapped his drawers. Smelled like Rome.

Hawked out a big gob, I did, right 'n 'is mouth. Sat with his head in m' lap for a while, feelin' all sweet 'n happy, bouncing his big head up and down on my lap.

Whacked off 'bout then—his left ear. Held it high, high 'nough ta hear the sound of revenge. Gaius' blood ran off my beard, dripping down my shirt.

Flashed on the only love of my life. Dumped me. Working on her fourth husband now, my very own Samaritan darlin'. Last I saw of her wuz by our village well, high noon, all by 'erself. Well, gonna pay 'er a visit real soon.

Looked around and got surprised. Rastus' boys were lookin' at me all twitchy, like they wuz better 'n me, or somptin'. I heard a voice like mine, real hateful and purdy, *pay that trash no mind.*

Me 'n Satan howled, danced a jig, holdin' Gaius' head up, jus' like David held Goliath's head up, or Samuel held up Agag's head.[11] Got high, we did—yippin' howls. Power streamin' through me, *both* arms holding my sacrifice high. Felt like 'xploshuns 'n earthquakes goin' off in my head.

"You boys don't even know the scripture, do ya? Prince hates all them holier and mightier-than-thou's. Judges 'n prophets be slicing up invaders 'n dominators since before dirt. Take yur lessuns in hatin' from me. I absolutely adore hatin'. Don't make demands like lovin' does. Don't make yur guts all squishy. Hate's my Hero."

They stared at me 'n Satan, who just done talked through my chops. I switched to practical stuff they could wrap their bitty ol' brains around. 'Okay, boys, work needs a-doin'. All the bodies, men and horses, an' that chariot—get' em put 'em down deep off the road. Feather out the trail. Leave everything like our Prince's kept it, pure dirt. Haul them rocks back to the top, tip-levers in place. Never know when we'll a good bushwhack all over again."

27

CLAUDIA

The setting sun was an unusual fusion of reds—pinks, scarlets, mauves, and magentas. They all bled together, dripped into the amphitheater below us to the west—an artist's palette made of reds.

I'd just left my bedroom suite. My slave girl had taken special care with my makeup, perfume, and dress. I'd told her, "Mother says, 'tell your maid to pluck your eyebrows. Can't have people confusing you with a caterpillar, dear.'"

She rolled her eyes but still plucked my eyebrows like a chicken. She used a killer kohl eyeliner afterward. The vermillion matched the sunset.

I stood in the outside courtyard of the palace on Palatine Hill. Here I was, dressed in my slinky black satin evening dress, waiting for Jesus to go with our families and see *Psyche*. Our very first formal evening date.

Out of the blue, a bolt of hot pain hit my neck, doubled me over, spreading from the left side of my throat and my left eye. Another crushing pain in my guts, like a tiger clawing and eating. If this was nerves, I was totally screwed. If not, I was dying.

Jesus ran over to me and sat cross-legged beside me. I rolled on my side and flopped my head in his lap.

He said, "Point to where it hurts." I grabbed my throat, moaned. Best I could do.

Mother and grandparents came through the palace door. Grandpa ran and knelt next to me. Worry and fear tangled in his eyes. I didn't even have to borrow Jesus' eyes to see them. This must be the thin place where Jesus lives all the time, where gods poked pain or pleasure into people.

Others gathered. I examined their ankles, heard their voices. Grandpa put his hands on my head. "What's the pain, Claudia?"

I rocked back and forth, head still cradled in Jesus' lap. Landslide of fear avalanched, random thoughts crashing down, crushing me. The vision flicked off and on and seemed to come from a lighthouse just inside my head.

Jesus shifted his weight and answered Grandpa, "Your granddaughter is seeing into the spirit world. Dim, narrow passage, and Death's in it."

I screamed, "Yes!"

Jesus said to Grandpa, "Someone just died. She's feeling his passing like it was her own."

Jesus put one of grandpa's hands lightly on the left side of my throat, the other over my left eye. He then put his hands over grandpa's hands. *How did he know that's where I hurt?*

He mumbled something into the wind, not to Grandpa, but maybe to *his* Father.

Soothing came into me, passing from his hands through Grandpa's hands into my body. I squinted up at Grandpa. His eyes rounded. My pain eased. Grandpa's hands stopped shaking. Grandpa looked at his hands, me, Jesus.

Jesus took his hands off of grandpa's hands, placed them between my shoulders. Gently pressed me up, sat me face-to-face with him. Grandpa's face hovered in the periphery of my vision, inches away. Mother stood just behind him.

Jesus' gaze melted into mine and our hearts' meld held. *Totally scary how he gathered together brokenness, darkness, and whatever else yielded to his pressure.*

Jesus swallowed hard. He said, "Your father died a few minutes ago, Samaria. Father told me, through Windy. I'm so sorry."

I bone-felt what he spirited into the moment. A mysterious truth-knowing, not like history or algebra, but knowing all the same. My brain fog started to clear.

Mother overheard Jesus' words. Her mouth pruned. She peered at me, face stony, "Gaius was devoted to duty, to war, and to *you*. His talent for killing included our marriage. Every day I was married to him, I wanted to walk into the sea."

She paused, jaw working. I closed my eyes before she said, "I'm glad he's gone. I'm putting him behind me, my little actress. Life will be far easier now."

Her ice pick stabbed me in the neck—same spot as before, but with cold, not hot. I raised my hand to neck to see if I was pumping blood. Nothing that an ordinary person could see.

I kept my eyes closed to her and looked to Jesus. I remembered how we both saw Joe-the-Jew die. Now, another way, we experienced *my* father's death and mother's attack. He saw. I felt. What he saw in spirit, my body felt. More complete together than alone.

I moved through deep waters, Jesus on one side and Grandpa on the other. Both kept me afloat in this fast-moving current of icy cold mixing with burning hot.

I said to Jesus, "Take me with you. I'm serious. I'll die without you."

28

WINDY

The crowds roared their love and approval when Augustus walked in. They stomped their feet, chanting, "Hail, Caesar!" The press of their adulation was overwhelming, intoxicating. Jesus felt the buzz.

The Vestal Virgins sat to Jesus' right; Claudia, on his left. Augustus, his wife and three daughters, all sat in the top row behind them. Jesus' family sat on the row below him, except John. When they left home, John was babysitting four-year-old Deborah, glad to be away from the press of people. Deborah was fond of muddy cats and questions no one could answer. The two were cutting out paper dolls, coloring them, and pasting them on a river baptism scene while she chattered on, and John scratched his head.

Bodyguards stood facing out, all around the elevated god-box. Jesus sat in this well-guarded space, in the middle of the god-box. He asked Father, *Aren't pedestals also prisons—like any other small, enclosed space?* He saw a cloud in the night sky, shaped like a big thumb pointing up, floating sky-high.

Jesus shook himself back into the theatre. The play itself threatened to yank him out of his seat and tumble him down to the stage. He said to Me, *A living parable! Maybe I should use parables when I explain stuff about Father to people?*

I tingled his spine, squeezed a 'yes' into his hand: *You will not teach at all without using parables, Son.1211* I moved Jesus' attention from the play to the people beside him. *Consider Claudia and Bathenia. Both are tunneling into terror, terribly unsure of their footing. Pay attention to these people right now. We'll get to parables later.*

Son immediately leaned down and whispered in his mother's ear, "Claudia's father was murdered an hour ago." Mary teared up, reached back, and gave Claudia her own black shawl. Claudia wrapped it around her head and rested on Jesus' shoulder.

The curtain lifted. Claudia's mentor from the palace academy appeared in the Psyche's role, reclining next to Cupid, her lover. Torches and candles surrounded both actors. Psyche was clothed from the waist down.

Her enormous green eyes, the color of ocean lagoons, peered at her lover over parted lips, like the folded wings of mating turtledoves. She reclined on emerald-colored grass, strumming a lyre and singing. Her song, airborne honey, flowed to her lover. Psyche soprano'd soulfully, and Cupid echoed back a breathy antiphonal. His only covering was a string loin cloth.

Cupid's mother, Venus, sat atop a wall, overlooking the lovers. Her gaze swiveled between Psyche and her cracked mirror. Gobs of green paint bled off her emerald dress, dripping down the wall. Both lovers were blind to her influence.

Up high in the god-box, Jesus leaned forward, elbows on knees, absorbed in the play. Claudia and Bathenia, on either side of him, were oblivious to the play. Tears dripped off the tip of Bathenia's nose. One hit her eternal flame straight on and put it out. Warthenia leaned over and lit her up again.

The pit orchestra wailed out a love song in a minor chord, alerting the audience to oncoming tragedy. The Greek chorus of ten singers, stage left, danced and chanted the truth of this scene with an apocalyptic rap,

"Jealous mother hovers.
Her shadow drenches lovers.
Lust-fires live to lie.
Who will love before they die?"

Lightning bolts flashed. Thunder crackled, and a cloud of white smoke covered the stage. Stagehands, in elegant black garb, blew out all flames. Fan-beaters chased away the smoke. Total blackness, scurry of departing feet.

After some time, the stagehands reappeared around the stage's perimeter, lit torches in hand, but now dressed in rags. Psyche also reappeared in this new light, now clothed in burlap, hair askew, tears streaking her face. She wandered left and right across the stage in a miasma of abandonment. She bumped into shadowy Venus, now dressed in black silk. Sharp, pointy collar surrounded the goddess' neck, half-covering her chicken-neck wattles.

Jesus mused, *wait a minute. Goddesses aren't supposed to age, huh? What's the meaning here?*

Venus challenged Psyche, "How dare you, *a mortal,* try to seduce my son, *a god! Anyone* knows he is faithful only to love itself. He discards lovers, like bones from a boar, after he's done feasting. Why bore him, mortal?"

Psyche bowed down to the ground and touched the hem of Venus' dress, "I'll do anything to wed your son!"

Venus filed her bright, pink nails and adopted an *oh-so-bored* look of fey insouciance. "You, mortal, age. Worry etches your face. You will totter into a nursing home before I choose my next lover. And, besides, a year or so of earth time is usually quite sufficient to cure marital affection."

She paused, appeared to reconsider, "However if you accomplish four, small tasks, I'll *consider* allowing you to marry Cupid since he's so fond of you in this moment. Come with me, wench!"

A submissive Psyche dragged herself after Venus. They came to a warehouse on the other end of the stage. Venus waved her arms. The front wall of the warehouse magically blew off its hinges. All manner of seeds exploded up and out—magenta, lemon yellow, indigo blue, lima-bean green, funeral white, wispy tans; big and little, flat and fat, speckled and solid—all of them flew, chaotic, onto the stage and over the first few rows of a gleeful audience.

Venus ordered, "Sort these piles by morning. Like with like. All of them, everyone; no odd seed in another's pile—and don't think you can get away with cheating. I can spot a stray seed from miles away." She waved her arms and vanished in a cloud of light, green mist.

Psyche wandered through the stacks of seeds and burst into tears, completely undone. She dived into a pile of seeds and disappeared from view, all of her courage in seed form. Howls of grief emerged from under the seed stack.

Unseen by wailing Psyche, an army of ants crawled out of the cracks in the ground. These synchronized seed sorters seemed to randomly switch directions but ordered piles magically grew all around slumped

Psyche. She sat cross-legged, seeds sloughing off her in organized clumps. Overwhelmed, Psyche realized at last what they had done for her. Her grateful tears bubbled up and out, bathing her low friends in her salty flow.

The Greek Chorus once again popped up, chanted the truth of this first act,

"Go slow, go low.
Close to earth, humbly grow."

I said to Son, *Claudia, unconscious, like Psyche, would marry up if she could—even while drenched in death. Her loss, ambiguous, has no closure. Help her live with grief, not revenge it or sleep through it.*

Mary had also heard My voice. She reached around, touched Claudia's leg, and whispered, "What a wonderful parable. Accept help from the lowly when neither life nor death makes sense."

Claudia stared back and forth at Jesus and his mother. Darkness filled her eyes, slammed her skull, ripping any clarity of thought, and throwing it to the wind. Somewhere, someone was figuring out how to push back Black Grief's cowl, but Claudia, for now, nestled in Mary's covering. I also caught her darkness and gave what was unbearable to Son.

He said, "Let me stay with you in this dark fire and ice, so you can bear it."

She didn't understand all his words but got his kindness. She put her head back down on his shoulder. Held on. Bathenia, on his other side, waggled her bent head back and forth in slow motion over her candle, fire almost leaking into her hair, but not quite.

Jesus settled himself between Claudia's icy fire from within and Bathenia's frail fire from without. Both flames singed him. Slow sweat rolled off his cheeks, over his lips, and off his chin. This play was more than he bargained for—wheels within wheels, on stage and off, burned and froze, burned and froze.

29

SLOW

I treaded the potter's wheel, working alone. Everyone else was off for the day, using the profits from our shop to feed homeless migrants. A tall candle holder, made from my own crush, was taking shape. It rose, a shiny, tilting pillar. Amazing what my hands could do with slippery clay. My hands pressed on the pillar, watched it grow tall. I made a rim around the top.

While I worked on clay, moods worked on me. A thought flickered, *this clay easily falls down and rises again. Why can't I?* This crumbled clay, *all my me's*, couldn't yet figure out a path to peace. Fragile and Escape hated the beds Harlot had made them lie in. Harlot resented Cutter scarring her body. Shame organized civil wars between them all when I wasn't looking.

Jesus had promised I'd come together. But he didn't say when. Maybe after I died. After all, I'd been reading Torah, marital scrolls Laz brought to me, and stuff written by holy men on how to grow up. None of that made any sense or any difference. Words *in*formed me, but they didn't form me. I thought wrong thoughts, a lot, but so what? I didn't want to *think* right. I wanted to *do right*.

I felt drifty, for the most part, a pigment of my own imagination. I made colorful, glazed pots with my own hands, not my head. All these fractured, mental-me's felt like cracked seeds.

Abuse memories seeded my imagination. Shame exploded them in a hot wash that made my face get blotchy red. My pubic hair prickled. These were my 'tell's.' When I didn't honor my wounds, I became them. When I didn't manage my moods, they managed me. When Laz was overly excited during Shabbat sex, Escape ran screaming from the room, without benefit of a door.

Laz bolted into the workshop with a cup of my favorite tea, still steaming.

I said, "Hey, buster, you're interrupting a private bitch session between me and my selves."

He said, "Talk to *me*, not your you's, Moody Blues."

"I have no words for you. My feelings are in seed form. The words I don't have, I don't have. My body holds my moods hostage, and my mind has nothing good to say."

He got down on his knees and hugged me. "For a woman with no words, you just said a *lot*." An adoring smile spread from ear to ear, making his auburn beard tilt 'n roll, like it was sailing on a stormy sea.

Outside, I grumped. Inside something shifted. He accepted, didn't fix. He knelt and adored, didn't advise, or quote scripture. I let his love seep in, maybe for the first time. My skin, not my head, felt loved. Today, now, he loved all my broken me's, even when I didn't.

I scooped up the wet pillar of clay on my wheel, pulled him to his feet, stripped, and mudded him head to toe. I smeared mud all over his face and beard. Plus, an extra. I made a halo for his angel head, slanting it off to one side.

Then I put my finger to his mouth, shushing Mr. Too-Many-Words. I sent Cutter and Fragile in a corner to cut out paper dolls. Harlot did a striptease. I might have helped. We stripped, mudded my whole body, and made devil's horns to fit inside his halo.

I lowered him onto his back, looked down at the candlestick that had grown tall again. I straddled him, laughed a wicked little laugh, danced in place, lower and lower, joining. Nailed his mouth to mine. Became a force of nature. The potter's floor thrust and churned, chaotic, dizzy. Shreds of color floated up, hot reds and purples, mixed with ripples of laughter between my legs.

Years later, I still smile to myself about that day. *That's the time we made our son, and I didn't kill him with morning-after tea.*

My body, all by herself, sorted Laz's seed. People like me sometimes don't need words. Our acts speak for us.

30

JESUS

Venus reappeared on stage for the second act dressed in a slitted, golden lamé evening gown, looking divine. She filed her carmine-colored nails and looked out over the audience. "I have to dress well for my lover—since I undress so often."

She then noticed all the piles of sorted seeds. Her mood changed in a flash. She stomped around the stage. "None of Cupid's rutters have routed me like this!"

She spotted Psyche entering at stage left and rearranged her dour features, pouring false praise like spoiled milk over Psyche. "Dear, dear, lovely Psyche. Well done! Now we must go on to our next task."

She led Psyche through creeping stage fog till they emerged out of it, both of them standing side by side next to a fenced-in flock of fierce, golden rams. These rams butted and ripped one another, jousting in a field of grass lined with huisache trees. The tangled thorns on these trees made a thick hedge.

Venus held in her left hand an enormous straw basket, woven with bright-orpiment wheat sheaves. Her right hand gestured toward the vicious sun-rams. "My dear Psyche, wander among the rams. Fill this basket with golden fleece by morning. Pack it down tight enough to weave a blanket for my lover, Ares. Vulcan, my husband, is out once again, cavorting with nymphs."

Venus flounced offstage, leaving the earthling alone. For the second time, in less than an hour, Psyche imploded with fear. She ran toward the riverbank at stage-back, away from the horny rams—away, away, toward a fast-moving river, apparently intent on drowning.

At this moment, the hollow, flexible river reeds came to her aid. They spoke to her in punchy bits of counsel:

"Night cools hotheaded fools;
Hope steeps when rage sleeps.
Forego death's greed; gather your need.
Walk the edges; harvest hedges."

Psyche heeded their counsel and waited till dark. She followed her feet in the twilight, picking shreds of golden wool from the hedge's thorns while staying clear of the raging rams.

Torches gradually dimmed and brightened once again, signaling a new day. Psyche brought a pressed-down, shaken-together basket of shimmering, fleecy gold and laid it at the feet of sleeping Venus. No more or less than what was required. She left, quietly.

The goddess awoke. Psyche was not to be seen anywhere. Venus stood and saw the basket full of golden wool. She fingered what she'd found, imperiously, and stomped offstage, yelling at the audience over her shoulder, "Who in Hades is helping this *ewe* of little brain?"

Windy whispered in my ear, *the wise woman wins by not showing up for a show-down—with rageful males or envious females.*

31

LEAH

We'd harvested our first barley crop and were planting another crop of late summer maize. I dropped seeds in Rabbus' furrow, as he had done in mine almost nine months ago. The maize harvest was far off; baby harvest, soon.

Cyrena worked alongside me. She'd taken a break from Jericho and Cy. "Need a few days to cool off, 'fore I kill that man." She trailed back of me, left hand on my shoulder. I'd say, "rock," and she'd pick up what Rabbus had riven from the ground, drop it in her back-basket. Sweat soaked her forehead cinching-strap. This woman was a workhorse. When I tired, she let me rest against her steady, beating heart.

We dry mortared our stumbling blocks into an altar on the eastern boundary facing Jerusalem. This waist-high wall had become our kneeling place, a space that bridged God and us, we and ourselves. Thorny vines twined in and out of the rocks. The rocks seemed like living stones, each nestling into the curves of another. On top of the altar, I'd fashioned a circle of thorns from two opposing vines.

I'd learned about the value of thorny boundaries from Rabbus. He'd mapped out his limits with clear eyes, knew each hillock and stump inside himself, knew who he was, and who he wasn't. He didn't talk about boundaries. He lived them. He was the place I stood when my feet were sore.

Our ex-lepers shared our one pit-fire for roasting fresh game, one iron kettle for soups and stews, one oven for baking bread, one well for drinking and washing, and one outhouse, downhill from our spring. They banged boards into houses easier than they built a home of belonging. Belonging happened only in fits and starts—three steps forward and a couple back.

Build a wall, break into a fistfight. We all struggled to get below common-enemy friendships into a firm, common faith in God.

Cyrena wasn't much different than these men. "Cy is impossible. Grumblin's an art form with him. He sighs contentment only after sex or silence. I tell him, 'Sex looks fire-red; silence, snow-white. I'll burn or freeze to death with you, Cy.'

"He don't know what to say."

I didn't either. Turned and hugged her. She wiped away some tears and told me, "Your hugs, they be golden."

Mid-morning, I looked up, saw a silhouette of a man on horseback. I said to Rabbus, "That who I think it is?" He nodded once, hardly more 'n a twitch.

The men all stared at Crispus. They'd recovered from killing Gaius' group of soldiers—but not from watching Crispus boil Gaius' skull and suck down the stewed brains.

Crispus bounced along with Gaius' skull jouncing on his belt. When I looked at him and his two skulls, my head suddenly felt poorly anchored to my neck.

Crispus jeered, "Come join me, men, not him. We'll burn Rome's ships to ash."

Ishmael, the Ammonite, studied his bare toe and dug it into the soil next to a tender shoot of early maize. His slow smile broke open like a comb of honey once a bear had got its claws in it. "Hey, Crisp, hain't finished murdering all them who don't like your brand of peace? That neighbor you luv to hate? Kinda stupid to burn yur neighbor's house down when common walls be holdin' ya up, *don't ya know?*"

"Nah." Crispus waved at the open hills all around. "Plenty of space to light fires. 'Sides, too much rage burnin' me up. Fires a-fixin' ta bust outta me anytime, here a fire, there a fire, little fires all over." He spurred his nag into the woods at the edge of our field, heading down toward Shechem.

Rabbus said, "Good to see his back."

I agreed. "Crispus isn't ready to *think* about changing—much less changing. He's untamed rage on the hoof."

Ishmael squinted into the sun. "This you bein' a prophetess, or you jus' bein' you, Leah?"

"Mixes together. 'Rightness' feels bone-bred when God's using my mouth. God talks to and through anyone who loves him. Act on the itty-bitty bit of God you know, and you'll get more."

About this time, I felt ill again. I heard the sound of hoofbeats and looked over my shoulder. Crispus had galloped back up the same trail he'd trotted down. He yelled, real excited, "I'd put it at two! Two centuries, Roman red, comin' up-trail from Shechem. 'Bout five hours off, them bein' way down-valley. We ken kill 'em all using the back door!"

I closed my eyes, resisted his blood-lust seduction. I whispered to Rabbus, "Not sure 'bout this, but I got an idea inkling, on the way to being sure."

I told him a story I'd read from the prophets.[12] Rabbus gave orders. Men took an hour to load up stuff. Three ex-lepers, leading Mercy and Goodness, trotted double-time down the trail into the teeth of their enemy.

Crispus was *not* happy. He stomped around in a circle, middle of our field. Then he circled our camp, poked his head into our stuff. Both eyes bugged out like someone'd stuck slivers of poisonwood in each eye. Neck looked hard, like a body could break a shovel on it. His face was tight enough to require letting out, just to make space for all his piss 'n vinegar. He spit on the ground, took off to the hills, alone.

Rabbus and another guy got a ram from our flock. They caught his horns in the circles of thorns on our altar, cut his throat, and set him on fire. We all got on our knees, burning inside while he burned topside. I'd hacked away the ram's thorny crown and put it on my own head. Felt like the right thing to do. My head, neck, and body felt as one.

I laid my forehead on the ground, arms stretched straight in front of my head, like a child praying before her father. The ground felt like music was buried under it. My body tingled, hummed with the vibration.

The men put their heads on the ground, looking over sideways towards me. Cyrena knelt flat next to me, touched my head, and let out an 'ouch' when she felt the thorns. She knob-kneed a few inches away and arranged her head in the dirt.

I begged God for our lives. I called on God as my altar rock. The men also broke into begging. Rabbus took my circle of thorns and had a turn with it on *his* head.

Once he'd taken my crown, I laid my skull down sideways for a long time, ear to the ground, tears hitting hard ground. I felt something like ground-weep rising to join my tears, a stream of hope rising up to water my roots that tendered down.[13]

Rabbus passed the crown round the circle. Each man wanted to wear it for some weird reason. We all did, blood dripping from our foreheads into ground where head met dirt. I sat up, took dust from the field, and baptized my bloody head, sprinkling it with earth. They did as well. I earth-baptized Cyrena. The field in this mid-afternoon heat trembled, fused with radiance. Wind sang an anthem in the thorny hedge.

We all stood and went back to work. Our lives were handfuls of squeezed sand in Rome's clenched fist.

I got tired with that small line of thinking. Lay down, looked up to see what God was doing. Windy blew clouds over our field in ranks—puffy cumulus down low, a darker layer of sprawling raincloud shaped like a spear in between, and then a skittering of cirrus. Miracles blew and brewed, minute by minute.

The heat of the day passed in this way. Late afternoon, the ground began to shake. Sound of heavy hoofs, the clank of brass jackets, on the move. Roman red marched out of the forest. Wary legionnaires prodded our men and mules on the tips of their spears toward where we all stood before the altar. These battle-hardened soldiers shaped themselves in a rough square around their commander. All of them faced outwards, eyes alert, helmeted heads swiveling.

The commander shouted, "Com-panyy, halt!"

Rabbus and I held hands. This man would hand us life or death. Ex-lepers circled us. Rabbus motioned with his hand. We all dropped to our knees, our small circle inside their larger one. Sun back-lit the altar and the hedges.

Rabbus said, "Commander, we're honored by your visit. My men brought wine, raisin cakes, dates, and loaves of honeyed barley to ease your journey. We have fresh lamb for your men to eat this evening."

A pregnant silence followed. *Pregnant with murder or mercy? I didn't know.*

The commander's insignia was foreign to me. One of his officers approached and addressed him as "Imperial Tiberius." Gave him a situation report.

The commander looked middle-aged, upwards of forty. Samaritan dust had bedded down in the furrows on his eyebrow ridge, over close-set brown eyes. They seemed to seek safety under the ridge of his brow. His jaws clenched and released, moving the skin of his acne-scarred face, like worms were crawling around in there.

Imperial Tiberius spoke in a stilted, formal tone that concealed his intentions rather than making them plain. His words came out slowly, stilted, "We're entranced by your offer, sir and madam. It soothes our invective and spurs our desire for further knowledge. Roman justice will be executed forthwith, summarily, rest assured."

I desperately tried to decode what he'd said.

Rabbus motioned over his shoulder. "Commander, our quarters are yours. Please billet your men in our home and house of worship for the night. Your servants will sleep under the stars."

Imperial Tiberius remained silent. Windy intoned, *Rome's next emperor tastes these words and tests for bitter or sweet.* I let out a sigh, gaining Spirit.

Tiberius leveled a steady gaze at my husband, then at my face and tummy, then at blind Cyrena, our rag-tag bunch with bleeding brows, then at the crown of thorns at my feet. His thin slit of a mouth softened. Lips went from compressed white to almost pink.

He said, "Today we will reconnoiter. Our persons harbor adamancy not dissimilar to an obstinacy of quadrupeds. Pertinent conclusions regarding tactical exploratories await. Our envisagement delineates on the morrow."

Huh? What in the world?

I collapsed on the ground, my head falling into the circlet of thorns. The insides of my head and womb felt like Vulcan's hammer was beating on them. Tears and blood hit dust beneath me like slow rain. Baby kicked bladder. Body leaked pee. I felt eyes on me—this bleeding, leaking, crying woman, on her knees, with dirt on her thorny head.

I looked toward Chariot Man. I hoped his words meant he wasn't going to kill us. Even while I prayed, peed, and hoped, a quick flash of reflected light came and went behind Tiberius' silhouetted head in the western hills.

Crispus had poked out from behind a tree on hillside, spear blade and skull catching light. Just as quickly, he disappeared.

That feral goat, caught in the thorny thicket of his own rage, waggled back into the wild. He and we got better than we deserved that day from our herd of Roman rams.

32

WINDY

The third scene opened. As the curtain rose, Psyche sat alone, high on the edge of a cliff. She craned her head, right hand shading her eyes. A river ran through a valley far below. Snow-capped mountains blued the horizon beyond.

Venus, dressed in a fuchsia silk gown, sauntered onstage and favored Psyche with a half-smile. "My third task, mortal. Go to that snow-capped blue mountain yonder, beyond the river and valley."

She pointed vaguely off into the distance. "Fill this one-of-a-kind crystal goblet. Fill it from a waterfall of forgetfulness that flows from a secret spring in a hidden, hanging valley beyond the mountain. Bring it back before dawn. Don't break this goblet, or you're done."

She sniffed and carelessly tossed Psyche the chalice. Psyche caught it with both hands, amazingly. Venus raised her eyebrow, blew a kiss over her shoulder, and sashayed back into her palace.

Psyche, predictably, felt undone. She staggered along the edge of the cliff, teetering on the brink. Her arms fluttered from her torso, her cloak flowing behind her in the wind. She closed her eyes to this cruel world and let go, falling to her death. A passing eagle, swooping up from below, caught her in mid-fall.

Both bird and Psyche flew up, up, into the blue dome of the stage's ceiling. Psyche melded with her rescuer, clawing her fingers into his feathers. She yelled, loud enough for even those in the god-box to hear, "Oh, I see a waterfall on the side of that mountain!"

The eagle dived straight through the waterfall. When Psyche turned her head and opened her mouth, water filled her mouth and her goblet. She promptly forgot her hopeless helplessness.

The eagle dropped Psyche back onto the stage, where she handed the full goblet to Venus. The goddess, looking mystified, sipped from the cup absently. She immediately forgot to be puzzled or angry.

The Greek Chorus popped up, floating their feet in perfect synchrony, arms roiling and flowing like eagles' wings in the wind. They spun as one body, clockwise. Hands and fingers rolled like a supple, velvet cloak. Then they snapped straight as rods, facing directly at the audience, stamped their feet twice. Poignant, pungent moment of silence, then slam-dance-chanting:

> "Cast bitterness aside, enjoy the ride;
> Let loss loose; anger, vamoose!
> Forget the pit, escape the grit;
> On eagle's back, sit."

It was intermission at the theatre. Rav Moshe swung his arm over his seat and looked up at Jesus, in the next row. "Jesus, your father, Joe, was so excellent at this. I splattered soul slime over him more than once. He didn't complain. He'd forget to be mad. Kindest thing he ever did was drink the waters of forgetfulness."

Augustus had leaned down, eavesdropping. Son leaned over Claudia's lap and said, "You must have had to ride the eagle many times yourself, Emperor." The emperor nodded, eyes closed, twitching. His unspoken emotion slammed into Jesus.

Jesus pulled Claudia up, gently. He asked Bath and War if they'd care to walk with them. They all moved down a side aisle, Warden Willie and Imperial guards fore and aft, as they drifted downwards to look at the stage and orchestra pit.

Meanwhile, the royals ate from trays of sow's udders, complete with bright, pink sow vulvas. These udders were stuffed with roasted flamingos which were in turn stuffed with boiled dates. Full flutes of champagne rested on silver trays. Wary slaves served, then scooted to the edges of the god-box, alert for a raised finger or cleared throat.

Julia looked spectacular in her flesh-colored silk evening gown, the color of the sow's vulvas. It was edged with gold brocade and saltwater pearls. Sexuality flumed off her like stage fog. Her half-sisters, Agrippina and Livena, primped over a shared mirror, too small to catch either's image fully.

The five royals finally pulled into a circle and filled themselves with stories not yet forgotten. Augusta said, "What do you remember about forgetting, dear?"

Augustus said, "There was a time when Tiberius was younger than Claudia and Jesus are now. When I defeated Mark Anthony and Cleopatra at Actium, my victory was his victory. He was triumphant. His chief qualities from your first husband were ugliness, intellect, and a gift for obscurity. I forget the rest of his childhood."

Augusta reached over and toyed with the wedding ring on her husband's finger, seeing if she could slip it over his knuckle. His shrunken finger still held the ring, barely.

Augustus continued, "Remember how he fell head over heels in love with… what's her name? I forget."

Livena said, "Vipsania. You let him marry her for a while, before you ordered their divorce and his marriage to Julia."

He replied, "Yes, of course. How long *did* they stay hitched?"

The women's faces and hearts hardened when Augustus stirred these ashes. The silent desperation of all they'd never before said aloud was *not* taking an intermission. Their past choked the present with unforgotten memories that refused to be exiled, father abuses of too much or too little.

Julia seethed, "How could you have forced me to marry Tiberius when he loved another woman and *also* preferred other men over me, Father? No wonder I found others."

Livia's hands were busy with sharp crochet needles. She hissed a retort, "I also remember when you sent him miles north to the battlefront in Gaul. Drusus was so surprised to see his brother. He galloped to greet Tiberius over a rocky plain riddled with gopher holes. His horse fell and rolled over him, shattering his leg, if you recall. He suffered horribly for two days. Died in Tibbie's arms. Poor Tibbie walked all the way home to Rome from Germany as penance."

She ramped up and rambled on, "When *my* son—now my *only* son—returned home, mourning, you had no time for him. You were embroiled in petty politics. Senators trying to stab you in the back, as they did to *your* adoptive father, Julius. But you abandoned my son! How can he or I forgive and forget?" If any waters of forgetfulness remained, they had long ago passed under *her* bridge.

Livia spouted more vitriol. "You ordered a few back-stabbing deaths, vicious divorces, and slippery marriages. Once the dust settled, you'd created a straight line of succession. That's all you cared about, now and then—politics and power."

The emperor forgot his urge to retaliate. He'd ordered Tibbie to Palestine just today. His strategy? Collect calm, gain an eagle's perspective, and release resentment on hapless Jews. Maybe they'd kill him. Maybe he'd kill them. Maybe he'd forget his likely plans for patricide, settle down with his male and female lovers, and become a reasonable successor. All was possible in this whirligig world, plays within plays, where nothing was as it seemed.

33

JESUS

The curtain came up on the last act. Venus sat on one side of the stage, pouring on makeup. Psyche, at the other end of the stage, sat on a tree branch, warbling an aria.

Venus finished with her cosmetics, exited her palace, and stood beneath Psyche. "Get down here." Psyche kept singing, swinging her legs. Venus yanked hard on Psyche's foot. Psyche tumbled to ground, splatting face down in a mud puddle.

I watched Psyche try to wipe away all that good, rich earth off her face. I thought, *we are always falling, from Adam till now—first, we fall down a birth chute into the light and then the world starts in on us—mudslides, rockfalls, falling into love or depression; all of us tumbling down somewhere east of Eden.*

Venus shook me back into the play. She ordered Psyche, "Your last task is to visit Persephone, Queen of the Dead. Get her beauty box for me, the one that breaks curses and spells. I must have it."

Psyche's response was collapse, of course. What else would you expect? Venus had commanded her to do no small task—die and resurrect. Psyche saw a tall tower made of stones mudded together.

She tramped to its top and teetered on edge. "Venus wants me dead? Okay. She'll get what she wants—minus a beauty box." She searched the air. "No eagle around to catch me this time."

Fortunately for her, help was even nearer than collapse. The breathing stones of this tower, none big enough to merit attention, gave her detailed instructions on how to survive herself. "Take two gold coins," said one stone, "and two honeyed barley cakes." Another said, "You'll encounter a ferryman, a guard dog, hopeless people, and even Death. We must all cope with each of these. Do not stop to help the helpless."

Another stone said, "Save the two honeyed cakes for Cerberus, the vicious three-headed dog that guards the underworld. Put the coins in your mouth to pay Charon, the ferryman on the Styx River. Do not look at the coins. Instead, spit them one at a time into his hand—one while passing through death into Hades, one while crossing back in resurrection."

Finally, another stone said, "Do *not* open Persephone's beauty box— Do. *Not.* Open."

Psyche did all these things—except one, of course. She said 'no' to all the helpless, hopeless people who will forever be needy despite whatever help they are given. She didn't succumb to the ravenous dog of fear. She spat out greed, gave herself up to Death. Then—right at the last moment— she failed. Something so simple. Itching curiosity.

Psyche looked at the audience. "Why should Venus hog all the beauty? I'll peek in her box and see what's there. Maybe swipe a wee bit of magic, just to keep Cupid interested."

When she opened the box, a deathlike beauty sleep enveloped her. Now she was as unconscious outside as she had been inside. Cupid happened upon his sleeping lover and stuffed the deep magic back in the box, as only a god could do. Psyche woke up, plucked an arrow from Cupid's quiver, and he pricked the two of them, each in turn. They fell in love again— forever.

Psyche also gave Venus her box of inner beauty. Venus dusted herself off and slowly turned around. Glommed-on makeup sloughed off, breaking the cursed trickery of another jealous goddess. Underneath was an unrevealed radiance. This glory came to only those goddesses humble enough to ask for help from a mortal. The beaten goddess was now a beautifully beaten goddess, like hammered gold.

34

WINDY

The final act was half-way over, and Claudia hadn't seen a bit of it—or, for that matter, any of the other three acts. She just wanted to keep resting her pained head on Jesus' shoulder. She nursed a prayer, *let me keep my head here. And, Jesus-Father-Amen, please tame that prickle of porcupines digging into my skin. I'll lay royalty down. I promise. Please, make a safe way out of no way.*

An alarm swept through the crowd. Claudia briefly roused, opened her eyes. Psyche was headed into Hades. She'd spat a coin into Charon's hand as she stepped into hellfire from off the barge.

A thought shuddered through Claudia—*I've spent my life running from the fire. Haven't yet burned. My passage, not earned. I'm paying for safety using Jesus' coin, not mine.*

She put her head back down on Jesus' shoulder. He shifted gracefully, easing her neck pain. Jesus' chest and shoulders rose and fell regularly. My wind whistled in and out of his lungs. His close-held breath rose and fell, rose and fell under her head, lulling her down, drifting her back into needed comfort. This was how she would learn to step through *her* grief and deal with fires she had yet to face.

At this moment Bathenia, on the other side of Jesus, rolled to her feet. When she bent forward to stand, her dress caught fire from her candle. I gave a quick blow, extinguishing both the fire and its odor.

Bathenia walked as if in a dream, passing below Augustus. The rustle of her feet startled the old man awake. She floated down the center aisle, down from the box of the gods. When she reached the grandstands of mere mortals, she delicately peeled off her outer garment. Stepped out of it, unconcerned. Her cloak dropped off her slight frame onto the floor of the center aisle.

Alongside the open-air theatre, branches from the black iron trees bent beneath my blow. They waved arms of invitation. *We outlast storms. Come down by choice, so others don't fell you. Root down to who you really are.*

Her bones, not her ears, heard their voice. She continued down, dressed in a silk singlet, living her dream. She held her thick, creamy candle straight out before her with unbent elbows, a hopeful offering for her hopeless lover, Romeo. The audience buzzed with whisperings, torn between the story on the stage and the story unfolding in the center aisle. What was this, a Vestal Virgin approaching center stage, *in her underwear?*

She stumbled. I caught her. Her virginal candlelight almost flickered out but then steadied. I guided this flickering candle along in her journey through shame. She'd been fired on a pagan altar. But now she lit the path for others, brave enough to finish what was left undone.

Onstage, I had breathed a deep sleep into Psyche. The actress lay half-naked under an oak tree, fingers and toes twitching, like a cat dreaming of opera. Bathenia walked past two guards to stage center. She didn't stop 'til she stood over Psyche, still holding her candle straight out, so all could see the woman she was becoming.

Cupid appeared stage left, unseeing. His eyes were forward, hungry for adoration. Soaring trumpets and harp music fueled his ballet. He swung between allegro and arabesque in twirling jumps, dramatic landings. He didn't hear the absence of applause. Finally, he looked for his paramour and saw a pair of *amours.*

He blinked hard, shook his head. Bathenia took four dainty steps and stood before him. She quickly let go of her candle. It fell and stuck to the stage, bottom down. Stayed on fire. Didn't leak.

She flicked the thin straps off her shoulders, and her singlet dropped. Cupid, and everyone else in the theatre, gawked. She bent, picked up her fallen candle, and gazed relentlessly at her beloved.

Cupid turned his head left and right, looking for someone to rescue him. Where was Mommy? *There* Venus was, on top of the stage wall, mouth agape.

Hmm. No help there.

The Greek Chorus leader, impromptu, sprung up, and the rest of his chorus followed him. They encircled panicked Cupid, brave Bathenia, and wide-awake Psyche—whose play had woken her up to real life. The chorus did a synchronized, syncopated improv. Wide-eyed, the leader chanted, directly to the audience,

"Don't look at the stage, study the stands;
Look to *your* heart, examine *your* hands;
Love's light is at stake. You must be awake."

At the words *stand* and *awake*, Bathenia herself woke up from her dreamy, detached state. She stood taller, separated her feet at shoulder's distance, somehow stronger in her stark nakedness. She took one step behind shell-shocked Romeo, kicked him in the back of his legs, and together they dropped to their knees facing the god-box.

Bathenia turned her head to him and cried out in a strong voice, "Cupid, take me as you took me! I've been yours since opening night. Your passion leaked into me. We set backstage on fire. Now I carry your sire."

"Marry me now, before the good citizens of Rome. Marry me before our divine emperor. Marry me before he justly judges us. We two lucky ones can be entombed together, husband and wife."

A groundswell of murmured astonishment swept the crowd, babbling amazement not far from panic. Who had unboxed *this* magic?

Bathenia shouted up to the emperor, "Divine Augustus, I beg your forgiveness for faithlessness. I have failed and fallen. I am guilty and deserve death."

Cupid shook his head furiously, in a panic. He sprung to his feet, pointed his finger at her belly, and pounded out a lyric to the audience,

"No folly from me, the liar's a she!
Don't trust her rap, don't bank her crap."

Bathenia glared at him. She spoke to the top row from whence she had fallen, a sleeping bolt of slow-motion lightning. "Your Highness, my Cupid is yet to be awakened to love. I entreat your mercy till he wakes up. And, please, our fellow citizens of Rome, forgive me. I leaked Rome's Light that night. Now it's gone." She used thumb and forefinger to pinch out the candle's flame, bowed her head and torso to the stage floor, arms stretched out before her toward the god-box.

Claudia leaned forward, riveted. Bathenia was turning into a woman before her very eyes, from a girl who had entered a hellish fire that night.

The crowd below, led by the head actor in the Greek Chorus, chanted,

> "True justice be cruel,
> 'til it weds mercy's jewel!"

Augustus consulted the captain of his Imperial Guards. The officer trotted down, picked up Bathenia's singlet, and led the two lovers off stage.

The captain returned and shouted, "All quiet! The emperor speaks!" The vocal cords of 2,500 theatre patrons were axed silent. Everyone turned, eaglets waiting to be fed by the Emperor Eagle.

Augustus pronounced, "Judgment will be rendered in three days' time, at noon, *Circus Maximus*. This play is finished for tonight."

I flashed Jesus forward to his own virginal fires. Father had given this last act as a preview parable of his own coming humiliation, death, time in Hell, and resurrection. The play also warned him not to unbox the mysterious but to leave hidden things to Father, as it is written in the law.[14]

Warthenia, abandoned, hung out in the aisle at the end of our row, cupping Rome's one remaining virginal flame with both hands. Claudia sat next to Jesus, left hand rubbing her neck. I prodded Jesus to lift Claudia's head and help her to her feet.

He leaned over and kissed Mary good-bye for the evening. I'd prompted *her* to rise and let her son go another way than her. She hugged Claudia and released the pair to join Warthenia. Jesus went left; Mary went right. Both left from separate exits, he into a bigger social swirl; she, into her family circle.

Jesus said to Warthenia, "Can we go to someplace quiet and get a drink? A lot happened tonight, before and during the play." Warthenia nodded, grateful. She took Claudia's hand, and the three moved toward a more peaceful place.

As they passed Augustus, he stepped over to his granddaughter and took her in his arms. He held her, rocking her back and forth in the night wind. After some time, he said, "I've sent Tiberius to avenge your father's death. He sails from Ostia, as we speak." After a moment, he looked at Jesus, "Tomorrow, ten o'clock sharp, throne room."

Claudia remained mute, starting her slide into a deeper form of grief. She'd felt a twinge of sadness with her brother's death. *This* death loomed, an assassin's sneak attack. I'd allowed her to be ambushed without warning, cut down from her high branch of entitlement, face in the mud.

Claudia was entering a swampish underworld, where maggots loved to feast. Jesus put his arm around her, so she would not be alone in her journey. Warthenia held her own Light. The three friends moved past all the exit signs, through deepening shadows, down toward the House of Vestals.

35
RABBUS

Tiberius had taken me with his soldiers as a hostage, allowing the others to stay on the farm. I led his men to and through the village at Pirate's Cove. We'd also covered the hills all around.

Tiberius, in a funk, queried me, "Rabbus, you've led us forthwith a merry chase for almost a fortnight. No culminative fruition. Mayhap we bring *you* and your familiars back to Rome. Augustus cares only that insurrectionists desist."

I heard myself say, "But *you* would know the truth. Aren't such lies about criminals like Huns dressed up in Roman red?"

"Schooled in ethics by a pagan? We, perhaps, may circumlocute later regarding apparitions of verisimilitude. For now, provide directive to Crispus' chosen place of obscurity."

"Commander, all due respect. I don't have any idea what you just said, but I think you want to find Crispus. I don't know him any longer, but the last I did know, he'd cracked under all his suffering."

"Philosopher joins moralist?"

"Not meaning to be any better than I am, sir. I'm an uneducated farmer, but I believe we carry the dead inside, like sacks of memories."

Tiberius mused, "Now a poet joins your crew."

I sat on my borrowed horse and watched Tiberius' men burn Pirate's Cove to the ground. Ash hung in the air. Smoke made silverplate of weak sunbeams. We headed back into quarry country through a narrowing valley. Judgment Cliff was in sight to my right. Legionnaires and cavalry surrounded us, scanning the hills above us.

I asked, "Don't want to be nosy, sire, but did you know Tribune Gaius?"

"Verily. He married into the royal family prior to my adoption by the emperor. We were civil. Barely. But I *do* harbor affection for his daughter.

She's effervescent, possessing an olfactory sensibility for dissimilitude. Thus, Samaritan, it's for Claudia that I embark upon this justice crusade."

These pointed words were no sooner out of his mouth than a volley of arrows swarmed down from the limestone quarry tops above us. Legionnaires dropped right and left.

Tiberius' gold marked him. Three arrows stuck in the shield he'd slung over his back, and two fixed themselves in his breastplate, one right below his neck. My horse was hit chest center, a kill shot. He whinnied and dropped.

We all scattered. The lucky ones reached shelter back of boulders. Those less lucky lay where they fell. Arrows silenced them in short order. By my count, maybe forty of our two hundred lay dead or dying in the open.

I crawled to Tiberius. He'd curled in a ball next to a boulder. "Sire?"

He grimaced.

"You wanted to find Crispus, Commander?"

He muttered, jaw grinding, "Crispus found us."

"Commander, the battle makes the warrior, does it not? Let's take this battle to open ground and fight, as you're accustomed, in a phalanx."

Tiberius grunted, non-committal. At that moment, I saw what I'd not yet noticed. A shaft was buried in his left flank, stuck through his side beneath his breastplate. The bloody tip hung out his back. Survivable if the arrow hadn't been poisoned. Crispus dipped his arrows in viper venom routinely.

I lightly fingered the arrow. "Commander, perhaps this arrow was unpoisoned, perhaps not. If I were you, I'd pull that arrow straight through and flush the tunnel. Otherwise …"

His eyes went wide, then scrunched shut. He nodded.

I grabbed the arrowhead using my shirttail, pulled slow and strong. The arrow slipped out, notched feathers last. One of the men who'd flogged me, Drenius, now handed me his skein of water. I chugged it into the wound, took a tub of balm from my pouch. "Woundwort might help."

Tiberius' eyes rolled back in his head. His grunt could have been a 'yes.'

I scooped out some of the liniment and poked my finger clear into the wound on both ends. He gasped for air.

I told him, "If I find some maggots, I'll lay 'em on top the entry and exit wounds, fore and aft. They'll eat the pus and leave healthy flesh behind. Whether I do or don't, those scars'll stay with you longer than most friends or family."

No response from Tiberius. Perhaps he was trying to bend his mind around maggots dancing in and out of his guts.

I took a strip of linen outta my field pouch and wrapped it round his waist a few times. "That'll have to do, for now."

Drenius looked up into the hills. "Those varmints don't play fair. We wear red, so the enemy can see us and fight like men. These weasels blend into the trees and rocks. *Ain't right.*"

I looked at my grey and green outerwear. "Might take a lesson from 'em."

Tiberius caught that, nodded.

Drenius seemed eager to play the hero. Perhaps no one'd taught him that heroes mainly come in two stripes—damaged and dead.

He asked Tiberius for permission to climb up the boulders, drop a rope, and pull his commander up after him. He pointed out a path that zigged and zagged up the hill toward the cresting ridge. Tiberius drew himself up for a look-see, poked his head around the boulder, and followed Drenius' pointing finger.

All was calm for the moment. Tiberius gave the nod, and Drenius started scampering up-hill like a goat. He got about ten yards up, looked down for a moment, and collected an arrow through his neck. He fell gagging at our feet.

Tiberius held him as Drenius suffocated and bled out.

He said, "I'm so sorry, Drusus." He seemed lost in time and space. I remembered from an earlier conversation that his dead brother, a famous general, was named Drusus.

I said, in the quiet moments that followed, "Sorry to intrude, sir, but this valley gives out into a plain around that bend up there. If we all stayed together in phalanx, we'd find more level ground to fight on."

Tiberius grimaced. "But we'd lose the man we came to get."

I nodded. "We'd live to fight another day, sire."

Tiberius fingered his waist wrapping. "Take five men, stripped down to tunics. Mud up and make your way into the hills. The main body of legionnaires will do as you said. Flush the enemy toward us. We'll see you in the valley."

He picked men to go with me. They stripped down and mudded up; nothing shiny. I had my sling, throwing-knife, and mudded short sword tucked inside my belted tunic.

Once again, I was in a party of killers—different folks, same strokes. We shinnied up between the crevices just as the square of soldiers began their shielded march down the valley. Fear was playing favorites again, and I was close to the top of his list. I took my next step up, throat quivering on my inhales, teeth clenched.

36

WINDY

The day after Bathenia's coming of age performance, Jesus walked out of Augustus' courtroom. The two cousins, Claudia and Postie, had observed the proceedings. Jesus had inquired of Me, and once again I had given him words to speak as he stood before a king and his court.

Claudia said, "You did as you said. When Bathenia was in the box of the accused, and Grandpa was asking your opinion about what to do, you walked away from him and stood next to her! You didn't have to say a word. Your actions spoke for you."

Jesus said, "I am what I do, not what I *say* I'll do."

Claudia looked left and right, at Jesus on one side and Postie on the other. "How odd to straddle the boundary between night and day. I feel practically sawed in two by the forces coming from each of you."

Postie thin-sliced the air with a retort, sharp as a knife-thrower's blade. "Night has its own kind of light when you're feeling your way under the covers, dear cousin— particularly now that *dear* Claud isn't around to service you."

I intoned to Son, *the Adversary is out—deadly, slippery. Register his presence inside your body. Knowledge of poisons is essential training.*

Claudia said, "Ignore warthog. He's busy rooting around in the mud."

"Sorry, didn't hear you. I was still reeling from your comment, Postie. Makes me want to cut back on what I take in—poison comes in such small portion sizes."

Claudia laughed, "For him to hurt me, I'd have to value his opinion."

She steered around a mud puddle, blinked hard. Her face went blank, and she rubbed her neck. She'd just felt a stab of loss, and it left her spinning inside, clutching for ground.

I directed her eyes back to Jesus. He would show her the right path.

Postie had no eyes for Jesus, not at all. His squat skull held sunken eyes above a clench of jawbone as full of odd angles as a twisted spider's web.

He looked at Claudia and Jesus. "The two of you are so chummy. You service her like dear Claud, now that he's dead in the Med?"

Claudia said, "Cousin, you obviously have death and sex on the brain. Amazing your skull doesn't shovel its own grave and bore into it."

Jesus looked at Postie and inquired of me, *should I try to make friends with him?*

I whispered to Son, *Do not entertain evil. Evil is the enemy. Don't strum its favorite songs on a lyre. Don't find a comfortable cushion where you recline and drink wine together.*

Jesus filled his mind with me and my words. I breathed him down the busy thoroughfare. The trio stood on a corner at the bottom of Palatine Hill, next to a fruit vendor's stall. Jesus' family apartment was caddy-corner to this stall, six floors up. He glanced up. Mary waved to him from where I'd led her out on the balcony.

When Jesus smiled back at his mother, Postie noticed. "Your ma reeling you back in, precious Jesus, meek 'n mild?"

Postie chuckled at his own humor, looked up at the balcony again, and stepped right in front of a loaded oxcart. He didn't see it coming. His sandal caught the sharp axle of the front wheel, and he went down under the black, iron-rimmed wheel. The cart rolled over both his legs. Sounds of brittle twigs snapping. One leg shattered below the knee; the other broke right at the knee.

A moment of stunned silence, then Postie's shrieks filled the air. He looked at his ruined legs, jagged white bones sticking out. Postie slapped about under the oxcart, covering himself and his coat of many colors with animal dung and street mud.

The young foreigner, ox-goad in hand, jumped down and saw he'd run over a nobleman. He thought, *I'm doomed.* His wife sat in the mud beside him with their small daughter alongside her. The child flapped her arms as if to scare off a swarm of bees.

A group of curious Vigiles, on their way to a fire, stopped. One bent over this incoherent stranger with blood pumping from his legs. *Ha! Leave this mudder to the Fates.*

A troupe of actors also passed by on their way to the theatre for tonight's performance of *Psyche*. They looked at this bit of street drama, moved on. *Can't be late for rehearsal.*

Postie whimpered, then howled—back and forth, beating his fists in the mud.

Claudia looked at Jesus, and he at her. Her eyes were twin wells of anger and resignation. *Let him die. I know you won't.*

Jesus looked from her to this young family. They were an island in a turbid sea of the non-involved. He felt compassion for this young man, in spite of his being gripped by so much darkness coming from Postie. Jesus remembered Lazarus's fall into a tomb, his broken leg, and how I had taught his hands to heal.

Father, he asked, *is this time now ripe for showing your glory to these strangers? You give sun and rain to everyone, even the casual and self-absorbed.*

Jesus asked, "Claudia, put your cousin's head in your lap, please. Pray for him. Pray for me."

Claudia propped Postie's mud-head in her lap. "Hey, God. Jesus'll do your all-seeing thing here—even though You know Postie's not worth a poop. He's cruel, piggish, and cares not a whit for anyone but himself. Besides that, his mom hates mine. But Jesus asked me to pray for this total hemorrhoid. I mean, he's not even an asshole. That has a purpose. Anyway, begging your pardon, God, that's all I got. Oh yeah, help Jesus. I forget that good-bye word, Jesus. How do I end this thing?"

"Say, 'Amen.'"

"Amen. What's that mean again?"

"Let Father decide what he wants done. As it is above, so let it be here."

"Okay, Amen. Can we go now?"

Jesus did for his enemy what he had done for his friend, not knowing what would happen. He placed his hands on both sides of the broken bones, pulled the loose ends apart, and then put them back together.

Bones knit, first in one leg and then the other. Broken ends reconnected. Bleeders stopped and rejoined the circle of life. Muscle, ligament, and then skin covered white bone. Pink scar tissue formed. *All fearfully and wonderfully done, in less than a minute, thanks to you, Father.*

Jesus said, "Father's given you one more chance to repent, Postie. What you do with your chance is up to you. Need help getting home?"

"What, your help, Jew? I do life on my own."

He stalked toward the terrified oxcart driver, dagger in hand, eyes black as hemlock seeds. "I'm going to execute you all for running down a royal, starting with your crumb-snatcher brat."

Son stood in front of Postie. "Most miracles don't change men's *habits*. But you're exceptional, Postie. *How much love can your unbelief withstand?*"

Postie moved toward the girl. Son said, "You're alive because you've been shown mercy. If you squander the chance to show mercy to others, worse things will happen to you."

Postie wiped a tiny bit of mud off his entitlements. The royal, fresh from exile, glared at the foreigner. "Get out of my sight, vermin, before I change my mind."

A Roan temple to Asclepius, the god of healing, silhouetted Postie's head. Its dome, opaque as tinplate, winked as a cirrus cloud flitted past. Head high, with an eye for the palace, Postie pushed away from Jesus directly into the path of a high-stepping warhorse. Son grabbed his shoulder and heaved him towards himself inside a bear hug.

Postie exhaled. Jesus remembered how some snakes fatally poison prey with their breath. He said to Postie, "School's still in session—for us all."

Postie turned his eyes away and huffed off toward the high places. He held both arms out for balance, like a tightrope walker clawing thin air.

This family, from Crete, knelt in the mud next to Jesus. Both husband and wife put their faces on the tops of his feet. Son bent one knee, popped their little girl on it, and put his hands on their heads in benediction.

The traveler looked up. "What is your name, lord, that we might worship you?"

Claudia piped up. "He's the god-man, Jesus, smokin'-hot-straight-from-heaven, trailing glory vapor behind him."

She amazed me with her fierce choice toward truth. Jesus smiled at her and them. "Father touched your life here. Now tell others what you experienced. Love justice, do mercy, walk humbly with the God of Israel."

15

Father's generosity now defined the future of this traveler, Titus.[16] Jesus pulled a hard candy out of his pocket and handed it to their child. She peeled off the wrapper, and merrily popped it in her mouth. Son held her, kissed her head. Titus and his wife got back into the cart with their child between them. They laughed with the giddy relief of an executioner's reprieve and went their way toward the port. Their ship sailed for Crete that very day.

Jesus lifted his eyes. Jude had joined Mary on one side; John, on the other. They'd watched the whole event from six stories up. This trinity of cheerleaders sent smiles to Jesus, bright as a spilled bag of sparkles. Mary steepled her palms together in gratitude. Ah yes, Son so loved being loved—by both his Father, mother, and Me.

37

CLAUDIA

Jesus and I were filthy. The road was a stinking salmagundi of poo—ox, horse, cow, and human. Jesus reached down to help me. I yanked hard, and he fell right on top of me. We rolled over and over, play-wrestling, smearing each other with animals' end products. I wasn't that much smaller in height than he was, but I could feel the strength of his arms. He was made like a cable, with knots for elbows and knees. His strength was like what held up bridges.

Once again, desire pooled warm in me. I wanted to melt into his skin and live my life within his beating heart. Maybe then, maybe then, I'd feel safe in this gladiator's ring that was the Imperial family.

I watched Jesus' family watch us from their balcony. James had arrived and stood next to John. He held a thin scroll and seemed to be fighting off a frown. Jude danced in a circle with two thumbs up. Mary belly-laughed.

We two walked away together, holding hands to steady each other's slippery steps. We laughed our way past the guardhouse and through the castle's outer courtyard. We passed under another archway where the sun danced over a sculpted, sky-blue angel. The angel practically leapt out of the arching fresco.

This inner courtyard was my favorite. Jesus had never seen it. It was home to a one-of-a-kind fountain and surrounded by fragrant ornamentals. Water straight from the mountain aqueducts flowed into the heart of a statue. The robed statue stood in the middle of the ten-foot circular marble basin. The silvered marble figure could have been male or female, any of Rome's many gods. This god bent low, both arms extended—elbows bent, palms up, and cupped. Water streamed from the god's chest into those cupped hands and dropped another four feet into the waist-high marble basin.

The Latin inscription at the base of the fountain read, "To the Unknown God."

I pulled Jesus after me into the fountain, and we collapsed in a heap, sorting ourselves out. After a bit of flopping around, we sat cross-legged, facing one another. Water streamed from Unknown's hands onto our heads. We rubbed each other's hair and face, directing the sparkling, warm water here and there. I've never enjoyed such a divine shower with a man.

How easy it was to let the water take me. Childlike and elemental, this surrendering to goodness—a splash of happiness against all that grief, but still the scales balanced. [17]

Jesus and I sat contented, connected—cleaned by the heart of this Unknown God. The lemony, gold sky shaded toward sunset rose. Pink rimmed silhouetted chimneys.

I opened my eyes after a few minutes of this bliss. A many colored coat, muddied, like a rainbow had thrown up on it, swept around a second-floor corner. Puddles of shadows splashed in Postie's wake. He'd been watching us. The warm water crystalized into ice and turned into daggers, back of my right eye.

Jesus hadn't seen him. His eyes were closed to this world, open to the next, lips moving, murmuring in the laughing tongue of this Unknown God.

38

RABBUS

*W*ait. *What was that?* A glimmer of movement.

Gray-green figures moved back of the laurel, up on that precipice. I looked over my shoulder at the stripped-down, mud-daubed legionnaires that crept up the crag behind me. I put forefinger to lips. *Still now; not a sound, hardly a breath.*

Another movement to our left—then another, above. A mockingbird hopped about, one branch of Tanglewood to another, leading predators away from her nest. Junipers, holm oaks, and willows moaned in the wind. Elder trees dropped lily-white florets, like confetti, into that same wind. A gaze of raccoons peered from under a granite overhang, so still I wondered if they were breathing at all. These were the places that held the sound of breath and the hollow plans within each hunter's chest.

The more I dropped into stillness, the more I saw. The hills crawled with camouflaged men, all creeping along the ridge, angling toward their best kill shot. Their men, my men, all of us looked alike, acted alike, one circling web of men, each with murder in his heart. The line between evil and eviler was fine as frog's hair.

My eyes had turned away from killing once Jesus and Leah had come along. That old life now reared up on its hind legs and claimed both parts of me—Barabbas and Rabbus. Jesus wasn't here now, only me with other hard men doing dark deeds. I took the next step forward, danced with the next set of shadows.

I felt like that heron who'd caught an eel too big for it. Even as heron gobbled its prey, the half-eaten eel thrashed about, slamming heron into the water again and again. Slippery question, this—who would die first, half-eaten eel or slam-danced heron?

143

Flash of moving white between boulders at ridge top. I caught my breath, held it. And now, between two great cairns, the size of barns, a bleached skull hanging low on man's belt. He drew his bow, let fly. I slid forward, looking for light, motioning my band of Italian killers to follow. We closed the distance to where I'd last seen Crispus in this godforsaken patch of ground that swallowed wickedness and burped up murder.

I stalked death; it stalked me. If I had a kill shot and didn't take it, the men behind would kill me. My sling appeared in my left hand, slender stone from creek ready to fly. Closer now, almost there, skull-crack zone.

Percussive sounds behind me. *Gurgling noises.*

I fell flat, peered over my shoulder. All the legionnaires were down, throats cut, bleeding out. Crispus leaned against a tree. He'd rolled up his sleeves and now showed off massive forearms the color of oiled olive wood. His men crouched in a half-circle, some with drawn swords, others with bows strung tight.

I dropped to my knees and threw my head back, looking beyond the forest's canopy above. I remembered something Jesus had told me. *Spirit gives words, Rabbus, but only in the moment needed. Ask, and you'll speak stuff you didn't know you knew.*

I inhaled. *Use my mouth, speak your words.*

I exhaled, "Do I get congratulations for leading the enemy into your grasp, Crispus, or are we going to act like strangers?"

"You wuz looking pretty chummy with the enemy. Makes me think you *is* the enemy. I'm a-thinkin' you done become a *real-live* secret agent man." Crispus rolled his idiot left eye round in a circle, hunched his shoulders like a cripple.

That always was a bad sign when he did his idiot routine. The unsuspecting laughed —right before he planted his dagger in their back.

I braved my way into the next sentence. "I had a choice. They'd burn my farm and kill everyone—or I'd become their guide and take 'em to Pirate's Cove. Leah and our workers are being held hostage. What would *you* have done?"

"Burn, baby, burn. Welcome to hell." His black eyes glowed from an inner fire. "You did the right thing in the wrong way, 'ol chum. Which makes it the wrong thing." Anger poised in his mouth, a poisoned blow-dart.

I took a deep breath, held it like I'd seen Jesus do. "If I hadn't done what I did, I'd be dead now."

Crispus stropped his dagger on an edge of Gaius' bleached head. Looked like he was planning further skullduggery. "I know 'bout precious, pious Jesus. Reform School of Samaria only takes you so far, 'fore the road leads back to me. Join me—not him—or I'll have two skulls on my belt before noon."

"Your plan?"

"Send you back to High 'n Mighty Tibery-Ass, lead 'im right through the back door, while you be sniffin' out our spoor. We'll be waiting with merry tidin's tumblin' to all."

His eyes sparkled. "You mess with me, Rabbus, and you'll wish *they'd* killed preggers Leah and your brat. But if you play our game with us, Mr. Secret-Triple-Agent Man, we'll keep whittlin' down the edges of their Empire. Friggin' Auggie'll realize somptin'—his packets of wind-up soldiers ain't a good investment, this part of the world. He'll stop sendin' 'em, when he figgers he's got a crap return rate. Then you 'n me can live all cozy-like in each other's hip pockets. Yep, we'll be livin' happy ever after, Barry-baby, hugs and cuddles for all."

Crispus sauntered my way, casually cut my throat, and stabbed me in the back. His voice swirled with glee, then growled, like it was soaked in lye. "Sorry, bud, gotta blood ya. Want 'em ta believe yur story 'bout bein' ambushed, everyone lost but you. Gotta wear your scars."

Neither wound was mortal, but they bled a lot and hurt like hell. My cameo turned shades of rust, green, and brown. Men bound my neck and chest with my own linen strips. Gave me no pain relief but relieved me of my throwing knife and sling. Left me my bow and a few arrows in my quiver.

Crispus said, "Get back to 'em wops, pronto, Barry-baby. Lead 'em nice 'n slow so we have a couple of days to get ready. My men'll be watching ya. Sniff down trails. Come back, shaking yur head, real hangdog like. Ramp up yur actin' skill. You always wuz good at bein' someone you weren't."

I truly wanted to relieve Crispus of his teeth. But survival instinct won, and I smiled, became a Crispus' lap-dog. Crispus rolled his idiot eye. "When you lead them up the backdoor defile, remember the moldy boulder. The one shaped like an Eagle's Wings—with a holler under it?"

I nodded, throat in agony, on fire.

"Get where you ken duck under the ledge, when the time comes. Sniff the air. Halt 'em with a raised hand. When I see yur hand, I'll pull the trigger. Spare you, but not *one* of them."

"If you've hurt my wife, I'll …"

"Help me cut your throat deeper? You should be praisin' me for my light touch, me bein' a neck surgeon and all. 'Sides, you're in no position to bargain, *l'il Jesus-wannabe*. For now, Leah and the Lepers are singin' a happy tune, dancin' a merry jig. How does that jig finish, at the end of a rope? That's up to you, *Barry baby*."

39

JESUS

It was high noon. Heat clamped down like an oven lid on everyone in *Circus Maximus*. Spectators chanted for blood. I sat between Warthenia and Claudia, on the row below the emperor. Ma and my sibs did *not* come today.

I looked down and to the right. Postie and three friends sat in a quartet of box seats. They seemed full of themselves and laughter. Claudia filled me in. "That one, on the far left, is Gemellus, Drusus' grandson. He's next in line for the throne after Tiberius."

Claudia continued, "And there, there's your childhood friend from Egypt, Julius. I told you his father died about the same time as your own abba? And the younger one, beside him? My cousin, Caligula, Germanicus' kid. He gets teased a lot about his falling out hair, falling-down sickness, and being so small. That's how he got nick-named after the soldiers' boots, their caligae."

Claudia called out, "Hey, Julius, come over here. Get re-acquainted with an old friend." Julius clambered up to our box and bowed respectfully to the emperor. He plopped down next to Claudia and looked at me, face screwed into a question mark.

I asked him, "Remember the two of us running up the tailpipe of the palace when we were six, Julius?"

He threw his arms around me. "Jesus! I thought I'd never see you again!"

"I also thought the same. After this ordeal, let's catch up over a drink, huh?"

He turned, touched me on the arm, and returned to his chair below.

Trumpets sounded all around the amphitheater, and the two bound prisoners were led to the sandy circle's center. Bathenia looked bedraggled; Romeo, defiant.

Romeo caught sight of admirers in the audience and fanned out a peacock grin.

Claudia said, "I can't figure out if that's a smile or a smirk, so I'm calling it a

smirkle." She laughed, and I squeezed her hand, but I didn't take my eyes off Romeo. He raised high his bound hands and shook them—a victor's conquering salute.

Augustus raised one hand briefly from his side and dropped it back, the spare wrist-flicker of a minimalist. Trumpets blared, and the crowds quieted. All eyes shifted to the emperor.

"I have consulted with your senators and my trusted advisors. We've made a decision in this matter of the Vestal Virgin and Romeo, the alleged father of her unborn child." You could hear a pin drop from the far stands.

"Bathenia will be exiled to Illyria. She will not return to Italy during her lifetime. Her family has chosen to accompany her. Guards, remove her. Her family awaits without."

Bathenia locked stares with Claudia, bowed deep from her waist, and mouthed, *Thank you.* She was escorted from the Roman kingdom to a whole new life. Windy whispered to me, *Father will rename, tame, claim, and aim her desires for his Kingdom. She will eventually marry and settle in Thyatira, Greece. She will become a merchant of fine linens, purple dyes.*[18]

Augustus continued, "Romeo remains. Guards, release his bonds." Guards unbound Romeo's wrists and ankles, withdrew. Romeo couldn't believe his luck. He waved at the crowds and danced his newfound freedom, whirling and looping, giddy as a parakeet. He burst into a lyrical flight of operatic aria. Such joy, under his new, blue sky! After some minutes of Romeo's flight into fancy, the emperor's head turned to the Captain of the Guard. His right eyebrow rose, dropped again.

Two doors on opposite sides of the arena quietly lifted. Two new dancers joined Romeo's party—dancers that tipped the scales at over six hundred pounds each. Romeo didn't notice. He still played to the galleries, eyes focused high, on the crowds. When he heard a collective intake of breath from the crowd and saw some fist-pumps, only then did he examine his stage. He found himself the intense focus of a couple—a couple of African lions.

Dinner was served. Romeo starred as the main course, the only course. First, an arm disappeared. Then a leg, from the knee down. Then, horrified, he stared as his intestines were ripped from his abdomen and devoured in front of him. The lioness finally showed mercy. She enclosed his head in her jaws and smacked down, cracking his skull like a raw egg. She gorged, chewed with relish, before the two tossed and tussled with what remained, ripping and grinding, gnawing their just desserts.

The crowds dispersed. A balance between mercy and justice had been worried and won by Rome's First Citizen. If the crowds could have carried Augustus out of the stadium on their shoulders, they would have.

40

LEAH

Tiberius had long since disappeared over the horizon with my husband. Two weeks had come and gone. No husband. No Romans. No nothing, but Cyrena, ex-lepers, and me. I'd decided not to fret, but my decider and my body hadn't been talking. My fingernails had worried themselves to the quick. Longing for husband sneaked out and trickled down my cheeks.

Our legionnaires had gotten bored after only a few days. One platoon had headed down trail toward Shechem for a little excitement in the bars and brothels. The other, into Sebaste. I wondered, *how could they know when their Master would return?*

I leaned on my hoe in the middle of the soybean field. Cyrena stood behind me, hand on my shoulder. Her back-basket was still held by the same sweat-stained head strap. I said, "Cy, two more rows to hoe and the field will be cleared. You wanna stay a few more day or return to Rahab's?"

She sent a grateful grin my way. "I might be blind, but I can see kindness. You gave me a choice."

A faint fragrance of burning hickory wafted my way from the men's bunkhouse. Someone smoking a wild hog they'd caught and butchered. My mouth watered, and baby kicked, watering my bladder right down my leg.

I yelled, "Ow! Gabe, stop beating up your mother, already!"

I turned to Cyrena, "Rabbus and I'd decided to name our babe, Gabe. Didn't matter, boy or girl. Gabriel or Gabriella would work. I put Cy's hand on my tummy, where she could feel the footprint above my belly button. As she fingered the foot, it slid under my ribs toward my back."

She said, "Wow. Kid's backsliding and hain't yet been born."

I laughed with her. "Truth is, Cyrena, *I'm* backsliding. The prophetess in me went on a walk-about. All I feel like today is a fifteen-year-old kid with a fat gut and a kid kicking the pee out of me."

I laid down in the field, cheek on the ground, trying to feel solid. Cyrena sat cross-legged next to me, rubbing my aching, low back. *Such a lovely woman.*

Ishmael, the Ammonite, emerged out of the woods. He trotted my way, "Hey, boss-lady, you better come with me and take a squint. Don't look good." Together we three made our way along the winding road south, toward Liza and Ben's store. When we were almost at the landslide trigger point, Ishmael said, "See anything weird here?"

I looked around. *Nope.*

"See here, and here, someone's smoothed the ground with a branch. Another's feathered it all crossways with a lighter touch."

We made our way into the woods. I was about to step past a spreading sumac when Ishmael held me back. Ishmael motioned for me to go around the tree to the right, into the bush, not on the beaten path to the left. He crawled back to where we were about to step, carefully removed a carpet of moss and twigs. Under the mulch, a deep pit. Sharpened stakes pointed up from the bottom.

Ishmael said, "An old trick. All those are planted solid in the ground, poison-tipped. If getting' stuck don't kill ya, poison will."

Ishmael said, "There's more. This was only a warning."

A few yards further on, we came to a pile of branch cuttings and felled saplings. Ishmael pulled some of the debris away and started digging.

A fist was first. Then a forearm, Roman red tunic, and the rest of the body, a shovel-full at a time. Different seeds from different farmers.

Gabe landed another kick. A low clamp bent me over, clenched my teeth. Lasted less than a minute. Went away.

I remembered Jesus saying, *when in doubt, reach out. Let Father love you.*

This thought of Jesus popped another into my mind, shaped itself into a prayer—*the sooner I figure out you're smarter than me, the smarter I am. Amen.*

We walked toward the farm. Ten paces, then hot tongs clamped my stomach again. I leaned over and rested my hands on my knees, heaving breathes, trying to recover.

I told Cyrena, "Being here without a midwife isn't smart."

All eight men, three mules, Cyrena, and me left our farm within the hour. I rode Mercy. Behind me, Cyrena rode Goodness, who led Kindness on a halter rope behind her.

The woods were unnaturally still, not a whisper of a wind through the trees. Our trail took us down through a narrow canyon. Something wasn't right—the men were jumpy, the mules easily spooked.

Cyrena said, "The sounds in the trees all have colors like black blood dripping off them."

Thanks, Cyrena, you just made spooky spookier.

And then, cheek by jowl with such stillness, earth began a-tremblin'. I moved a floppy eucalyptus branch to pass, then ducked under a weeping willow branch near Eagle's Wings. Mercy stepped slightly off trail, through a scratchy patch of nightshade. Leaves whispered in the breeze, goose-bumped my skin. I smelled bitterbrush growing on the hills. Mercy shivered beneath me.

I said a word beyond my knowing, "Ishmael, please take Cy back home. I forgot my swaddling clothes from when I was a baby. I need 'em bad. Cy knows where they are." Cyrena grumbled but turned Goodness and Kindness around. They headed for home, a couple of miles back up the hill.

I said to the other men, "Drop back now, fifty yards or so. Stay close to the rocks, quiet as mice." I tightened my cloak around me, rode 'round a bend in the trail and ran smack into a beam of sun. I turned my head toward a patch of hemlock on my right. There it was, the backdoor trap looming above me.

Sunlight dodged behind a pregnant cloud, one that looked like its water might break any second. In some places four or five feet deep, the dry creek bed paralleled my path to the left. My imagination flash-flooded with visions of deluge. A gush of warm liquid spilled down my legs.

Guts squeezed, cramped. I threw my head back, hoping to distract myself. There, between cloud and forest, Crispus. He lurked on ledge's edge, behind a lichen-covered boulder. Perfectly camouflaged, index finger over his lips.

Earth quaked stronger, pounding, clomping sounds below me. I swiveled my head down trail. Rabbus had just come 'round a bend. He trudged toward me, maybe thirty yards off, walking in front of his horse, bending over, stopping and starting on the trail, searching this way and that. He was point man for a ragged bunch of Roman foot-soldiers, plus half a dozen guys on horses. They all ground upward on the sharp, rocky incline. Tiberius was in the middle of this group, slumped in his saddle, eyes fixed on his saddle horn.

Rabbus saw me and instinctively raised his hand in greeting. His eyes saucered. He screamed, "Leah, for the love of God, *get under Eagle's Wings, now!*"

Crispus right arm swung down. Rocks began to roll down both sides of the pass. Crispus yelled a victory cry, right before the ground gave way beneath him, and he joined the avalanche headed directly toward me.

41

JESUS

The honky-tonk bar in Rome was loud, the evening cool. This disco on the edge of the Forum was the "in-place" for Rome's avant-garde. The four of us sat around one of the circular wooden tables fringing the dance floor. Smudges of candle wax, drink stains, and... I blinked and saw what wasn't there. A puddle of blood, dripping from table to floor? *Ack! Windy, what is this?*

No words, but a deep breath heaved through me, another kind of answer. I welcomed winter's pure breath whenever the front door banged open and shut, a snatch of respite from the bar's smoky atmosphere. I struggled to hear my friends over the music. People at the next table sucked smoke from bongs and blew out blue streams, heads nodding to the band's dance rhythms. Couples—men with women, men with men, women with women—did their bump and grind on the dance floor.

Claudia and Postie seemed lost in thought. Claudia gave an order to the bong-waiter who'd circulated our way with an assortment of stuff in little jars.

Postie sucked down his fifth brew. He studied himself in the mirrored wall. Wall mirrored his face, and drink mirrored his soul. Drink and drugs had whittled his face to bone and shadow, his body a husk he couldn't shed.

He was made even less attractive next to Julius. My childhood friend from Egypt had a chiseled square jaw, sparkly blue eyes, and muscles on his muscles. He looked like all the statues of Roman gods I'd seen in museums. A blondish beard was filling in nicely.

Julius hunched forward over his drink. "Catch me up, Jesus. It's been, what, a decade?"

I sipped my glass of wine. "Last we saw each other, we were boys with living fathers. Now we're men with dead fathers. We men don't live overly long."

Julius agreed, "True enough. Maybe all this thirst for might ain't right, huh? Our panting after certainty and security." He shook his head, laughed.

I said, "Hard to resist snake oil peddlers selling certainty. Beats not knowing what's coming around the next corner, for most folks."

Julius prodded Claudia. "So, do women handle not knowing what's coming 'round the next corner better than men?"

She said, "Oh, Julius, I suppose it's true. We've had more practice being helpless, but not by choice." She rolled her eyes. "Truth is such a hag. We all pretend to love her. She has long snaggleteeth, a burning eye, knows better than you, and doesn't play nice with others—so what's not to love?"

Postie chortled. "Love it. You and me, just alike. We're good at lying easy and fightin' dirty, cousin. Smear half-facts on a label. Make 'em believe snake venom is snake oil, right before you stick 'em."

"Postie, put a plug in it—inbound and outbound. Drinking booze and talking crap. You're drunk."

I turned to Postie. "Want to know a truth that's hard for all of us? Dead fathers—some long gone, other graves are fresh, or not yet dug. As for me, I've been like an oak tree with a hole through the middle since my abba died. I'll always go through or around that hole all my days."

Postie hiccupped. "I'd rather get drunk than yak with a Jew about getting dead."

I refused to take offense. "A Jewish pastime. Sit around, drink, talk about death. Makes us happy."

Postie moved his face to within inches of mine and said, "You Jews do suffering the best."

The waitress came, stood with her order sheet. Claudia motioned to Postie. "Nothing stronger than a spritzer for him. He's beyond buzzed."

Postie let loose his impersonation of a smile. Reflections of fire from the wall torches danced in his eyes. He said to me, "Makin' fun of my father, 'cause he died early, huh? And this from the bastard son of a whoring mother who claimed God screwed her. I hear those stories."

I took offense. Felt the urge to retaliate. Windy, now a male warrior, whispered, *Stay put. Shut up. Sit back.* I obeyed. Sat back, right hand on the table next to my glass.

Postie bled hatred my way; Claudia, desire. Julius looked back and forth at my companions. "Well, here I am, face-to-face, with the wounds and wants of the human race."

Postie whipped out his stiletto and stabbed my right palm, between my third and fourth fingers. He let go of the dagger, and it quivered over my hand, stuck firmly to the wooden tabletop. He pushed his chair back in a tumble and cawed, "Let's see if he *wants* more of my *wounds*. Happy to help."

Everyone around us was struck dumb, hushed. Bouncers looked the other way.

Claudia pulled the dagger straight up with both hands, freeing my hand. She threw it on the floor under Postie's upended chair. "I'm *so* sorry, Jesus. I'd have him locked up, but he's used his status as a royal to intimate everyone."

She put her nose in Postie's face and shouted, "Grandpa will find out tomorrow what you did to his seer tonight! I'll tell him about Clemens, your look-alike servant—how you sneak away while he fools everyone into thinking he's you.[19] Grandpa will backhand you onto Planasia and lock it down tight."

I couldn't believe what had just happened. A stream of my blood puddled on the tabletop and trickled to the floor, *just like the vision I had when I'd entered the bar.* Claudia poured some of my rose' on the wound, wiped it off with her dress, leaving a red stain. Then she took a snow-white silk hankie from her shoulder bag and bound my bleed. She whispered to me, "Not everyone wants to be saved by you. Many are hell-bent, no matter what."

Postie eyed her taking care of me, chugged the rest of his beer. Devil, drink, and a damaged soul mingled seamlessly together. He yanked up his discarded dagger off the floor, got in my face, and made a show of licking blood off his blade. "Yum, Jew blood."

I took a deep breath and stared back into the face of evil. He turned on his heel and stomped out into the dark, rolling the night up after him.

Once Postie had gone, the noise in the bar resumed. Inside, I felt the pain at a distance, like someone else's hand had been nailed. Both hands, both feet, screamed. I had to look and see if someone had pierced them as well. Tears welled up from both eyes.

Julius cut in. "Here, Jesus, take a pain powder. I keep some with me for headaches—a gift from my father. He enjoyed ill health so much he couldn't keep it to himself." I slugged down his powder.

Julius shook his head to clear the madness. "My father didn't finish well. Do you remember how thin he was? I encouraged him to eat, but he'd have little of it. Counted the peas on his plate. One night, toward the end, he muttered, 'All those people I disappeared into mass graves. So many women, so many children.'"

Windy helped me clear my mind with a deep inhale. Then He said something from my mouth, teaching me what I didn't know, even as the words came from my mouth. "I remember playing too rough with James in Alexandria—about the time I met you, Julius. Ma walked into the room, looked at me, and didn't say a word. A warm wash flooded my face. I busted out crying and hugged my brother, telling him I was sorry."

Claudia said, "Ahh. You're the sensitive sort, stuffed to the portholes with creamy light. Postie feels no shame. Shame would be an improvement for a sucking hole like him."

I shrugged. "Postie's captured territory. Shame washed up on his shores on a tide of drink and drugs, then slipped into a disguise of entitlement."

Claudia said, "Sounds like someone gave him a box of darkness, and he thinks it was a gift."

"I suppose. Father does send darkness as a gift. But this isn't that." I looked at Julius, "This darkness is an assassin. When my Father sends the dark, and you don't run away, it leaves your face radiant."[20]

I looked at both of them. "We're all in warrior training. Spirit warned me tonight, in a vision and a word in my ear, but I got distracted. I left my hand on the table too long. The result? This." I motioned to my bound hand.

"We all need the courage to listen carefully and deal with what's in front of us. Now, at the outset, we're free to choose our journey. Once begun, the journey chooses us."

Julius said, "How come I felt a cold finger ice my spine right now?"

None of us had a reply. The band started up a tango. Tables emptied, everyone around us in a dancing mood after darkness had vacated the premises. Claudia grabbed my left hand and swept me onto the dance floor with her.

She said, her face a grin, "Careful with your wounds, my love, but I don't want to miss this one. After all, I'm *entitled* to be your partner."

I followed her onto the floor, stayed around the edges, right hand to my heart. Our last tango in Rome.

42

LEAH

Rabbus' cry was no sooner out of his lips than I kneed Mercy's ribs and bolted toward the Eagle's wings. My wet calves and heels dug into her sides. Mercy skidded to a rough stop with stiff forelegs and delivered me over her head into the space beneath. I fell hard and rolled to the inner wall. The thunder of falling boulders surrounded me. I was left in total darkness, stunned. A thought crept into the silence after all the clamor— *you're safe in here.*

My hands groped along the rocks in all directions. My feet rested on Mercy's cooling head that poked through the rubble. A whiff of fresh air came from a crack in the wet limestone to my left. The wall also leaked a dribble of water. Air and water both. I licked the wall. My tongue captured the water but also felt a pattern underneath it—not just water on flat rock. I traced it with my tongue, then my fingers—a carving, simple lines. My tongue and fingers could see what my eyes could not—soaring eagle's wings with claw feet hanging below, a sharp beak above.

I remembered Rabbus telling me that he'd done an eagle carving here when he was a boy. Without knowing it, he'd carved his presence then, for now. Also, I felt Another hover.

I listened for other voices than my wild imaginings. Heard nothing, felt nothing but Gabe's pressure within me. This babe was bottom diving, his water dribbling between my legs.

I settled myself. *Spirit Mid-wife, what to do?* Heard not even an echo of my whisper. Hands stripped me naked, my hands. I put my dress—a homespun fiber sack—beneath me. My cloak overlapped the sack and stretched to Mercy's head. I squatted upright, feet splayed, knees open. Inhaled slow. As much air as I could hold. Exhaled hard, strident huffs and ragged pants. A giant hand squeezed my guts. My bottom was splitting in half. I felt like a womb within a tomb, blazing pain from the bottom up, crapping out a turd the size of Jericho.

Ohhh! Windy, Doula-from-Heaven, mid-wife my child, and me, from this grave made for two.

43

RABBUS

My wife pitched under the ledge thirty yards away from me. I plastered myself against a closer, shallower ledge. Boulder avalanche smacked the ground hard where I'd been standing two seconds earlier.

To my left, in the rockfall, I caught sight of a person. The face and white-skulled belt got tangled with grey and green limestone. Crispus had stood too close to the edge.

An eerie quiet fell. Cool breeze blew the dust away. Moans from men under and between rocks on the edge of the avalanche—keening, pleading. A single man stood, limping toward safety. I took a step out from under my ledge, peeked up in time to see another boulder, the size of a horse, reach a tipping point. It hesitated, decided to pack it in.

It rumbled as it rolled, gathered speed. I flattened myself back against the mountain and became one with the wall. The boulder careened off the pile of rock in front of me. Wedged into the gap where Crispus stood and crushed his leg.

I rock scrambled toward Eagle's Wings past Crispus. He wasn't going anywhere. The newly arrived boulder had wedged his leg like a vice. Gaius' jagged skull had splintered and lodged in his side. Crispus' guts oozed out around Gaius' laughing jawbone.

Limestone rocks sprawled outward from Eagle's face. I screamed into the scree, "Leah! Can you hear me?"

No sounds at all from inside the Wings or under the center of the avalanche. I hopelessly tried by myself to tunnel into the cliff. Esau-the-dwarf jumped out from under the trunk of a juniper on the northern edge of the avalanche. He joined me. Ishmael also joined in, then another, and another. All had somehow been saved from this disaster.

I pieced it together. When I'd held up my arm toward Leah, Crispus triggered the slide. Crispus' band along the ridge had all melted away, in ones and twos, back to their farms and families—and into Tiberius' trap. I'd told Tiberius earlier of Crispus' plan. We'd lured the pirates into position. He'd placed half his legionnaires in a ring around both sides of the woods, all stripped down to under-tunics and mud-daubed. He'd marched the rest of us up-gulch into the valley of death. His soldiers did not question him. Best to do and die—this was the Roman rule.

Neither of us knew what would happen, but I'd told the commander, "God will get honor from this, somehow."

Now I wasn't so sure. Half-dozen of us clawed a tunnel into the hillside, all of us covered with beggar's lice. I called Leah's name and begged, "Please God, keep her alive, don't squash her flat and any hopes I have for happiness."

Down the hillside to my left, I heard another voice, weak but clear. The voice called my name, "Rabbus …"

Tiberius?

I told my men, "Keep digging here. I'll check that cry over there." I raised my shield in my left hand, carried a Roman's short sword in my right, one I'd picked up off the avalanche. I headed toward that last gasp.

I yelled his name back, "Tiberius!"

A reedy response, "Rabbus!"

Our voices bounced each other's names back and forth. We narrowed the gap. *There.* Under this particular pile of rocks over *this* bit of creek bed. I pulled rocks apart, headed down into the rubble. Felt a warm, unmoving flank of a horse, Tiberius' horse, Rex.

Voice underneath, weaker, "Rabbus …"

"Commander. I'm coming." I slashed with my sword, disemboweling the horse. I cut straight through to the other side, piercing and peeling aside hide, ribs, intestines. Rex's insides flowed over whoever was beneath. I reached down, through Rex's guts.

Halfway between the two sides of horse's ribcage, out of the grave's entrails, a trembling hand, wearing a Roman signet ring, poked up and out toward me, fingers trembling.

44

LEAH

I grabbed a round rock that lay beside me. I felt its cool, smooth surface with my right hand, a comfortable handful made just for me, it seemed. I balanced, my left hand fingering the eagle carving. Gabe banged furiously at the gate.

I dropped the rock between my bare feet, picked it up again. I got into a rhythm—holding and squeezing, breathing and pushing. At the end of each contraction, I dropped the rock between my feet. I rested, felt held, backed up. Suddenly, a thought. *This is the comfort of Windy's womb— not death's tomb. She wants to deliver my faith into the outer world, even in darkness.*

Someone spoke from behind me, but without speaking.

The rock I put in your hand? Your teacher. That stone drops to the earth, effortless. The rock needs no help falling. I pull it toward the heart of the earth. Become like this rock. Trust your heaviness.

The Unseen underlined the unsaid. I felt Her weight as I squatted, knees open. Pain came in hot waves, an expanding ring of fire. I leaned back into the one Who held me upright. Her open arms and legs behind me made this stretching between my legs endurable, barely.

I screamed out my guts in the dark. "O God, help me bear this white-hot ring of fire." I felt Her say, *Breathe, push, breathe, push. You're not alone. Now... now! Let him drop.*

Thump on cloth. Wet movement against ankles. I leaned into my Backup, exhausted.

Now other voices, faint scrabbling sounds of rescue, closer. I screamed again, but now my scream shaped words, "Here! Here, I'm here! Help!"

Wails from between my legs. I prayed over Gabe's crying and my wailing, *Spirit of Jesus, thank you for my life, my breath, baby's life, baby's breath. In life, or in death.*

45

RABBUS

Ishmael called out, "Rabbus! We heard Leah screaming. Come quick."

I was twenty yards away, holding Tiberius' hand. I yelled back, "Trade places with me. Un-earth Tiberius. He's here, under his horse in the creek bed."

Ishmael pressed one gnarled finger against his nose and blew out a snot gob at my feet. Then he moved to help his enemy.

I rock scrambled over to the tunnel beneath Eagle's Wings, swapped places with Esau, kept digging. I passed rocks from night toward light, a miner's bucket brigade, wary of rocks on top collapsing and crushing me. I propped up tippy boulders with tree branches that others had cut and passed forward. Finally, I climbed over Mercy's cooling corpse.

Empty space. "Leah?"

Leah croaked, "Rabbus? Oh, please, God, let it be my husband."

I pulled alongside Leah, holding fire in my left hand. I knelt on all three's, laid my face on hers, and spiked the torch down between two rocks. My arms encircled her, rocked her.

A whimper. I looked down and saw the very best part of myself at the end of his mother's rope—squalling, kicking, waving tiny arms. Gabe was slick, streaked with red in the torchlight—tiny lips, tiny toes, splotches of orange on his cheeks, hands cheesed, and crinkled with God's fingerprints.

I wiped off my throwing knife on my tunic, cut the cord, and a few hairs from my wife's head. I tied off the cord with those hairs, placed my squalling son in his mother's arms, his mouth at her breast. I lay next to her, one arm around her, the other on her stomach. The air in that tiny space was suddenly too tiny for words—not enough room for even one word—just the sound of quiet lapping over us, like milk. And our son, sucking.

Leah's stomach contracted, a final push. I put my hand between her legs. A sticky blob flowed into my hand, mingling with the residue of horse guts still on my fingers. Afterthought hit afterbirth. I tore off my shirt, wrapped up the goop. Someone had told me this was sacred in some way—wasn't sure. Maybe mothers ate the stuff.

I thanked God he'd made me a man, laid Leah and Gabe back on her garment, and covered them with her cloak. Ishmael passed forward Leah's swaddling clothes that he and Cyrena had brought from the farm. We swaddled Gabe, lifted and pulled mother and child out, feet first, on her coat. We pulled over and under rocks through this dark tunnel.

Before we got all the way out, Leah said, "Rabbus, go back. Right where I was squatting, where my right foot was, a smooth stone. Get it. That stone felt alive. Helped me be heavy and drop Gabe to ground."

What? Heavy, crushing stones surrounded us. I went anyway and found a red, round handful of stone by the imprint of her foot. Took it with me and birthed my wife and son through our rickety, ribbed birth canal into the light of day.

We came from her mountain womb into another, of sorts. The remaining able-bodied legionnaires had formed a protective, double-layered enclosure around us. All of the men on the outer layer looked up, shields held high to protect from any stray slingers or archers. Tiberius stood resurrected in the midst of them. He was bloodied and bowed, but still present for the birth of my wife and child from the mountain.

A cry came from above, "Sir! We've captured thirty rebels, all bound hand and foot. Your orders, Sire?"

Tiberius said, "Stay encircled. Send a turma of men and horses for two more centuria from Capernaum."[21]

I said, "Commander, you might be interested in something. I found Crispus, alive. He's over there." I motioned toward the debris over my left shoulder.

We walked over, Tiberius leaning on my arm. Crispus stared straight ahead, unblinking, head lolling off to one side, and guts spilling out around the jawbone beneath his fifth rib. Anyone would have taken him for dead.

I said, "The man's faking, sire. A born liar, in word and deed."

Tiberius ordered soldiers to pry back the boulders and dig him out. Once the boulder tourniquet was removed, blood spurted in jets from his leg. The ooze of blood from his torn side also increased in flow. Gaius' splintered jawbone hung out of his guts, mouth unhinged, like he wanted to have a last word with us.

Tiberius commented in his hifalutin' style, "What a cacophony of catastrophes! Morning's mist evinced afternoon's indisputability!"

The stern general, for some unknown reason, bent over to examine his enemy's leg. I caught a blurred sideways arm movement from Crispus' right arm and thrust my shield in front of Tiberius' bent, bare head. Crispus' throwing knife buried itself in my shield. I plucked out that knife, that same razored dagger he'd used to stab me in the back, cut my throat, and severe Gaius' head.

Crispus glared at me, croaked, "Traitor! Sold out to the Roman whore!"

Before my mind knew what my hands were doing, I took Crispus' knife and snubbed him. Even as I stood there, holding his cut-off nose, Tiberius kicked Crispus' bloody face full-on with his hobnail boot.

Crispus didn't have to pretend unconsciousness. Better for him that he was out of it. I removed Gaius' jawbone, pushed his guts back in where the jawbone had been, and field-dressed his open injuries with wound-wart and dittany from my side pouch. Sewed up his guts and bloody nose openings. Maybe he'd make it to Rome, so they could kill him there. Maybe he'd die on the way.

Tiberius watched me work. "Not bad for a simple farmer."

I didn't tell him my experience in such matters had come from thieves and murderers like Crispus. I finished my stitchery without speaking.

Others moved unconscious Crispus on a rough litter to join the wounded, worn out, and newly born. Leah's left hand was in my right hand; my shield held high in my left hand. Our square moved up trail as one—back toward home, Jericho, Capernaum, and Rome.

46

JESUS

Julius and I walked Claudia back to Palatine Hill, through the outer gates. We passed under the blue-angeled arch and sat on the fountain's edge. I gazed up to the Unknown God, who still flowed over us. My fingers trailed in these waters that came from Father's heart.

I played with a parchment scroll with Augustus' personal sphinx signet imprinted in the royal red wax. It had arrived at our apartment this morning.

I said, "Want to hear what I got from your Grandpa today, Claudia?"

Both Claudia and Julius leaned in.

"To the Jewish Seer. I require your counsel. We will stay at Nola, in the shadow of Vesuvius, the Erupter. We leave in three days' time. Leave your family here in Rome. First Citizen."

Both Julius and Claudia tried to speak at the same time. He won. "Wow, traveling in style with the Emperor! I'm impressed. But I wonder, why now?"

I replied, "Good question, I don't know. I do know that little faith in Father trumps big faith in small certainties."

Claudia sighed. "You're as close to your Father as two planed planks in a carpenter's vice."

I said, "We *are* close, but I still don't get why your grandpa wants me to go along on this 200-mile trip to Nola."

Claudia mused aloud, "You're going to the very place where Grandpa grew up. Fig doesn't fall far from the tree. You know, maybe he wants you to see where he's been or where he's going. You seers are good at that kind of thing."

She turned to me. "I bet Grandpa wants you to help him see and secure his successor. He eternally wants to be secure."

She stood with her back to the Unknown God and faced the only God she knew. "You see things he doesn't. You have powers he doesn't have. For example, you could tell him if you see demons floating in and out of people's heads."

When I arched an eyebrow her way, she fought off a smile. "Seriously, Grandpa hasn't figured out how to true people's hearts. For that matter, he can't create loyalty out of artifice. That's what you do by…" She furrowed her brow, "being present. I think maybe he wants to learn your brand of Presence before he steps into his own Circus Max where the lions prowl."

Her words washed over me. I wanted alone time with Father and Windy. They were Lions I didn't need to defend. When set loose in anyone's heart, their truth would defend me. I was so lonely for them. This lonely hunger panted in me, like a living creature, wanting home.

Windy broke in, *Son, this is what all exiles feel as time passes through them.*

Her statement stuck in my windpipe, close to my heart. *I feel like I'm passing the time in exile, or time is passing me by. Either way, Windy, can you hurry future into history? Sometimes these times are too much to bear, and I want to be done with it.*

I felt a soft breeze cuddle me, whistle through my nose into my lungs. I felt Her presence, but I hardly felt present for either Her *or* my friends. I sighed and turned to catch up with my friends' conversation.

Claudia was in mid-laugh, joking with Julius when she saw my attention return to her. In a blink, her eyes, like blue glass, lit from within, saw my sad. "Why so blue, Jesus?"

"I was flirting with an exiled feeling. Thinking of going steady. Wanting to be home."

"I'm jealous. But I know you came a long way to be here with us, and I love you for that."

She flipped back to Julius—an effervescent, quick-change artist. "Even though I'm Grandpa's favorite, Grandma might talk him into socking me on some lonely rock. She's put Julia on Pandateria; Postie, on Planasia; and her daughter, Julilla, on Trimerus. Revolving door exiles, all of them, based on her whims. Grandma thought Julia would learn loyalty from *Psyche*, so she brought her up for a visit. Guess Julia didn't pass muster, cause now she's socked back on a rock. The older Grandma gets, the more family ends up dead or on some lonely rock surrounded by water."

Claudia dances so lightly between moods, Father. Now chipper, then solemn—a quick study for any acting role.

As if to prove my point, she pulled a face, bent over, elbow on knee and chin resting on her fist. She angled her face for the best light and postured regally. "Do you think this is my most "August" expression? Empress *is* the role of a lifetime, you know, but the lifetime for that role is very short."

47

WINDY

Slow waddled a tray of glazed vases, slow as you please, out to the street shop. The purple pottery shimmered in the noon sun and rested on her baby shelf. A tear bottle almost slid off the tray. Someone gave her a hand, steadied it.

She muttered, "Good catch, Fragile. We're in this together. Not the weight that's important. It's how we tote it. Mother, baby, and bottles need balance. Be reasonable. That way, none of us gets left behind."

Harlot grumped, "You leave me behind all the time. I have fire in my belly, and all you let out our mouth are puffs of smoke. Little flakes of ash. No passion."

"You're always on some slippy, feeling path, Harlot, stable as a mudslide. Never reasonable."

Shame weighed in, "All your you's are a woman bites dog story, but no one can agree who's the dog and who's the woman. You've chewed you up. Should be ashamed of yourselves."

Slow was so focused on her in-fighting that she walked right into her brother in law as he entered Rahab's courtyard. Leah followed Rabbus, riding on Goodness. Kindness followed on a halter, tied to his mother.

Slow put her tray of tear bottles down. Duck-waddled herself over to Leah, who handed her Gabe-the-babe for the very first time. Auntie Slow goo-goo'ed at him. He gurgled back, happy as a seraph tap-dancing on the Ark.

Leah enunciated her next words carefully. "Sis, ever heard of anyone getting buried in a landslide, then delivering her kid in a cave, in the pitch black, with Mercy for a midwife? And, oh yeah, Mercy had passed."

Slow looked up at Leah, wide-eyed, confused. Thoughts argle-bargled in a tangle through her mind. Maybe her ears had gone wonky. Perhaps

Escape had sucked meaningful speech through a wrinkle in the air. Or maybe Shame had crumbled all her cookies, disconnecting self from selves.

She said, "Say all that again, and real slow, so I can get it."

Leah hugged her sister and repeated her news, adding, "And Someone held me from behind while Gabe dropped out of me, heavy as a stone. Held me, I tell you, even though I was alone."

I whooshed around the sisters, whipping their hair around. Leah paused long enough to pull her hair into a bun. "After I dropped this load, Rabbus and our men birthed Gabe and me from under Eagle's Wings through a ribbed tunnel."

Slow quipped, "One of us has taken leave of our senses. Or did I miss a recent childbirth class—*Invisible Midwives, Ex-Lepers, and the Eagles?*"

Gabe started bawling, and Leah took him to her breast. He kept crying. She sniffed his diaper and wrinkled her nose.

The two sisters whisked inside Slow's apartment for a diaper change— plus lunch, afterward. Garden fresh cucumbers, tomatoes, and chickpea falafels were just the thing, with a wine spritzer. Together, they caught up with life in the Jericho fast lane.

As they disappeared into the apartment, Tiberius cantered into the courtyard on a blazing white stallion. He led his band of ragged legionnaires. His face matched the color of his horse—dead white.

Rabbus said, "Commander, perhaps you should lay down after your journey."

A soft moan escaped Tiberius' mouth. "I need to secure the prisoners."

"We'll secure them, Commander. Can I take you to your room now?"

"Our persons need-be reconnoiter with yon captain." He cantered over to a junior officer.

Laz turned to Rabbus. "Something strange is happening here. Help me out."

"Laz, you're looking at 'strange,' over there." Rabbus pointed to a delirious man on a stretcher who flopped back and forth, side and leg oozing blood.

Rabbus added, "Another Cynico situation, except different. Two men broke bad. Cynico became Cyn, who became Cy. That man grew up as his name grew down. Crispus burned and grew badder."

Laz looked scared. "We *have* to keep him from going up in flames if he lights himself on fire?"

Rabbus said, "If he and his buddies die, so be it. But Crispus is still dangerous, even in his current state. He'd do to you what some Bedouins do—cut their enemies' heads open while they're alive and eat their brains with a spoon."

Laz said, "A guy to be watched, for sure, but not while he's eating. Let's put him over there in that shady corner between garden and stables. And, by the by, how'd he lose his nose?"

Rabbus said, "His own knife turned on 'im."

At this moment, Tiberius collapsed. One moment he was talking to a centurion; the next, he was down and out.

Rabbus yelled for help. "El Roi, send for a doctor, quick!" Roy dispatched a runner.

While we waited, I lined up the two men's litters, stripped them naked, and put them in the shade of a courtyard corner. Each unconscious man leaked green, putrid pus from different holes.

Slow and Leah emerged from Slow's apartment and stood in the shadows, scrutinizing the action outside. I gazed adoringly at both sisters, both coming together slowly, piece by piece, into all Father had designed them to be.

I popped a strange image into Rabbus' head. The image caught fire—a golden microburst flaming down toward Leah, gentled with gifts unseen. This vision surprised him, but Leah surprised him more. She was complicated—sometimes a frantic kid, chewing her nails. Other times, a mystic prophetess. Now Father and I had added motherhood to the mix. I stirred well. New parts of her were being birthed, more or less at the same time. Rabbus thought, *if I don't watch careful-like, I'll miss the next delivery, like I missed Gabe's.*

Meanwhile, two respected physicians in Jericho, *rophe* from the tribe of Levi, arrived. The men kneeled beside the patients on litters. One was a surgeon, an *uman*. He still wore his bloody surgical apron. The other doctor nodded solemnly and pointed to the ragged edge of Tiberius' abdominal wound. Purplish-black streaks stretched from his wounds, front and back. He held both hands up with palms out, beard wagging about Tiberius being poisoned. The medical men also talked ever so learnedly about black and yellow bile being out of whack with phlegm and blood humors.

The senior man gave orders, "Move these men to the *battei shayish*, right away!"

This marble hospital, by synagogue central, was where surgeries were conducted. Zac and Rastus' abba had donated the money, earning extra points that he'd present to St. Peter at the Gate, hoping for more elegant digs.

These physicians were respected in town, true. But folks also knew that when people went in the front door of the *battei shayish*, they usually came out the back door on a straight path to the charnel house.

Rabbus thought, these doctors looked sober and serious. Most doctors do. If you were going to kill a person, you might as look studious. Reputations needed maintaining. Rabbus tried to stay as jaundiced as possible with these sorts of things, but it was hard to keep up.

48

LEAH

Rabbus and I walked behind the litters, inside the cordon of legionnaires. Windy's voice blew around inside my head—snatches between distractions. The look and smell of those men's wounds nauseated me. How did these physicians ever do their work without vomiting all over their patients? I took a deep breath, quieted my stomach, dropped my rock right hand to left, steadying myself, getting heavy like the ground.

Windy's voice, surprisingly clear, deep. *Leah, watch and learn. This is your calling. I called your mother to be a court musician. I called you to be a prophetess and healer. I will guide you. My voice will touch your ears. My touch will guide your hands. My breath will fill your lungs. Stay small in your own eyes.*

I let my shoulders droop. Made myself smaller.

Windy snapped, *Not like that. I'm not interested in appearances. Square your shoulders, girl! Walk boldly, outside. Stay humble, inside.*

Windy, you sound different, like with a man's voice.

Does the Wind have gender, child? I'm neither male nor female. Beyond gender. All you need do is listen and obey.

I racked back my shoulders, listened. Felt less like vapor. Windy continued, *You are not your parents' shadow. And even if you believe this lie, a shadow isn't owned by those who cast it. You're my child more than theirs.*

The further we walked, the better I heard. Windy counseled, *both of these men have a great capacity for cruelty and suffering. Crispus has murdered scores. Tiberius has and will order the deaths of thousands. Both are rambling wrecks, sexually, faithful to nothing but pleasure and power.*

El Roi glided over. "Watch the doctors work, Leah. Pray. I told them that you were sensitive to the Spirit world and could help their outcome. They asked if you were a witch. I said no, you were a prophetess."

My sagging shoulders squared once again.

The senior Levite changed his bloody apron for a fresh one. Both men washed their hands. The table had been scrubbed clean. Both prayed for guidance, and then the senior *uman* looked straight at Rabbus and me.

He said, "Wash your hands, then come over here, both of you." We did. "Hold this man down by his shoulders, gentle but firm." We held Crispus down.

They used clamps to stop Crispus' blood from squirting so bad when they cut to bone. Got out a saw now, not a scalpel. Their patient moaned, opened his eyes, and flailed around. Alarmed. Rabbus and I held tighter.

The guy with the saw looked at me. "Speak comfort. He will hear your voice."

I lowered my eyes. I prayed, *Windy, men are in charge here. I'm only a teenage girl from a foreign country speaking with a foreign accent.*

I heard sighing. Then, *stop looking at you through their eyes. Own the vision, hearing, and feeling Father gave you as a woman. Speak when and what I say—no more, no less. Remember the source of your skill and training.*

Thanks, Windy. When I taste your mind, like now, I know what I've hungered for.

A strong wind whipped through the open window and blew my hair back from my eyes. Close clouds, nearly black in their centers, muttered rumblings. A bent-over nurse poked her head in the surgery door. The strange glint in her eye weirded me out.

Tiberius yelled, "Drusus! I come!" His chest went still, eyes open and staring up at the ceiling. The doctors checked his vital signs. The senior *uman* draped the sheet over his head.

Both men went back to work, separating Crispus from his leg. Windy said, *Speak this to Crispus, 'God has use for even you, if you repent. The choice is yours.'* I said these things in Crispus' right ear. His eyes popped open. He was clearly focused on me for a moment with both eyes—not one wandering eye, like a loose die rolling around in a casting cup. I knew he'd heard my word to turn around and let God use him. Before he could speak, he chose to let unconsciousness claim him once again.

I knew the doctors and Rabbus had heard me speak to Crispus. I wondered what craziness they thought of me. Then I remembered Windy's words. *Use your eyes, not theirs. Listen with your ears, not another's.*

The surgeon made it through most of the thigh bone, took a white-hot blade from an assistant, and touched it to the bleeders. Blood vessels seared shut. The smell of roasting meat filled the hospital room.

49

JESUS

John and I were on one of Rome's seven hills, walking a ridgeline. I was to leave early the next morning for Nola. Below us, a crowded city teemed with a million sheep. Lambs from many flocks, all belonging to Father, Windy, and me.[22] They stayed busy, busy, busy, searching for home.

Windy said, *see these lost sheep, Son? I've mingled their longing for home with yours. But for now, pray for one found sheep who's feeling lost. Leah.*

I immediately stopped in my tracks and turned to John, "We need to pray for Leah."

John said, "Okay, but pray for what?"

"Not sure. I feel waves of nausea. I'm getting overwhelmed. Maybe this is me, maybe her. I see her face, hear her voice. She's calling for help and trying to keep from vomiting. Let's pray that Leah will allow Father to work through her mouth, her hands."

We dropped to our knees along the path, face to the ground. We rested there, as simply and honestly as we could manage, listening for Father's reply.[23]

After a few minutes of silence, another word came for me to request Father—*empower Leah, now.*

I told John to pray for her, and then I too went to work, each of us, apart-together, focusing like a ray of sun through a magnifying glass. Catching fire.

I imagined power surging through Windy's breath into Leah's lungs and tissues. I rehearsed and remembered Windy's lightness and largeness, how She would slip through a crack in time, a rift in the fabric of a soul, a crossroads at the edge of life and death. I picked up echoes of His power. Stayed focused. Energy arrived and then left me like I was a relay station. I collapsed flat out, prone on the rocky soil, arms stretched out over my head. I was dead tired, for no reason at all.

50

LEAH

Windy said, *Leah, take the sheet off Tiberius. Lie down on top of him. Put your hands on his hands, your legs on his legs, your stomach on his, and your chest on his. Put your mouth on his mouth. Breathe into his lungs. Believe he will live again. Don't wait. Do it now.*

I complained, fumbled, crumbled. I told Him, *I'm a stray tumbleweed blown across the Negev from Moab. I've always lived my life on the skinny side of miracles. This resurrection stuff is way out of my league. It's for someone like Jesus. Not me, Windy. Not me.*

He said, *a weed is something unwanted, unclaimed. It drops from bird poo or a wanderer's coat pocket. You're not a weed. You're a wonder. I blew you here with my own breath for you to do my good works. I have no bodies on earth but those who believe in me.*

My thoughts and feelings weren't fit for human consumption, so I gave them back to God. I grumbled, "I'll look so, so *stupid!*" I didn't want to hear His reply. My already teensy ears shriveled further into my head. I could practically feel wax filling them.

The Voice continued anyway. *Leah, if you say no to Me, I'll find another and pass you over. By your own choice. Choose your life, and choose it now.*

When I emptied myself of pride, I felt heavy—like my deliverance rock was ready for further employment. I pictured and heard an oval, clay jug chugging life out its mouth. I pulled back the sheet that covered Tiberius. Laid down on top of him, head to head, chest to chest, feet to feet.

The surgeons still fiddled with knives and saws over Crispus' bloody body. No one noticed me, except Rabbus and the two guards. All three men stared at me, wide-eyed. I whispered to Rabbus, "Hold my hand and pray for us."

Rabbus grabbed my right hand, even as my hand grabbed its rock. He dropped to his knees beside the stone table. I lowered my head toward Tiberius' head. My mouth was dry as a stale cracker. I opened his clammy jaw and cool lips. I put my lips on his and breathed a little puff of air into his mouth. Energy-charge tingled my bones. My right hand, the one gripping my stone, quivered involuntarily, passing a bit of lightning Rabbus' way. I scrunched shut my eyes and silently prophesied, *Live! Through Windy's power, with Jesus' kindness, for Father's glory, come alive again, future emperor of Rome!*

Windy said, *Yes! You did your part. Now I'll do mine.*

I raised my head a couple of inches and looked down at Tiberius' face. He spluttered, laboring air up from his lungs, as if raising water from a deep well. His eyes flickered open. He looked around, leaned his head to one side, and said to Rabbus, quite reasonably, "Why is your wife lying on top of me?"

51

SLOW

I suspect slow resurrections are more interesting than quick ones. Not that I'd seen either one, just heard about that one down in the surgery—from Leah and everyone else in town. This was my first resurrection to see with *my* own eyes. I watched it dawdle along for a year or two as Cy and Cyrena each learned how to love, resurrecting one another from a cruel past of abusing and being abused.

This morning they sat in the early morning sun after a night shift of work, before bedtime. Cyrena sputtered, "Cy, let me feel your head." He plopped his head in her lap.

"Oh my, what a tangle! Let me comb your mane, my lion in winter." She soothed his wild hair and beard, first with her finger comb and then with one Cy had carved from the bone of an ass. Once his hair was presentable to her fingers, they toddled off to bed.

Each was busy bringing the other into a life neither had known. Slow trickles of laughter flowed from him, in spite of himself. The two showed up at synagogue when Roy was speaking and sat in the back row. Cy's lips slightly moved when the congregation sang. I know, because I was in the back row too, a few seats over, on the other side of Laz.

Later, Cyrena told me something that brought tears to Fragile and leaked out my eyes too. She said, "You know that new temple Zac's father paid for? The one with the spire that points the path to heaven, without trying to poke a hole in it? Well, we know the night watchman. He's blind, like us. He rings them bells so purdy. Mellow, round, and silver-colored they be.

"Anyway, we wuz alone together, us two, silent, when the bells rang for the third hour. Cy was at the wheel. I'd bent over, hands gloved, taking a pot out of the kiln. He stopped his treadle, hands still in the spinning mud.

"He said, 'Cyrena, I've been a silent bell my entire life. Never knew it. Never knew it at all, till you struck me, and I could hear who I was.'

"I dropped my pot, Slow. Splat. I shattered it. I sat and cried. I knew then we'd spend the rest of our lives bein' two bells together, even if we wuz broke."

Laz and I watched the Cy's learn to live presently. They were sensible enough to make peace of their pieces. Theirs was a slow process that instructed all my me's. They taught Cutter how to use her sharp edges profitably. Cracking and crumbling happened less since they weren't so quick to take offense. Cyrena forgot, more often than not, how to criticize. She taught Fragile by example to be fragile like an orchid, not an explosive. She learned the value of a good cry, without Shame—that showers, not thunder, grew flowers.

Cy showed Escape how *not* to 'yes-but' Cyrena into Thursday of next week. Instead, he learned what he called 'nine-hard-words' from El Roi— 'I'm sorry, I was wrong, please forgive me.'

When they did get into a screaming-meemie, knock-down, drag-out fight, both took their cutting fragments to the grinding ground and started over, fresh.

After a wheel or two of seasons had passed, El Roi saw it was time. He turned a couple of new pots off his workshop wheel and made one pot from it. This double spouted vase, Cy1 and Cy2, graduated in commitment from just partners to husband and wife. Their love story—a blinded, reamed-out Italian mercenary and an Arab demoniac ex-whore—caused people in Jericho to scoot out of the way and make room for possibility. After all, it wasn't every day an ordinary person got to breathe deep and enjoy a Double-Cy.

52

WINDY

When the two cousins learned about their grandfather's trip south, both of them took action. Neither knew what the other was doing, but Father had arranged a fateful meeting for the two of them.

Claudia promptly lied to her mother, "I'm spending a week with Rosa at her parent's cliff house on the way to Nola, Mother. She's got a stable of new men to entertain us." The week with Rosa and the men was a lie—the villa, not so much.

In fact, the abandoned villa was perfect. Right in Jesus' path on the way south. Claudia rounded up her maids and guards, and they left the next day. She wanted to arrive in plenty of time to get her banquet ready. A banquet fit for a king, you might say.

Once they had slugged up Grandfather's famous cut through the mountains and pulled into the estate, Claudia set her servants to work. She ditched both servants and that cobwebby dump for Jael's Spike. This tip-top of Strider's Ridge offered such a serene view. But the view from Homer's *Iliad* was much better.

Like Augustus' road engineers, the Greek playwright also used a pickaxe to cut rock. But his ax cut into stony, soul-soil. The story of Helen being loved by Achilles bled from Homer's mind to hers, fertilized her fields, and popped up crops of imagination—enough to feed friends and poison enemies. She folded her body like a piece of origami and settled in, cuddling with Homer and wishing he was Jesus.

The other cousin, Marcus Vipsanius Agrippa Posthumus, aka Postie, had a different idea of a good time. He'd escaped his exile isle once again with the help of Clemens, his servant. Clemens had stashed a boat in a hidden cove for him. Elba, on the Italian mainland, was only nine miles northeast from Planasia over open water.

Postie rowed hard with a tailwind pushing him toward his destiny. Clemens had left a horse for him in the usual place. The saddlebags were laden with special assassin's toys for young Postie. He cantered south for a few days along dusty country byways, finally turning north on his grandfather's new cut through the mountains.

He tethered his horse deep in a wadi and climbed through a hidden series of mountain caves to a perch he'd discovered on earlier escapes. These caves always fascinated Postie. They were dim, interlocking chambers, one on top of the other, threading through the hollows. Not too different than the hollow hearts of hungry men such as himself. Ambition slid down his gorge like a ripe fig, a sunrise in his mouth.

As a matter of habit, Postie had located himself precisely at that intersection of his ambitions and loves. He dragged this intersection with him, step for step, wherever he went, so he was never lost. His creamy rose habit, complete with hood, was his good luck charm that mother had made for him. He blended with the niche perfectly, a mix of shadow and sandstone.

Postie's mother, Julia, had never lacked fire—she was equally hot in bedroom or throne room. Now, in her later years, her cast-off, exile years, Julia's fascination with her father's throne was not unlike a magical inferno. All she had to do was fire a mystic gaze north from her exile isle, Pandateria, toward Postie on Planasia. He would feel her fire and ignite, crackling into a curious complicity with her.

They had plotted to take over the empire. Julia masterminded the coup, drawing in past lovers from among upwardly mobile politicos. She'd appointed Postie as her backup hit-man, if her primary strike team of assassins failed.

Now the day was at hand. Postie's perch was impeccable. The sun had dropped below the ridge and was no longer in his eyes. The range to his targets, easy. And his quiver of arrows, the ones Clemens had packed at the bottom of his horse's saddlebags? Ah, yes. Poison-tipped, sent special delivery from mother, whose aptitude for strange fire was only exceeded by her skill with poison. She'd always been an excellent student, sitting at *her* mother's feet. She'd observed Augusta, taken notes, and prepared these arrows for father, special delivery from her son.

Families do these things for each other.

Postie fondled his mother's arrow, the one she'd painted bright red, and grinned. He fantasized as he stroked the arrow's shaft. Grandpa and the Jew would be sitting next to each other, close together. Maybe if Gramps and the Jew were sitting close enough, and the angle just so, one arrow, this very one, would spear both of them. Sweet! Even if he had to spend two arrows on these maggots, Jeez-the-Jew had to go. He'd soon join his carpenter father and become a fading memory, courtesy of Postie.

53

JESUS

Emperor Augustus, Senator Paullus Maximus, and I had bumped south all day in the open-air carriage. The senator rested on a velvet cushion next to Augustus. He appeared to gather displeasure about himself, like the silk cloak he wore. I sat across from both men on a wooden board pitted with knotholes, a few inches lower than their covered seat.

When Claudia found out that Max was traveling with us, she'd told me, "Grandpa and Max have been the best of friends and enemies over the years. Right now, they share aging bodies and hardening of the perspectives."

Windy said, *Max trusts you in the same way a thorn bush trusts an approaching scythe. Beware.*

Augustus had handed me a portable desktop when I first arrived. Inside lay an empty scroll with a stylus and bottle of ink. He said, "You're our scribe for the day. Take notes." Emperor and senator began a discussion of current crises across the empire. I sat up, leaned in, and scribbled what they said.

We'd passed Via Severiana junction a while back and taken a turn up through the mountains. Toward late afternoon, both Augustus and Maximus had run out of conversation, and leaned their heads against one another, napping. That was fine with me. My Latin script was scraggly, with all the bouncing around, and my hand was cramping.

After some time, Maximus jarred awake and looked around. He took the occasion to ask me one question, his only question. "You Jews are different than everyone else I know." He tipped one hand sideways at an angle. "What makes you so off-kilter?"

I replied, "Maybe because we Hebrews are always crossing over." He looked confused but said nothing more.

I braved my way forward. "That's what the word *Hebrew* means, Senator, 'to cross over.' Father has pushed us out into the world, crossing borders of countries, darkness to light, naïve to innocent, being born to being born again. And all who cross over to my Father must go through me."

Maximus refused further questioning, though I'd left plenty to question in my statement. Windy said, *Max sees you as a pale, permitted shadow— transitory, precarious as a vivid dream, gone when the morning comes. Watch him. He's looking up at the eastern cliffs, straining his eyes.*

I argued back, *I wasn't solid enough to make an impact. He ignored me.*

All you said was true, Son. But you said too much, too soon. Timing was off, a little forced. But no worries, you're learning through mistakes and the things you suffer.[24]

Okay, got it. Thanks.

I turned my eyes to the mountains. The sun splashed the corrugated rocks in a moving tapestry of color: yellows, honey-orange, pink, tangerine, and the darker shades of magenta. I'd look at one bright orange spot, move my eyes away, and then, a few moments later, that same spot had fired to burnt orange. The immense darkening blue cistern of the heavens beyond was trimmed with gold.

Windy said, *isn't is great, this surrendering to color? No need for you to control what I do with the mountains or the sky. These men are no different— surrender to what is present. Be attentive and available. I'll produce change.*

I slipped out the side door and began to jog beside Augustus' closest bodyguard, the one who'd been double-timing beside us for miles.

"The beauty is astounding, Sergeant!"

Sergeant Petrius replied, "Indeed, there *is* beauty in how we Romans tamed this stone. My two elder brothers helped dig this bit—something like emptying a city of gravel with a teaspoon and then smoothing it out with a butter knife."

I nodded and noted the different beauties that lodged in each of our eyes.

Petrius, after another mile or so, offered further comment. "My brothers started it after the Emperor took office and then took most of their lives to finish it. Young man, there's no substitute for perseverance." I determined that one day, this would be said of me.[25]

I looked up to the hills. *Father, from whence comes my help?*[26] A moment after this prayer had flickered through my mind, the reply came back. *Your help comes from Me. Your trouble comes from the hills.*

I looked up again. The late afternoon sun had dropped below the western wall and now shown through a hole in that wall, becoming a focused pinpoint of light on the opposite, eastern canyon's face. This pinpoint highlighted one crag in particular. As I looked, in that moment, a sliver of silver light, like metal reflecting, winked on and off. The glint was almost over us. What *was* that?

I pointed out the spot to Petrius. "I saw a flash of metal up there—an archer?"

He squinted up into the hills. "Maybe the sun playing on a vein of quartz in the rock. Sheer rock up there, not even a goat path to the top—and a killing drop straight down. The light this time of day tricks folks into seeing stuff that ain't so."

Indeed, I *was* seeing things. But things that were so— a hooded man in a rose habit. He stood, hunting bow fully extended, aiming at our carriage. I leaped over the door and landed on Augustus, throwing him to the ground. I looked over my shoulder in time to see Max slump sideways, an arrow diagonally through his neck. His lifeblood spurted out and he rasped, "He missed. Our man, Pos…". He didn't finish his sentence before his eyes glassed over.

The Emperor was now thoroughly awake. He squirmed beneath me. I rolled off him just as another arrow anchored itself in the wall of the carriage. Petrius jumped up on the running board, shield up. He yelled for help, pointing to the shooter's niche. Archers in Captain Pontii's squadron returned fire. Their arrows bounced off the sandstone, some of them pinging down on the rocks around us.

The senior general of the Imperial Guard, Trattatori, charged his stallion our way. I wondered, *Windy, why is his short sword out, not his long one? And why is he holding it under-handed for close-in fighting?*

The Emperor, head still tucked down, asked me, "Is it safe?"

"Momentarily, sire."

Augustus popped his head up, judging his seer's sight. He drew his jeweled dagger from his inner tunic, slid it up his sleeve.

Trattatori closed the gap quickly, horse snorting as he skidded to a stop. His face was rutilant, and his broad, flat nose was as red-veined as the back of a gladiator's fist. His fingers pressed white around the hilt of his sword.

I whispered to Augustus, "This man means harm... to *you.*"

A shadow passed over the Emperor's face. He left the carriage, stood next to it, glanced past me to Petrius, and nodded.

Trat dismounted and ran toward Augustus, his eyes on the hills above, motivations moot. A second later, his killing move was complete with a downward gaze, flashing smile, broken teeth, and eyes rolling wild as a frenzied wolf.

Augustus saw the strike coming. He fell flat at Trat's feet, letting the short sword pass over him. Petrius' throwing knife landed in Trat's stomach, doubling him over. On his knees, Augustus thrust his dagger upwards into Trat's crotch, pulled out, and planted his dagger again, this time in his enemy's chest. Twisted the dagger, probing for heart meat. Trat fell to his knees beside his boss.

Augustus, lungs toiling in his chest, growled, "*Et tu,* Trat?"[27]

The general's searching eyes went wide, as though seeing into horror beyond a thin veil. His eyes held the horror for a moment and then went dark as guttered candle wicks. Augustus sucked his lower lip, his own eyes flushed with victory over yet another assassin. He stood, right arm dripping blood from his dagger, and saluted his loyal sergeant.

I said, "Emperor, the enemy still crouches at our door."

Augustus dropped to one knee. Another arrow thudded in the carriage door. He kept his head down and yelled orders to the troops around him. "Trattatori, the traitor, is dead. Those who are loyal to me, climb that cliff. Bring me the assassin.'"

Pontii's armored archers began climbing, quivers slung over their shoulders.

I also moved to obey. I checked with Augustus, got my backpack from below his seat. It contained all I owned and was almost empty.

I took a few steps away from him, sling over one shoulder and backpack over the other. I moved toward the cliff's face. Augustus cried out, "Wait!

Jesus, you're a seer, not a soldier. Leave this to the professionals. That rose sandstone is as treacherous as Trattatori."

I replied, "As you command, my Emperor. However, my seer is wedded to my warrior. I've fought lions and snakes with the weapons Father gave me. I'm at your service."

Augustus hesitated, looked me up and down. "All right, Pontii can always use a good slinger to round out his archers. But if you must go, take my armor in the back of the carriage. Traitors' arrows fly by day and night, and shadows are lengthening."

I remembered my ancestor, King David. "Your armor, sire, doesn't fit me. Father has given me all I need."[28]

Augustus seemed to shrivel before my eyes. He shuffled back to the carriage. He turned back, handed me his blooded, jeweled dagger. "At least take this."

I tucked it under the rope belt that held my cotton tunic tight. I cinched my backpack strap, bent over, and found five smooth stones. Foot soldiers hoisted me on their shoulders. I reached my first handhold and began to climb.

54

LEAH

I scooted off Tiberius and moved to stand behind my husband. Roy helped Tiberius off the table. The physicians looked him over. His entry and exit wounds were thin, even white scars, only slightly puckered around the edges. Purplish-black streaks, gone. Temperature, normal. All three pulses in his wrist were in harmony.

The one surgeon, a sly Jew with a ready wink, said, "Commander, you sure fooled me. I couldn't feel a pulse or breath. But all you needed was a pretty woman on top of you, and up you came!"

An annoyed smile flickered across Tiberius' face. "I did not implore resuscitation. God, if there is a god, brought back my soul, if I have a soul. Now I'm here again in this strain and slop." He strode out the door without looking back.

The operating surgeon picked up Crispus' bloody leg and handed it to an assistant. This man went to an adjoining room, dumped the limb in an incinerator, lit a match, and dropped it in. The banked fire danced afresh, licking its chops.

Crispus himself remained mercifully unconscious while they cleaned out his side wound, applied ointments, and laid the long flap of skin and muscle open over his gut. They'd agreed to let it air dry and reconnect layer by layer, in its own good time.

Legionnaires carried Crispus to a closely guarded infirmary unit. They shackled him to a metal cot, fastened to the concrete floor.

Rabbus and I left out a side door. Husband and I wandered the bazaar, stopping for a cup of tea and some sticky-sweet baklava.

He commented, "First time you've ever brought anyone back from the dead, or am I missing something here?"

"Wasn't me, sweetheart. Windy and Father, pure and simple. When you make everything that is, bringing life back to a fresh husk is nothing much. Spirit uses whoever pops their pride balloon and comes to ground. In my case, pride was disguised as a whine."

"Jesus has given you gifts I don't have. You hear Windy, same as Jesus."

I savored the sticky baklava, confidence newly resurrected. "When my small spirit is clear, Windy is there."

Rabbus asked, "What's clear? This is all clear as mud to me."

Spirit gave me speech, "I'm clear when light goes through me clean, without worry or pride to block it. Mystery, pure and simple."

"So, light went through you in that pitch-black cave?"

"Sometimes no light, only faith holding on. Face it. God's edgy."

These words were no sooner out of my mouth than I had a vision of Jesus on some edge; trembling arms held high, strength failing. I took Rabbus' right hand, and raised it with my left hand, raised it high as I could. "Jesus needs us to hold his arms high, up to Father, right now. He can't hold on by himself like I couldn't in that surgery."

I screwed my eyes shut and then popped them open wide, looking up. *Strengthen Jesus' grip, Windy. Father, calm His spirit. Protect the Emperor.*

55

JESUS

I stretched far enough to grip the tiny knob of rock above me. Yes, now I had a firm grip. I scrabbled my left big toe toward a waist-high chink in the rock, jammed it in. Then I looked down. Over a hundred feet below me, Augustus craned his neck upwards, hand over his eyes, gazing my way. Empty air, without cushion, between us.

Father, keep me from falling. Thank you for hearing me, even when I can't hear you. In that moment of silence, only the wind whipping around me, I heard, *pull up with your right hand, transfer weight now to your left foot. Hold. Pull up now with left hand. Speak strength to quivery muscles. Now, pull, pull—yes, yes!*

I'd made it to the next ledge. Both elbows were on rock, feet still dangling in space. My eyes closed, head tipped high to heaven in praise to Windy and Father. I looked down. Augustus raised both arms over his head.

The voice came from my right. "Hi ya, Jeez. I sent for you, and va-va-voom, here ya are! So eager, rock scrambling to greet your long lost other half. A precious sight—watching you impress dear, doomed Auggie."

Satan lounged on his side at the entry to a cave, velvet green cushion beneath him. The cushion was an exact likeness of Augustus' tufted carriage cushion, only thicker and more luxuriant. He wore a flowing, black thawab. A naked female demonette, an exact look-alike for Claudia, crouched beside him, knees splayed open. She dropped a blood-red cherry in her boss's mouth and bent down to snort a white line of powder off a mirror. She sat back up, fingering her razor. The sun's shadow cut them in two. Both were lit from the chest down, eyes sparkling in the shade.

A thin rock bridge of blood-red shale connected Lucifer to me. The cliff I had climbed was a veneer, maybe ten feet thick, over inner shafts of emptiness.

On the other side of the bridge, Satan's cave was made of harder stuff—granite, scarred with anthracite. Behind him, on the wall of his cave, shadows of flames flickered, then blazed, subsided, back and forth.

I pulled fully up on the ledge. Looked at my friend from before calamity, before earth time, before he tried his coup. In a blink, he went from Old Friend to Old Enemy.

Lucifer oiled out his patter in a droll tone, "Such a smooth Glory Hound!"

I stood, took a step onto the shale bridge. "Your mix of truth and lie is a mistake. I do want glory, but this splendor reflects Father, and is for Him alone."[29]

"I make no mistake. You're *way* more than another failed messiah or a populist politician with an ax to grind against Rome. You're striving for more, much more. Why settle for being a failed insurrectionist? Your secret wish—if we're honest—is glory. Your name ringing down the halls of history—'Jee-sus! Jee-sus!'"

He snorted, "*I* need to take lessons from *you*."

I replied, "Wrath is cruel and anger outrageous, but who can stand before envy?"[30]

Lucifer laughed, "Ah, I forget. Pious *is* your trademark. But appearances aside, who's the envious one here? *You're* the secret glory grasper—but one with a big fall in store, second Adam."

I took a deep breath, *stay on the path, stay on the path*. Took a step forward and stood in a puddle of bright light angling through a tiny rock window in the opposing western wall.

My foot slid forward, knocking a pebble off the bridge. It echoed off the cliff walls, down, down, falling, fading. A terrible stillness followed, like the silence after an executioner's ax has fallen.

Satan peered over the edge. "A long way down, for those who long to get high."

He mirrored my exact image. When I changed my expression, his face effortlessly took on my shape. A sling rested over his shoulder, as did my own sling over my shoulder. I picked my five stones out of my pocket and nervously trickled them, one hand to the next. He picked five identical stones from his pocket, calmly mirroring my actions, all the while gazing unblinkingly at me. *Totally un-nerving.*

"Wanna sling a little string, Son of David? Your way of gettin' high was *so* much work." He grinned. "Let's see who can smack Auggie in the noggin first. I'll even let you try first."

I ignored his jibe. "Lucifer, I climb toward light, astonished with the beauty of Father's world."

Satan opened his mouth to speak, but Windy's sword flashed off my tongue. "You, meanwhile, recline in the shade and risk nothing, refuse vulnerability, churn out addictions and shame."

"Your halo's slipping, Jeez-the-Pious. The Emperor can't see your itty-bitty temper tantrum—only me. I know you better than you know yourself, White-Bright-Light. I tolerate a thousand shades of grey you refuse to deal with. Father sent me to educate you about yourself. Same as he sent me to Job."

A great lethargy hit me. *Father, my words feel like soap bubbles. No consequence, none at all—no currency anywhere in heaven or on earth.*

The Enemy continued his quiet, suave patter. He pointed down from whence I'd come. "You know, we could really fool him, manger boy. Such a cuddly fable, by the by, even *you* believe it.

"Ah well, back to business. We can shake up history today. Ya know, bud, during some millennia, nothing happens but the primordial slop bubbling away. That's it. On other days, millennia can happen. Like today."

I stood, arms crossed, started to speak.

Satan cut me off, temptation-quick, "We'll start with Auggie's empire and go from there. You do your sweetness and light gig. I'll handle the down and dirty side of things. I'd get most of the work, but you'd be a great front man. Skin-deep, true, but such a glowing radiance! You sucker sheep through the front door. We'll share the glory, right down the middle of all time, and beyond."

"Stop it, Satan. You well know it's written, 'Don't tempt God.'"

"Did I forget to tell you? God's not here. It's just you and me, junior."

"I'm One with Him, not the fallen aspirer. I'm in. You're out. You tried to steal His throne, divide His kingdom. Failed miserably. You're nothing more than a fizzled lightning bolt, left with only its sputter. Then total darkness, for all eternity."

Satan hissed, "And you, what of you, power-climber, tryin' to get high on such a fragile bridge. You're dust over dark. You, tiny you, must be so, *so* desperate for a father, now that I took poor dreaming Joe out of it. He didn't even see me coming."

I hadn't seen *that* attack coming. I staggered under his blow. The blast of grief almost caused me to lose my footing, tumble into the void.

I whispered, "Help me, Windy, Father. I need you now."

"Oh, stop whining, Jeez. I heard you calling in the Troops. Forget it. You're on your own. I got a head-nod from Pops. He told me to crush you like a bug like I did with Job. That was so much fun."

He flicked his gaze up from playing with his stones. "No more drivel, little man. At least Job had no God pretension. Let's see what the great God-Pretender is made of."

I took another step forward. Now in the exact middle of the bridge. I didn't know what to do, where to go. I breathed, lifted my arms up and out, palms toward heaven. My right palm began to bleed in the spot where Postie had driven his dagger through it.

I waited and stared steadily into the eyes of Evil. Evil stared back at me, implacable. I felt the cold, uncoiling of a great snake in his belly twining into my intestines. Hundred-pound lead bags weighted my arms. Windy and Father were silent. My eyes stayed locked on Satan, arms trembling. The air sizzled.

Then, after another minute of nothing but quiet, my hands grew lighter, my arms grew stronger. Flickering image of Leah, Rabbus, holding my hands up.

Confidence surged. I said to Satan, "Even in the shadow you cast, Father protects me. I know El Abba lives, and in my mortal flesh I shall see him once again."[31]

Even as I quoted the patriarch, I remembered Claudia and muttered to myself, "He had sex with her." I flinched.

Satan said, "Ha! Sainted *Jaay-sus*, now you're pondering precious Claudia, that lust bag of gyrating hormones." The demonette licked her lips and stared at my crotch, a residue of white powder rimming her nose.

Satan chortled, "What a consummate, conniving vixen, your Claudia. A murderess as well, scheming her way to the top. She's been in training with me, you know." He said no more, caressed his demonette.

How to tell lie from truth with this guy? I knew Windy and Father saw all I did—but I couldn't sense their presence. *Were these my next lessons in growing up—living in silence, depending on the kindness of strangers to hold me in their prayers?*

I told Satan, "Father and Windy's *hésed,* their kindness, always chases me."

Satan smiled a devilish smile. "Let them chase you now." He tapped the bridge where I stood with his pinky finger, ever so delicately. The bridge crumbled beneath me, along with the outer cliff wall behind me. It fell away, all of it, a couple of yards from his cushion. He gave me a finger wave, mouthed the words, '*bye-bye.*'

I dropped like a rock, like Abba had dropped. Wall flashed by me. I stretched out both hands, both feet, reaching for a handhold, toehold, anything.

The wall picked up speed. My right hand clutched at a jagged edge of flinty rock. Rock ripped forearm, slowed my fall. Right foot smashed another bit of crevice, slashing. *Oww!* Right calf ripped. Impact slowed me. I grabbed a knobby edge. Hung on with my left hand. I'd been snagged by a knob I couldn't see, dangling in the dark. Outside walls crumbled, avalanching toward Augustus.

56

CLAUDIA

I was bored, my mind shuttling one thought to the next. I rolled up Homer's *Iliad* that lay beside me, napped, leaning against a shattered Ionian column of Apollo's temple. I dreamt in the sun, picturing me as Helen and Jesus as Achilles, rolling into Troy inside his Trojan horse. Helen and I were quick-silver shallow, loving life on the edge of sunny porches. I was so shallow, I got right down to the skin of things. We needed rescue, Helen and me, from our surfacy selves.

I couldn't go back to Rose Villa without Jesus to rescue me from myself—*and* that gloom. The place reeked of love lost. I imagined Rosa's Jewish father and Italian mother popping out of the walls—fingers pointing, cords in their necks popping out as they yelled at each other.

The late afternoon sky was a watery blue with streaky rooster tails of cirrus flitting high into the darkening royal blue bowl above me. A murder of crows wheeled across the sky, cawing like rolling thunder. They reminded me of a single, black scarf that folded back on itself and then stretched out long again, expanding, contracting. I watched them till they dropped into the canyon beneath me.

I stared into the empty bit of blue that once held them, daydreaming of Jesus entering this abandoned temple, seeing me and saying, "There you are!" I knew that if the shoe were on the other foot, me sighting him as I entered a room, I'd say something like, "Here I am!"

I was distressingly like my mother in that way. I had to find that quick-silver, shallow, 'look-at-me' bitch and stomp her into a grease spot. Because drama fueled her life, I didn't have to show up for all her performances. Maybe I could shape her into a pickaxe and smash her face into the stuff of things. Go deep; yeah, that was the new me, hiding out behind a new god in town, one whose temple was not yet in ruins. Regardless, I wasn't going to spend another moment, not a candle-flicker-moment, dwelling on my mother. She made me wary as that wing of crows.

I started at the sound of a rasp behind me—a clawing, scrabbling sound on the temple steps. I turned in time to see a shadow slip behind a column. Then, nothing but silence. Tingles shot up my spine. Me and whoever owned that shadow were alone together.

I crowed, "Come out, come out, whoever you are. Or do you want me to come get *you?* Hide-and-Seek is always such fun!"

Postie dragged himself into view. I don't know who was more surprised, him or me. His bow and a quiver of arrows were slung over his right shoulder—and why was a black arrowhead embedded in the meat of his right thigh, close to his crotch?

I stood with my arms wide out to scatter my tingles. I said, "You found me, cousin! Well, here I am!"

"You have to help me, Claudia. I tried to kill grandpa and that friggin' Jew. Instead, I shot Max, mother's lover. Not my fault! The Jew jumped on top of grandpa and forced my arrow to hit the wrong guy. Then grandpa killed Trattatori, real sneaky like, after the Jew whispered something in his ear."

A huge sigh escaped him. "Everything went wrong today, spoiled by that Heebie. Mother is going to be *so* pissed at me!" He slumped into a frump on the step next to me and immediately yelled, "Ow!" He'd forgotten his new, third leg, the head poking up further out the front of his thigh.

"How'd you collect that arrow? It's a stand-up addition to your catapult artillery, I must say."

"A lucky strike by one of grandpa's archers. I was slipping through a crevice when it speared my behind. I hauled ass up here, a secret pathway through the hollows behind the canyon wall. But this did slow me down." He pointed to his poke-a-haunt, inhaled.

"You're losing blood, cousin."

"I'll be okay. But I need a hideout, a place to recover for a day or two."

He paused. "Forgive me, cousin, for being snotty to you in the throne-room, on the road, in the bar, in Vestal's house. I'm not my true, loving self when that Jew's around you."

He thought furiously for a moment, smitten by a brainstorm. Then he kneeled on his wounded leg. "Claudia, help me get back to Planasia. I won't miss next time. Gramps, a wrinkled-up old prune past his prime. And Jew-boy has to go too—for both our good, dear, both our good."

A rumble in the distance, the rushing sound of rocks, or a cataract of waters.

I said, "What's *that*?"

Postie put his most ambitious foot forward. "Ah, nothing at all. Maybe a rockslide. Happens all the time around here." He paused, fingered his new shaft. "We two could rule the empire, you know. With your beauty, my brains and brawn, anything is possible. We'd make a great emperor and empress."

I put a bright expression on my face and broke a smile into shards. "Postie, do you *really* think the two of us could live happily ever after?"

"Oh, yes, my true love! It will be as you say. I've always loved you, even though you've been..." His brow clouded. "Grievously seduced by that slime-ball Heebie."

I said, "Never mind him. Come with me. Grandpa doesn't know I'm here. I'll hide you in Rosa's basement so you can gain your strength back. I think I, ah, *we* can pull this off."

I helped him up. He leaned on my right shoulder. We hobbled together, past Jael's Spike. This, in turn, led to a side path not far from the back door of Rosa's compound. The name over the door was in Hebrew script, *Lo-Ruhamah*.[32] Rosa's Jewish father had hand-carved it.

Postie said, "Do you think you could learn to love me, dear cousin?"

I said, under the lintel, "I've never truly loved anyone, really, except...."

He cut me off. "We'll figure it out. Meanwhile, stay clear of the arrows in my quiver. One small nick is fatal, my queen. Mother gave me the poison, distilled from her snake venom. She milks them, you know, the snakes' jaws."

We came to the back-bedroom door on the lower floor. I slid the bolt open and turned back to help him. He sat, ogling me. I turned round and round, as if roasting on an open spit. My wounded paramour took me in his arms and began pressing us together. He groaned, forgetting he'd been shafted.

I said, "Postie, that was so hot! But let's get you inside first. Then we'll see where our passions take us." An eager shine swirled around his face. I sat him down in the hunter's basement bedroom. I yanked the sheet off the bed and tore it in strips. Looked deep into his eyes. "Let me bind your wound."

I pulled his pants down and took off his shirt. Postie was naked as the day he was born. I held my arms out, palms up, and tipped my head to one side. He lurched toward me, wanting what he wanted. I said, "First things first, my feathered friend."

Overhead, the floor squeaked, guards and maids moving around. Bedsprings squeaked, rhythmic, directly overhead. *My maid, Bella! And that was to be Jesus' room for the night. Okay, part of the night.*

Postie looked up, a worried look on his face.

I said, "Ignore them—hired help, having a romp. We royals are safe together."

I took the long, straight shaft in both hands. "I've never done this before, but maybe this is how it works."

I forced the stiff shaft away from me with a strong pull. The straight arrow came clean out the bloody hole. I salved the wound with a tin of pig grease. Added a little more on his other arrow.

I said, "Before we get to the main course, let me satisfy your other appetites." I gave him my best salacious smile. Postie weakly smiled back, exhausted by his failed efforts at regicide and Jewicide.

I went to the hunter's downstairs kitchen and rooted around in his cool, dank cellar. Smelled of decomposing flesh. I flipped a joint of aged ham and two half-boiled potatoes on a plate. Then I tipped a tanker of cool wine into a goblet, adding a full measure of clearly marked "Sleeping Powder" from the medicine chest.

How ideal! Cousin Postie certainly needed rest from his labors.

When I returned, he greedily gulped the food and wine. I plastered my silky smile into place. He finished gobbling down his meal and let rip a long burp, looking very pleased indeed at his contribution to Latin oratory.

As an encore, I slowly undid the buttons on my dress. Postie helped me along. He became a wee bit impatient, ripping off my last three buttons. He went right to work. But alas, his quivery arrow collapsed.

After some time, I said, "Your wounded leg. The pain must be intense."

His face burned, beet-red. I didn't look at his eyes. Instead, I watched his wispy beard. It agreeably bapped up and down again and again, warbling noise from that hole above it.

"Cousin, you must be exhausted. Besides, if we give into our passions with a rough 'n tumble, you'd bleed. We couldn't have that now, could we?"

He relented, laid on his back. I leaned over him, sang him love songs from *Psyche's* popular ballads, the ones faithless Cupid sang to Psyche.

His head lolled, then jerked up, now and again, rising and falling more slowly as the minutes passed. I massaged his chest and ran my fingertips over the pulsing, triangular hollow in the middle of his chest, below his breastbone.

I covered his loins and stroked his sweaty, black curls away from his face. So peaceful, soon snoring. I stood up, looked around for my torn dress. There, in the corner where he'd thrown it in a heap. I put on an old hunter's toga that hung from a nail on the wall. I smoothed out the leather, arranged my hair just so in the sliver of cracked mirror on the wall. *Nice.*

Some hunters hunted for personal glory. *Well! Those hunters need hunting.*

Once I was properly dressed, I raised my chin and practiced looking predatory. I reached down and took one of the poisoned arrows from Postie's quiver on the floor. I stroked the shaft absent-mindedly, wondering how Aunt Julia milked a black adder's little head. Did she suck the poison out directly?

I ran my thumb lightly across the flat, poisoned blade of the razored arrowhead, bringing it to my nose. Did poison stink? Huh, nothing, not even a whiff. I covered the length of the arrow with a strip of bed sheet and held it firmly with both hands. Postie was sound asleep when I plunged his own arrow straight down, right into that pulsing hollow below his breastbone, fastening him securely to the mattress.

57

WINDY

Our Son had disappeared over the top of that ledge. Augustus, left alone without his seer, felt vulnerable. His *auguren*, the discerner of life and death, was gone.

He mused, *how best to remember Max and Trat, the heroes they once were or the traitors they'd become? I, too, have a bit of each yeast baking within me. Hero and traitor vie for supremacy. Whatever I let rise today will feed me tomorrow.*

Augustus' father had schooled him to assure the powerful of undying loyalty until it served him no further. That's where Augustus had introduced traitor to hero within himself, had them shake hands—his own Truth and Reconciliation Commission.

The emperor looked at the sandstone mountains, the very one Petronius' brothers had spent their lifetimes blasting and carving with legions of other engineers and workers. Now his highway ran through these same mountains. How different was his life from those cliffs? His decisions, like all those grains of sand, had compacted, coalesced into character—lighter layers of hero blending with blood-red traitor, husband lying on top of cheater, friend folding knife into enemy. Now all was set in stone, immovable.

He prayed, without knowing it. *What if that cliff was more scree and sediment than hard stone? What if his whole empire was going to come down on him? Hell, everything, everyone looked unstable. Hadn't the seer said his foundations were slippy?*

I answered his prayer by moving him out of his carriage, walking him twenty-five yards or so, toward a blackened overhang. He thought, *this obsidian is the only solid thing amid all this flaky shale.*

His troops fanned out in a loose cordon around him. He eyed them all, searching for signs of betrayal. Petronius stayed by the carriage, holding the horses.

The overhang was unusual, glistening, jet-black—a shelf shaped and colored like a crow's head with a hooked beak—a crow embedded in roses.

Augustus sat under the crow and laughed with the felt force of irony—he'd always believed if a man hung with crows, he'd learn to caw.

Just then a murder of crows swooped down from far above. This scarf of birds was shaped like a swirling, black beak that cawed its own chorus.

The Emperor thought, *I just laughed at my worrywart self. Now, these wretched crows appear while I sit under the beak of another crow. Is this, or is this not, a laughing matter?*

Augustus stepped out from under Crow Rock to better scrutinize the birds. No sooner had he done this than the whole cliff over him began to crumble.

Augustus blinked hard and shook his head. Was he going crazy, like the lunatic that fell madly in love with a cauliflower? *Perhaps a touch from the trickster goddess, Trivia?*

From the top, the cliff avalanched down, at first slowly, then gathering speed and resolve. Augustus bolted back under the jet-black beak and plastered himself against the wall. The earth collapsed around him. He turned his face outward in time to see Petronius, his carriage, and most of his men, get obliterated by rose-colored boulders the size of palaces or parliaments.

58

JESUS

The roar of falling walls had stopped. Choking dust streaked dim, slanting sunbeams. I grabbed the rounded knob with both hands now, not just my left one, and pulled with all my strength. As I pulled up, blood from my right arm blinded me. I closed both eyes and elbowed over a dim ledge. I sat cross-legged, closed-eyed, my face a sticky sheet of blood.

I wiped my face clean with my left hand. Satan wasn't showing himself, for the moment, but a cliff wall had gone missing. I looked around me. Dim, honeycombed passages wiggled like tubes into the mountain's guts.

I looked my body over. Eyes and fingers both filed a damage report. No broken bones. Skin gashes, deep and long, on right arm and calf. Right ankle and left wrist swollen, aching. Ribs wracked with pain, maybe cracked. I took off my belt rope, cut it in two using Augustus' dagger. Cinched half the belt above my right elbow, cutting blood loss in that arm. The other half, applied in the same way, slowed outbound blood traffic from my right leg.

I sliced my singlet into pieces—the largest piece made a loincloth with a small pocket. The others I used for ankle support and wound bindings. Wounds screamed, heart pounded like I'd plugged my ears, and dizziness swamped me when I tried to stand.

I decided it was best to do something, not nothing, so I climbed toward a snatch of blue heaven, ready as I'd ever be for all I didn't know. After fifty paces or so I came to a sloping rock three times my height. Carved niches in the stone made steps. They led up to an outside perch. I felt like Jonathan stalking the Philistines with his armor-bearer—uh, minus the armor-bearer.[33] I climbed slow, looking up. When I crawled out onto the ledge, an empty perch greeted me—only a few spent arrows and a spray of blood on the ground. An arrow careened off the wall to my right.

I yelled, "Don't shoot! It's me, Jesus!"

I peeked over the ledge. Pontii and his men were on an opposing ledge less than a hundred feet away. In between us the highway had filled with a fallen mountain. I yelled, "A trail of blood angles up into the mountain. I'll look inside. You search outside. And, does the Emperor live?"

Pontii hallooed back across the chasm, "Yes, but many were not so lucky."

I called back, "Tell him that I'll meet him at Apollo's temple."

I carefully reversed course, down the carved niche steps, into the mountain. The trail of blood stopped after a shallow bend in the tunnel. I looked around, bloodstains going up the wall. I spotted an inside gap in that wall, a window of sorts. Another ochre smudge glistened on the lip of this opening.

I leveraged myself up the narrow chimney, feet and butt edging each other upward in a bent-knee slip-slide. My strength belied my wounds. Someone must be praying for me.

Father, I said, *You're not in my ears, but my wounds. Thank you for catching me as I fell, for marshaling my energies now.* Quiet calm grew, even while my right calf screamed at me. I edged my way up-chimney, popped my head through the gap. Nothing but another blood smear on the floor. I pulled through this window of opportunity.

I kept speaking to Father in the dimness. *Thank you for enough light to see your rose cathedral inside a mountain.* I crept forward, praying with my feet, a stutter-step-prayer.

Trickle of water moved around my feet, flowing from the mountain's heart. I followed one branch for some time before the light dimmed out entirely, and I was in total darkness. I practiced repentance, turned around.

The light was so dim I couldn't see the ground, so I crawled. I saw clearly when the trail was a few inches from my eyes. Fifteen feet along, or so, a bloody drip on the wall, to the right of my hands. I kept moving, crawl-hunting.

Father, We are equal. Yet I submit my will to yours. Both. Guide me.

A song of worship, smooth as a silk ribbon, rose in my heart, becoming my strength. Windy tuned me, tested me, harmonizing with my notes. Father soothed with comfort more felt than telt.

Then a question-prayer flickered, flared: *Am I to be a hunter of people or only a seer and savior of souls?*

I didn't know. I wanted to be like my hero, King David—the warrior, king, poet, and lover—hunting down my own Goliath, a thousand years after David had been gathered to his fathers. If not David, well, okay, maybe Jonathan.

I prayed, *Maybe Satan was right, Father, when he said my pride was at work, currying favor with the Emperor, showing off?* Silence without any strengthening surety in my bones.

Father, David was a bloody man. You didn't let him build your temple for that reason. And now, I am also a bloody man, but with my own blood. I'm your temple, your road, your bridge. Faint tingle of energy in my hands—tissue witness within.

Father, what must I do? Fight for the Emperor, or be his bridge to you, true Emperor?

In my seeking-after Father, a calm comfort like dew descended. I remembered King Saul. He'd failed to inquire after Father, to his demise.[34] I splashed forward, little ripples spreading out from hands and knees—singing, praying, inquiring, listening.

My right calf complained. Didn't like being dragged through mud. I pulled up to my feet. I steadied myself, both hands out, touching the wall to balance out my faint-headedness. I shuffled along with enough light for the next step, no more.

Now and again, I stopped to let my eyes adjust to the light—now dimming, then brightening, back and forth. I followed the course chosen for me and reversed my course often, both. A word written by King David came into my ear. *When I walk beneath the earth, even here, I cannot escape your Presence.*[35]

Father's answers were not audible most of the time. Instead, surety pulsed through my feet and fuzzed into substance.

Words condensed out of pain. *Son, I set King David on an exterior course, warrior-king. Look around. You're on a more difficult, interior journey. Use Windy's sword to slash past regret, future dread, and present Evil. Hunt Loving-kindness—don't let her escape you.*

Did I have to be ripped head to toe at the enemy's hands for this sort of learning to root? All I knew was this—as I tolerated this mysterious dark, a bright right lit my way. This rightness, if I moved with it, produced a sort of mental acuity.

Father's words were distant mumblings for the most part. Occasionally a clear sentence condensed out of mystery. This one rang in my ears like a bell tolling the night hour—*Others will spill blood, both your blood and the blood of those who will follow you, Son. This is for them to do, not you.*

I bled into the earth. Learning bled into me. I listened hard and got so absorbed in what wasn't being said that I almost stepped into empty space.

Windy caught my foot before I fell into the abyss. She said, *Whoops! Sense alert. Stay awake.* I pulled back and kicked a pebble over Surprise-Edge. It careened off chasms below. I turned, thankful I'd taken a turn from 'Warrior-King' to 'King of Thorns.'

Another intersection appeared. Gloom glowered less. Father spoke from Nothingness another snippet that I could clearly hear—*Son, I give life. I take it away. I am the Lord Militant, Ruler of Ambiguity. I prepare in darkness and mystery, triumph out of emptiness and mist.*

Father's majesty stunned me. *Son, live in the shadow of everyday not-knowing. Show courage with vulnerability. Bless people with your one wild and gorgeous life.*

Windy's wisdom flowed to and from Father's heart. She was a circulatory system, complete. Once I "got" the lesson, immediately I acted. I laid my sling down in this mountain, so honeycombed with Holiness. I reached inside the pocket of my loincloth, fingered my slinger rocks. I picked these weapons out, one at a time, and released them, and a whole other destiny. I tucked Augustus' dagger in a crevice and crumbled scree over it. The jeweled hilt winked out beneath its burial cover.

Father, take these tools. Let others take the kingdom of heaven by force, not me.

My life's course altered irrevocably, inside Father's classroom, the good earth.

59

CRISPUS

I woke up and looked down. Right leg, gone. Gaping gut-hole, present. I inched up a gut-flap on my flank. It was a hand-width wide and twice that long—sticky loose, shaped like a jawbone. Underneath, my ribs and guts. Hmmm, something funny on my face. Hurt bad. I felt around with my fingers. Nose, gone missing. What happened there?

A fuzzy memory, but I cut it off. Better not to remember too much. I found a leather nose piece with a silk ribbon on the table next to my bed. A little note, signed by Leah, *try this on for size and see if it fits.*

Crispus the Crip—under guard, in chains, whittled away. Idiocy had only adopted a new face—missing leg and nose holes joined goofy eye. The rage charade just got better. Ya don't drown when ya fall in a river—ya drown when ya keep yur nose underwater. Even when it ain't there.

Fanatic, sainted Leah and her Roman lap-dog husband visited during those days of my feelin' poorly. They did their Jesus yammering. I threw in a few Hallelujahs and Amen's. Told 'em, "I'm working hard to believe." Didn't say, believing in what, mind you.

The starry-eyed radical fringe from the scripture-pounding, religious right—always the easiest to fool. Emperor worship, Yahweh worship, hocus-pocus Resurrection worship—pabulum for the pathetic. Spare me that crap.

I'd get gone tonight. Felt it in my bones. Night was my stompin' ground. I knew night so well I should have been brought up by a family of bats. Not meaning to brag, mind-cha, but I was a top-notch enemy. I let regret go like oiled pasta, shucked remorse like an oyster. That's power for ya, the power of an *absolutely* vacant conscience.

Someone called my name, "Crispus!" My head jerked to the right. I trimmed both eyelids down to slits. An old crone, hair white as dandelion down, shuffled along past the guards. The nurse set the basin down and began to wash and salve my stump and side.

Huh! I knew her. She's ma to my homie, Ben Hadad. He'd glommed goop enough on her so she'd look twice her age. She flattened a thin stiletto with a three-inch blade under my fresh stump bandages, faintly nodded a vague smile, and left. Then, seeming forgetful, she turned back to retrieve a bloody cloth on the floor.

She took the moment to whisper, "Tonight, after the second watch. They come for you. Be ready."

Yes sir, Crispus-the-Crip! Captain Darkness, at your service. Another stab at freedom, coming up.

60

LEAH

Tiberius had invited us for dinner at his corner quarters over the street shop. Singers and dancers had entertained us, all brought in from Jericho's finest restaurants.

Now everyone else had gone. I slipped into another chair, nursed my sleepy son in the shadowed corner by a window where I could watch the full moon. Rabbus and Tiberius gazed at the trio of fat, creamy candles that flickered on table center. Tiberius said, "Dying was laden with portent, yet ineffable."

Oh no. Here we go again. I can't understand this man.

Might have been a stray moonbeam, but Tiberius saw my confused expression. His words tried to untangle themselves. "Ah, Leah! Unwitting, me; 'twas waxing crepuscular. Hence, no further obfuscation.

"What I meant was this—all I had to do was take one more step across a threshold. We brothers, Drusus and I, would have once more been inseparable, as when children."

I kept my eyes on the blue moon and my shy ears on Tiberius.

He continued, "But this wrecked, wretched flesh, slammed into that narrow creek bed, under the bridge my horse provided. Fate fought me and won. Like the moon summons the tides, this earth called me back. It was your voice, Leah, and Another, who called me back.

"Drusus' last words burn within me, 'I cannot come to you, brother, but one day you will come to me. Till then, think of me as your bright jewel of loss.'"

"Commander," my husband said, "Your destiny is to rule in each present emergency, each burning moment, till your candle blows out. Your destiny is like a huge Roman wall, like the one you told me about in China.

This wall is enormous but mortared with small stones. My wife and me, we're pebbles, called to hold you up."

Tiberius' face glowed unevenly in the flickering candlelight. He leaned over the rough wooden table, eyes pooling with sadness. "Not to appear ungrateful, but I didn't choose my destiny; it chose me. Death's crush fell like a millstone on a robin's egg. But, unreasonably, the wheel turned, and the egg dropped into a hole beneath it. A new hatchling cracked open that same shell from within." Quiet fell on the three of us.

Then, again, he spoke, "So strange this freedom I feel to speak with you. I've never felt this freedom in Italy. The empire's maw had swallowed me. I've been eaten by abundance while I thought I was eating it." His eyes reminded me of a confused child, lost in a bazaar crowded with stuff, looking for mother.

He continued, "For years, I've watched Augustus trudge sideways from drudgery to grudgery. He tolerated the parfait of darker feelings that are always launched at rulers. The groveling, glad-handing, greedy. He knew inside every grovel was a shovel, quite ready to bury him. And there's this other poison too, first cousin to greed—some moot feeling that lurks between longing and loathing, envy's stretchy shadow. Thinking of it makes my skin crawl."

One of the three candles flickered out, wick smoking. Tiberius' face became a study in deeper shadows. Light and dark etched salt-and-pepper beard over pockmarks. His slight frame appeared spun from the same wind that Windy blew through candles' flames. She blew a forelock of hair across his face.

I said from my corner, eyes still on the moon, "Commander, as you well know, kept goodness has the shelf life of a day flower. It's like the Israelites of old—their uneaten manna would turn to worms overnight. The best place to store your goodness is in the stomach of a hungry person."

Before he could answer, there was a knock on the door.

Tiberius ordered, "Enter."

An officer popped his head in the door and said, "There's a problem here. We went to check on Crispus after the second watch. His guards, murdered. He's gone."

61

CRISPUS

The bell tolled for the second watch—the sound just as crisp as my name. I started gasping, thrashing, and calling for help. The cretin they'd assigned to watch me was dumb as a mouthful of cow pies—also, *dead* asleep. I'd fix the asleep part of that shortly. Revved up my cries. How much thrashing did it take for this idiot to wake up?

Finally, he came over. I gasped his name, soft, garbled, "I'm dying, Titus…"

He leaned over me. Quick as a wink, I pulled him down with my left arm. In the same movement, cut his throat with the stiletto in my right hand. Shoved his face in my chest so his gurgling wouldn't cause no alarm.

Shadows came for me. They'd left a quiet trail of bodies behind them, took Titus' keyring, unlocked and loaded me on a litter, covering me top to bottom with a sheet. Like they were taking me to the charnel house for burning.

We left Rome twitching on the ground.

They carried me out of the hospital with all the honeypots of night soil. Real fragrant, I wuz. This was the same wagon, drawn by the same gray mules, that came every morning to pick up sewage.

They say, "the divine, devilish, and dung all pool in low places." Well, glory be, and hallelujah, amen, I hadn't lost my nose for filth. Move yo' ass over, cuz I be slidin' by on my way down.

My personal physician, Raouf al-Qudwa, slapped the reins on the mules. I called, "Come here, Abu, my stump pains me." He handed the reins over to his companion, swung back into the wagon, threading his way 'tween the overflowing chamber pots.

"We'll have you into the hills 'fore long, Commander. And your stump? It'll pain you for some time. That's the way of the world, pain coming like a phantom, itching what's not there. Take this powder; it'll ease your discomfort."

"My body, Abu, may be slow, but my brain runs wide open." I slugged down the pain powder anyway, with a long draught of strong wine.

Abu said, "We'll work north into our strongholds near Mount Ebal, and from there, to the coast." He paused. "A couple more things. A polished silver nose, got it right here. Fits you exactly. Much sturdier. You look distinguished now, my captain. Much better than before. Also, here's a crutch with a false bottom and hidden trigger in the handle. Poisoned blade pops out when you press here. The tip's pregnant with venom from white oleander and black adder. Fits you perfect, Captain Crip."

62

CLAUDIA

Postie surprised me. He'd startled when I stuck the arrow through his chest. Woke him up. Eyes popped open, went wide. His face grew a death mask of horror, the kind you see on theatre playbills. I sat above him in my hunter's outfit, examining my prey. His eyes fixed on the feathers of his mother's shaft, still sticking out his chest. He blinked hard and said oh-so-sweetly, "My love! Cupid's arrow?"

He never was the sharpest arrow in the quiver. Even in death's classroom, he was slow to catch on—and Jesus wasn't here to save him this time. He quivered and shook, snot streamed out his nose.

I studied his ears. They were pinkish-white, pale as a newborn pig. And his fingernails! Blunt as sunbaked goat scat. I held his shoulders down with stiff arms. "Don't fight your fate, lover!" He kicked his two big legs a bit. His breath shallowed, fluttered like he was skimming a dream.

I said, kindly enough, "Postie, you should never have tried to kill Jesus. You were *very* naughty. Now, please hurry up and die. And don't make such a mess. I have things to do today. Grandpa and Jesus are coming for dinner."

He stared at the arrow's flocking and the red shaft. Recognition dawned, "Mother?" Her poison took him. He guttered a last gasp and was done with it.

Well, finally! I left him stripped naked there in the hunter's room and tip-toed my way upstairs. I experimented walking like Diana the Huntress—a tough 'n sexy, swagger-sashay. But I had all that messy blood and Postie snot on my hunter's outfit. I slipped upstairs and into my bedroom, unseen. Then I washed, re-applied my makeup, and put on my rose-tinted, chiffon frock with the lovely *palla* I'd stolen from mother. Draped it just so around my neck and over my arm. There, all beautiful!

I went to the kitchen area. Bonita was an excellent cook but possessed with an incurable case of prudishness. I'd bet her woman parts were made of cast iron. Bella, two years younger, gave indolence and whoredom a bad name. They'd both missed their calling—Bonita would have been a much better Vestal Virgin than Bathenia. Bella could easily star as a languid harlot in a sheik's harem.

I went outside and looked down the road toward the canyon cut. The road turned 'round a bend in the woods and dived down into the canyon beyond Jael's Spike. I strolled down Striding Edge along the middle of the ridge that dropped off so sharp on either side. I lost myself in the crisp, razor-cut sunbeams that played with soft forest greens. And that pond! A layer of rosy dust streaked the pond, almost the color of my dress. How did all that dust get there? No matter, it was lovely. Jesus would have absolutely adored this view. Where was he?

Before long, a further puff of dust clouded the clear air. Men came 'round a distant corner, marching in unison. Ah yes, Grandpa and Jesus, almost here! I put my hand on my chest, right where it pulsed between my breasts, felt my heart jumping around in there. *Alive! Yes, I was very much alive—thank you, Zeus. You have birthed me full-blown from your head, like Athena, or Jesus.*

But maybe god-man had a different delivery? I forgot. These myths were all so tangled up.

I walked to the temple and arranged myself fetchingly. Grandpa's brigade came 'round the last bend in the road. The Imperial Guard looked ragged, and some were limping. And where were all the cavalry and chariots? Strange, indeed.

I ran to meet them, arms holding out my frock to either side. My *palla* flowed behind me in the breeze. Couldn't have it dragging in the dirt; no, that would *not* do, not at all. Grandpa raised his eyebrows, eyes wide in amazement, as he watched me race across the lawn toward him.

"Grandpa, I wanted to surprise you! I rushed down here two days ago to plan a surprise party for you at the Rose Villa. I couldn't bear to be apart from you any longer."

With his grandfatherly smile, the endearing one, he said, "I can never predict you, my coquette. You're such a blend of grace and grit, an ever-changing vista. Today's been full of bad surprises before now. And, oh yes, Jesus will come another way." I twirled a full circle, trying for a Jesus' sighting.

Grandpa waited till I'd done my twirl. "Two disasters fell on us, granddaughter, one after the other— assassins and an avalanche."

So that's what all the rose dust was on the pond—and the rumbling noise. "I'm *so* glad you're alive, Gramps," I said, and I meant it. "Thank Apollo! But what happened to Jesus?" I meant that even more.

"Jesus free-climbed up a hundred feet or so, straight up, slipped over the top of a ledge, and I saw him no more. A few minutes later, that whole part of the cliff fell. Blocked my road, killed my men, almost killed me."

He fell silent and then put his arm around my shoulder. We moved toward the temple in the fading daylight. After a hundred or so paces, "Today has been the worst day I've ever lived through in all my years. Apollo knew I needed consolation, sent you to me."

I figured I'd better not tell grandpa just yet about Postie.

63

JESUS

I followed the trail of blood inside the mountain all the way to the top through tunnels and wall windows. A mix of light, shadow, and blood flowed around and under me. The cave's entrance loomed. I alternately moaned and sang warrior songs. I imagined Windy's sword at work, slashing my enemy to bits.

Father had kept guiding my feet in the dim light, right and then left, all the way to this entry. I got the feeling I was in training for future dark-walking. His teaching was now also in my ears. *You'll dark-walk in different ways all your earth years. In all your walks of life, clarity comes with commitment. But now, a final lesson from hollow mountain's classroom. Get on your knees. Look at that moss over there.*

I obeyed. Got back on my knees and examined a narrow weft of crisscrossing. Almost invisible green threads gripped moist soil near the cave's entrance—beads shimmering in the dark.

Watch this. Goblin's Gold, Son. I leaned forward, kneeling in a child's pose with chin on fists over bent elbows, my rump up in the air. A brief ray of sun, day's last gasp, hit the moss and lit it up. Pearls of moisture glowed like lights from a faraway city set on a hill. Then sun's brief beam passed on after no more than five seconds. Faint glowing still remained inside the moss in the darkling. Enough light to live, and live well, though so brief. *Thank you, Father! You open your mouth, and miracles fall out.*

I poked my head out of the mountain, looked to see if Satan was visible, waiting to trip me up. The mountain ridge was empty of enemies, for the moment. I teetered on top of the catacomb haven where I'd been crawl-walk-singing. At that moment, the tippy-top edge of the sun winked out with a greenish smudge into the western sea.

'Sunset' was a weak word to describe all the beauty this sky held. And all so silent. The sun's going, and my coming were quiet as a whisper. A warm breeze blew my hair back out of my eyes. *Thank you, Father and Windy, for preserving my life. Now, where is this Apollo temple? Guide me.*

I got down on my hands and knees and began crawling into twilight's far edge. Yes! A faint bending of a twig here, broken bracken there. And a darker splotch, right in front of my nose. I wiped it with my finger, tasted it—tang of bloody iron. I put my head in the grass, resting, listening.

A gibbous moon rose over the eastern cliff. I stood and followed the faint bends in the grass, bit by bit, in the dark. Then it hit me. This is how all of my days would go. Nothing more than my next step. That's what had been given to me.

I walked, kneeled, crawled, lost the trail, picked it up again, all by the light of the moon. A distant David melody, from a psalm, was on Father's playlist for me.[36] I hummed along. Light reflected off the moon from earth's tiny star, one among trillions that Father had spoken into being and now called each by name.

I made slow progress. The uphill gradient flattened my strength. A little further now, that's all, another crawl, another slide.

Help, Father. I'm drained. And there, ahead, the silhouette of ancient columns, darker black on grey sky! The temple. A few torches lit within the columns.

My ears couldn't believe what they heard next—Claudia's laughter, so light, lyrical, unmistakable! That girl could seduce every bit of salt out of the sea. But she was supposed to be in Rome. I walked up the outer steps of the temple, suddenly felt light-headed, and collapsed.

64
WINDY

Claudia strolled between the torchlit temple columns with her grandfather. She regaled him with stories and loved him with her eyes. Augustus thought, what would I give to be her age again? She loves the old curmudgeon, the despicable toad, and the elegant emperor within me. This is truly sufficient for me to have a good flirt with contentment.

Faint thump in the dark. *Son had arrived, but they knew him not.*

"Guards!" Augustus called out, alarmed. He unsheathed his sword, fight besting flight. Captain Pontii and the guards came running from the temple's four corners. Augustus pushed Claudia behind him, then moved cautiously toward the inert lump on the stairs.

Two guards stood over Jesus' body, torches flaring against the dark. When Claudia saw him, her hands flew to her face. Jesus, in her eyes, looked not only wounded but weary, beyond her ability to measure weariness.

Augustus called for his physician, Hippo. He and another man loaded Jesus onto a litter. Then Hippo left him alone for a moment to get his medical bag. Claudia filled the moment. She nestled in beside Jesus and put his head on her lap. She bent low to linger a kiss on his lips, and became a longing filtered through a woman's body.

Hippo arrived and scooted her off to one side, but not before she'd taken off her *palla* and pillowed his head with it. Pontii and another archer carried him to Rose Villa. The villa had been partially built into the side of Strider's Edge. Its two-story western walls and mouth were exposed to the light of day and dark of night.

They converted the large entry room into a make-shift surgery. The walls of this pink sandstone room were veined with dark red iron. Brighter red obelisk quartz arteries glittered in the torchlight. Jesus waited, unconscious, still as a corpse, inside this room that itself resembled the inside of a corpse. Father and I were giving Son practice for a long weekend yet to come.

Claudia was Jesus' first memory after regaining consciousness. He remembered her kissing him, her warm hand resting on his bare stomach. He remembered hearing moans in the air, groans that sounded like rusty nails being pulled from dried hardwood. It took him some time to realize the moans were coming from *his* mouth.

Hippo gave Son a draught of powder with sweet red wine. He said, "It'll ease your pain, and what I'm about to do." Hippo whispered something to Claudia. She nodded. He snipped a few long strands of her auburn hair, threaded his needle, and began to sew, joining layers of muscle first, then skin. Pontii and another archer held two torches over Jesus' shoulders for the physician to see more clearly his work. Claudia, sitting at his hip, also held a torch for Jesus.

Hippo said, "I like to stitch muscles with human hair. Hair dissolves within a week or so. After that, the tissue holds. Only Claudia had hair long and stretchy enough to work. She will be inside you, slowly dissolving. I'll remove the outside silk stitches in a week or two."

Jesus held Claudia's right hand with his left while Hippo worked on his right arm. Claudia and Son examined each other's faces.

He said, "Satan did his level best to kill me, even as he'd killed Abba at Sepphoris. His effort to murder you at the well was no less real—a soul-stealing attempted murder of your true self."

Claudia studied their hands, fingers wound together. I said, *Son, see how she's absorbing your words, even as your body absorbs her hair. She's letting herself become more than skin deep.*

Jesus closed his eyes, *thank you, Windy.* He said to Claudia, "Truth be known, often I can't tell who's the real you. I have a memory of Satan's demon on the ledge. She was your exact imago, except she inhaled a white line of powder off a mirror that left her nose all reddish and did sexual things for Lucifer's pleasure.

"I ask myself, 'Are you… you, or her?'"

Claudia was shaken, her panache gone missing. She replied, her mouth to his ear, "I come and go; the real deal's always on the move. But I'm no demon. I'm a real person, not a phantom—but I do feel Satan's presence here, now—though I can't see him. He brings this creepy sizzle that prickles my skin."

Son whispered, "This deeper, newer, brave self—the part without pretend? She's more truly you than the *hypokrites* you spin across the stage.[37] The *new* you, and me, together, we can beat the Old Enemy."

Hippo finished working on Son's right arm and did the same stitchery on his right calf. Like all careful healers, he worked from the inside out, in layers. Finally, before wrapping his wounds with linen strips, he massaged Jesus' skin with frankincense and myrrh, his gold ring flashing in the light.

Son had been lying on his back, eyes resting shut. When he opened his eyes, two things. Claudia's tender face hovered over him, lit by her torch. Directly above her, suspended below the cave's ceiling, a leering Satan—now appearing a skeleton. Jesus' eyes widened. Claudia followed his gaze. Both could see. Both stared at Satan, glassy-eyed.

He motioned with his finger in a circle, like he was turning an invisible dial. The lights dimmed. The room felt like it belonged solely to Jesus and Claudia, like they alone had entered a different virtual reality. Focused light on walls and ceiling projected from Satan's eyes, moans and groans flowed from his tongue. Silky, sensual friction flew off his fingertips.

Two humanized demons were going at it. One of them looked just like Jesus; the other, Claudia. Sexual sensations penetrated every inch of the couple's skin. Surround-sound, surround-vision, surround-sensation. All they could see and hear and sense was sex. Sound and sight and skin slammed their senses.

Death rode Sex in the dark.

I allowed this exposure so that Son would know first-hand the power of such a seduction. Then I took on the form of pure light, shimmering bright. I washed away Satan's virtual non-reality and replaced it with myself. I cleaned Jesus and Claudia's minds and hearts, leaving them clear.

Satan had come to tempt at Son's low point, as he was wont to do. He came to seduce when Son was vulnerable, exhausted, and sick. I strengthened and soothed Son, commended him for enduring the strain of such a test. I also murmured a word of encouragement in Claudia's ear and soothed her skin that still ached with hyper-arousal.

In those same moments, I pointed the way out for Satan, into the dark, readying him for a dim future. Satan unzipped a space, bowed with the mock flourish of a showman, and disappeared.

65

JESUS

A blaze of light washed out Satan's otherworldly sex-trap. The room was as it had been before he dimmed the lights.

Immediately, a flash-forwarded vision from within replaced the sex sensorium imposed from without. I saw my body prepared for burial, wrapped in linen strips after being anointed with frankincense and myrrh. My left hand, the one Claudia held, trembled.

She looked at me, "Did you see what I saw just now? It felt real, vivid, like what I felt at the well in Sepphoris. But now, almost entirely gone."

I nodded. "Satan, doing his usual job. He's very convincing, making lie seem like truth, evil like good. Always have to be alert."

As if to confirm my words, Satan splashed back into view, a disembodied miasma behind Claudia's face inside a floating frame. His syrupy voice was hardly more than a whisper. "I'll give you another chance, Junior. Touch *her* velvety skin like she's touching yours. She's more than willing to tend *all* your needs."

Claudia cocked her head. "That you, Jesus? I felt weird just now—turned on, but with a creepy skin sizzle."

I looked at Lucifer and said to Claudia, "That was Satan again. Mate those sensations with your heart's knowing, so you recognize when he's at work."

She said, "He's a real showman with his razzle-dazzle. I didn't know what was real and what wasn't. I thought we were making love, but we weren't. I wanted you, but it didn't feel right. Weird. I'd always thought the only difference between performing and lying was if your audience was in on it, but I knew what he was doing and still got confused."

I said, "He's a master liar. Even now, hear his whisper?"

She cupped her ears, bent her head, and tried listening to the mist. She shook her head, hands raised with palms out. She reached out her right hand and stroked my face with her fingertips. "You hear. I feel. I got nothing now besides what my eyes and fingers tell me."

Her confused expression matched my wondering spirit. She looked at me, touched me, and perhaps sensed that I was the Jesus demon that she had seen before. I listened to her and didn't know if she was Claudia or a clone. Such was the magic of Satan's trickery.

Exhausted again, I asked for help. Windy, now a male warrior, policed my boundary. He pointed Satan toward the cave's mouth. Satan gave me a one-finger salute and stepped through the ripple in the air.

I turned on my side and vomited all over the marble tile, dry heaving after the first couple of splats. I laid back. Claudia wiped off my mouth, made soothing noises, and summoned Bonita, who wiped up my mess with wet cloths.

Claudia left to check what was going on in the kitchen. I flopped my head back down and wanted nothing more than sleep. I dozed.

Claudia's voice woke me up. "Anyone hungry besides me?"

Augustus also roused from his sleep in the armchair over in the corner, moved ever so slowly to the table. Hippo helped me hobble, at about the same pace as Augustus, to a long plank table.

Claudia snatched a black theatre mask off the wall, one of a matched black and white pair of *hypokrites*. She play-acted the role of chef, with an impressively deep voice. "And here we have my marvelously prepared meal, finished with my very own hands! Roast beef, stir-fried bowls of eggplant, broccoli, and corn-on-the-cob, each spiced differently with saffron, peppers, cinnamon, cloves or rhubarb, pomegranate or citron juice. And over here, mashed potatoes with the trimmings, and crusty sourdough bread with virgin olive oil for dipping. Italian red, at your place setting. Save room for dessert." She bowed with a flourish and returned the mask to the wall.

Augustus sat to my right. Claudia took her place opposite me, and Hippo to my left. All three of them feasted. I took a bite or two before I started gagging. Put my fork down. Sipped the wine and hoped I could keep it down.

Claudia's maidservants attended us. Bonita, the older one stood in a corner. Her shoulders were pulled up, tight as a winter rosebud on a frosty morning. She looked straight ahead, but when my glass was a swallow short of full, she refilled it.

The younger handmaid had an eye for the Imperial Guard outside the door. She flirted with him whenever there was a spare moment wide enough to squeeze through. She motioned with a wink toward the lower floor, and the two of them slipped away.

Augustus, between bites, queried, "Why did you pull the earth down on top of me?"

I answered, "Emperor, that power is not mine, but Father's. He allows another to run on a short leash for a short time. Satan sat out of your view, just beyond the ledge, lounging in the mouth of another cave than this. A thin shale bridge connected the cliff's false face with its weeping inner wall."

Augustus coughed up a bit of roast beef. "Can you ever speak simply?"

I continued, "My enemy and I had words. He got mad, tapped the bridge with his forefinger. The bottom dropped out. The cliff's outer skin, riddled with inner flaws, could *not* hold up."

Augustus was alarmed, "Who's this Satan?"

Claudia said, "Jesus' dark counterpart in the underworld, Gramps. They're old enemies. You gotta choose one side or the other—True Faced or two-faced." She looked at the masks on the wall. "Black and white issue."

Augustus' tone turned strident as he looked at me. "So, was this disaster from you and your all-powerful Father—or this Satan-on-a-leash?"

I said, "You battle evil every day, don't you, Emperor?"

Augustus nodded. "Within and without. I know both battlefields, also the false and true faces. I got your meaning, but not you. Perhaps you are the Prince of Darkness, and your allegiance is to Satan."

I replied, "I am many things, but the Prince of Darkness is not one of them. My Father wears darkness like a cape and allows, even causes, calamity.[38] He afflicts the comfortable as easily as he comforts the afflicted."

Augustus got half my intention, the lesser half. "Aha! You admit it. You and this father of yours did try to kill me."

"Father tells me very little of what He does, just what's good for me to know. Mainly He tells me to be content, journey one step at a time with Him. Compared to Him, what I know is nothing piled on nothing."

Augustus fidgeted. "So, I'm doomed to crawl into obscurity while the empire goes to hell in a handbag? What good are you to me as a seer?"

"I was sent to serve people by walking or crawling in the dark toward unknown destinations, as I did tonight. Father uses his truth to comfort and afflict. No one escapes his truth, including you."

Augustus grimaced. "You dare talk to your emperor like that?"

"What I just said was true, Sire. In fact, I am Truth."

I shifted my gaze from Augustus to Hippo. "In some ways, I'm like you, physician. You repair torn flesh with your needle. When I repair torn souls, that process is equally uncomfortable."

Augustus said, "You have an interesting way of repairing. Have a duel with your archenemy. Bring down a cliff on my head. Wipe out my men and my road. All with your father's approval. None of that is high on my go-to repair list."

Augustus tucked in a forkful of potato, dripping with sour cream and bacon bits. His expression hardened. He glanced at Pontii and glared at me.

Windy counseled, *He wanted plain speaking with plenty of ear-tickling. What you said is not that. Now he wants to kill the messenger of bad tidings.*

A groundswell of tension trembled throughout the room. My aches increased. Claudia's feet frantically tapped under the table. Augustus' hand tremor worsened.

Out of the corner of my eye, I saw Pontii. He had washed his hands in a silver bowl by the kitchen door and was now drying them with a towel.

Augustus gave him a flicker-nod. Pontii drew his sword, took a step toward me.

Before Pontii could take another step, a loud scream broke out from below our room. It wasn't a soft, short yelp, but one that increased in volume and panic. Augustus pushed back from the table. Pontii and the other Imperial Guards rushed to protect him.

Claudia said, "I know what this is about." She stood up and motioned us all toward the outside door.

66

CLAUDIA

We walked outside. I ducked into the gardener's shed and pulled out a shepherd's staff with a crook on the top of it. I shoved it under Jesus' right armpit. He hobbled, holding onto my right arm with his left. Hippo, Pontii, and a dozen Imperial Guards hovered before, around, and behind us.

We went down the garden path to the villa's lower entry door into the mountain. Bella stood by the door, red-faced. Her boyfriend had melted into the flood of Roman red surrounding us. We all trooped into the musty, lower apartment that was an even deeper, darker cave than the house above. Pontii opened the bedroom door off the main living area. He and his men opened a space for grandfather to approach the bed. I trailed behind. Soldier's torches, all around, seared the air in hot waves. Postie's body lay as I left it, stuck to a bed that now resembled an altar surrounded by a sea of wavy fire.

I faced Grandpa and held both his hands. "Grandpa, he was the archer. He told me he was going to try to kill you again. I got him to come here and lie down. I tended his leg wound, gave him a sleeping powder. Then I took that poisoned arrow from his mother into my own hands."

Grandpa sat down next to his dead grandson, shaken and shaking.

Jesus said, "Your granddaughter was as good as the woman-warrior, Jael, in our Hebrew Scriptures."[39]

Augustus looked at Claudia. "You were better even than my own Imperial Guards." He glared briefly at Pontii, who lowered his eyes to his hob-nailed caligae.

Together the group of us went back to the dining room for a casual post-murder, after-dinner coffee and dessert. We settled down by the fireplace. I scarfed the chocolate mousse. Grandpa nibbled at crème brûlée, served with a side of his favorite whiskey.

Jesus said, "I still feel like throwing up. I hurt all over."

Bonita wafted into the room, bringing a small pot of chamomile tea on a silver platter. She poured the tea through a wire mesh into a porcelain cup. Hippo put a pouch of powder beside the tea. Commented, "Painkiller and something for your stomach, if you like."

Jesus took the tea and the powder. He looked at Grandpa. "When you were napping in that corner chair over there, Satan arrived. He magically dimmed our lights and projected porn on the walls and ceiling. He kept grinding out this very sensual, convincing virtual reality before Windy ran him off."

I said, "My body still feels all that sexy stuff he packed into me. Makes me lust you as much as I love you. But I'm afraid. Will Windy run me off too?"

My royal heart, now a beggar, began to plead.

Jesus looked kindly in my eyes. "I too struggle. Managing all that sexual excitement wears me out—and I'm already weak. But no, Windy won't run you off. Father lifts up those who lift me up. Satan lifts only himself up."

Grandpa said, "I can't lift anyone up, including me or my throne. We're both too heavy. Besides, my hands shake too much. But I still have a choice or two remaining."

Jesus said, "Sire, your last exhale here precedes your first inhale in heaven or hell. We're *all* immortal. "

Grandpa turned his head halfway toward the dying light. I caught his wave of unbelief. We'd all been schooled that we humans breathe but briefly, then turn to worm food.

I lifted a log to the fire, stirred the embers. Was this my destiny— empress of three logs and two twigs?

Jesus said, "Satan claws for power. But he's in a losing fight, and he knows it."

I looked at my empire falling to ash. "He's winning a lot of battles for a loser. He almost killed you. One little knob, sticking out of that dark chute, was the only thing that saved you."

Jesus' face gladdened and saddened at the same time, if that's even possible. "Father gives handholds or toeholds in the dark. When we grab them, they become strongholds for faith. If he hadn't stuck that knob in my hand, he'd have saved me another way—maybe flown an eagle beneath me, as he did for Psyche."

He tapped his finger forcefully on the table, "Father owns every inch of this universe. He rightfully says, 'Mine, all mine!' And that includes the Roman Empire, Sire."

Grandpa said, "So, my empire isn't mine? It's your father's, is it?"

"It's yours to manage, Sire. Father owns it."

Grandpa said, "I half-believe maybe half of what you say. I do seek control and power—you're right about that. But the more I age, the less I control. I can't even control my hands these days. They shake as we speak."

Jesus looked squarely at grandpa, "Satan's hook is in your jaw. He seeks to satisfy you with control over *when* you die. He takes away hope for the life hereafter and sells you control over your suicide, wrapped up as the grand prize."

Grandpa said, "In this, you are well-sighted, seer. Augusta waits in Nola to assist me in my chosen date with death."

Jesus said, "Bend your knee to God. Refuse the lie that once you die, you're one and done."

Grandpa guzzled the last of his whiskey. "Almost persuaded, young man. Almost persuaded. Time now for that little death, sleep."

67

SLOW

Tiberius and his men marched toward Caesarea. A few days later, I was almost ready to dump my load—nothing dramatic, like Leah. I was at home, at Rahab's, with Lydia keeping watch over me—not in a cave with boulders collapsing around me. Laz was five miles away at Herodium for a few days. He'd heard there was a new teaching rabbi there, a younger man with a wife and small child. El Roi and Laz were intrigued. New blood in the neighborhood. They went to argue Torah with him. Jewish men, making friends.

Ow! That hurt. Another labor pain, fifteen minutes now after the last one. Lydia said, "Not long now. Let's walk this baby down, take a turn or two around the courtyard."

We'd done one loop, me leaning hard on her arm, when the front gate burst open. A herald blew through the gate, tooting his own horn. He cut through the clot of merchants and buyers, like a hot knife through butter.

"Make way! Bow before the King! Herod Antipas, your potentate, has arrived."

This pudgy man dressed in purple. A crown of gold olive leaves adorned his head. A slender woman and an albino trailed behind him on foot.

Herod Antipas barked, "Chuzo, how much was a whore at this dump last time we were in town?"

The man called Chuzo flapped his hands helplessly. He turned to the veiled woman, "Joanna, dear, tell the king what he wants to know."

Her voice was crisp and clear. "Fifty shekels. And that included a certificate from the *uman* at the hospital. She was clean of disease." She lifted her veil momentarily when we passed to get a better look at me. The lines on her face and jaw were angular, skin pale and rose tinted. A jagged, white scar ran from just below her right eye to mid-jaw. She looked me up and down, nodded pleasantly. Then she dropped her veil.

I heard a voice within me. *Be glad you're obviously with child. The king didn't give you a second look.* A chill went down my spine. Escape slipped out the back door. Fragile collapsed. I straightened my back, poked my stomach out another mile, and walked by the camel and its high rider.

I'd remember that inner voice and come to trust it more as time went by. For now, the king came and went, and the baby came to stay.

Laz and I named him Michael. If my sister was going to have one archangel, I would have the other. No sibling rivalry here, mind you—just an angelic choir in the making. The only problem was Tiberius had taken Leah, Rabbus, and half our angelic choir with him on his warship. Guess he wanted his resurrection specialist close-by.

Leah had the gift of divine interiority. I'd been given the gift of mediocre exteriority that covered a splintered self. She had stretch marks in her mind and heart from carrying Jesus' Spirit. I had stretch marks on my gut. She grew God in her imagination and prayers. I grew fear of Rome, Crispus, Herod, or whoever else looked dodgy or dangerous. I was a mother struggling with milk flow and sore nipples. She was a mother ship carrying God's cargo.

Really, now, was this fair?

My friends, Cornelia and Maltesa, both childless, were dry wells in the mother department, but I didn't have to exhaust myself with them, pretending to be normal. Esmeralda was fear-shopping most of the time, cramming herself with stuff against the day Zac might sell her. Rastus was here today, gone tomorrow, still waiting for an attack of common sense to break out. Meanwhile, he aimed himself, like an arrow, at whatever in his path needed killing.

The only ones I could count on for comfort were El Roi, Lydia, and Laz. Together they were like boulders that anchored a field to the ground.

I thought of Jesus. I was glad his body was gone. That way I didn't get reminded so much of the person I loved and was meant to be like. Instead, I settled. Living loved by Jesus, body present or body gone, cost more than I could pay.

I told myself, *It's okay to shape a life far below where the masterful live. Let your sharpie shards be your weapons and armor.*

Cutter surfaced now and again to cut skin or yank out another eyelash. Escape floated above it all and looked down on the rest of us. Fragile routinely enjoyed headaches or diarrhea. Harlot seduced others into liking her shiny, fake self. And Shame kept reminding us all we weren't worth a poop.

I felt like a frantic juggler in a traveling circus troupe. My busyness helped keep others, and me, away from me. Separately, we had nothing good to say and kept on saying it. Together we probably had something good to say but couldn't wrap words around it. None of us wanted to become the beating, beaten blob of compassion that someone had stuck in Jesus' chest. Nope, that wasn't for us. Better, being broken.

We kept puttering with pottery in spite of ourselves. Roi showed us how to do free form sculptures. He let me play with mud on a corner table beneath an outside, western facing window. I played and flopped, got blown around inside.

Then, when I wasn't looking, a blob with limbs rose out of my mud. Like a person pulling out of the mud, but losing. That was the first one. The next half dozen became more and more human—not so much jagged pieces smacked together by accident. The faces all looked a little less tortured, one to the next, as they tried to rip themselves out of the earth. The first looked like Achan, Leah's abba and my first abuser; the next, Cyn; then, Cyrena, and a couple more.

I slowed and stopped my work. A hot wind had started up from the west and heaved dust over Jerich as if the surrounding hills were skinning themselves and blanketing the city in red. I watched the dust hang inside converging sunbeams that slanted through the windows. Fragile light dazzled dust into beauty. I reached out to collect what dust I could and include it in my mud.

I started work again, gathering Escape and Cutter into my consciousness. Shame sat by herself in the shadows, but looked lonely. After a while, Roy popped back into the workshop.

He looked at my seventh sculpture and said, "That, my dear, is the spitting image of Jesus' face and your body. He beams from out your mud. Like there's a true home for him in there."

We set my Becomers under an overhang in the courtyard, halfway between the back wall and the synagogue. One day two visitors stood looking at them. One said to the other, "My, my, whoever did this, surely did it with love."

I remembered Jesus' blessing so long ago. He'd said my pieces would slowly come together, becoming someone good.

68

CLAUDIA

We passed through rolling pastures dotted with grazing flocks of sheep. Stone and briar hedges separated the emerald fields. Young shepherds waved to us as we passed.

Grandpa got gloomier as he swam upstream to his spawning site. He kept one hand on his knee and used the other to hang onto the carriage. A royal courier, on a lathered horse, handed off a message to a guard. He passed the sealed scroll to Grandpa, who scribbled a reply. The courier galloped back toward Rome.

I looked out of the carriage from where I sat next to Jesus—Vesuvius was to the south. A dark crown glowered around Vesuvius' dome, puffing out a drizzle of vog that began as a finger pointing upwards and then slouched across the valley floor toward Pompeii. Vog swirled around us in patchy drifts, making it seem like we were driving through a dream.

Grandpa said, "The scroll was informative. Tiberius died and resurrected—if the message is to be believed. A friend of yours, Jesus— woman, name of Leah. She brought him back after he'd stopped breathing."

I said, "The Leah I know? The dark, brooding, fingernail-worrying, ugly duckling sister to gorgeous Go?"

Jesus nodded and turned his gaze to sulky Vesuvius. "Yes, Leah didn't run away when the heat got uncomfortable."

I gave Jesus the stink-eye, but Grandpa perked up, as though pliers had pried him from his dour mood.

Jesus launched into another one of his frigging parables. "Once upon a time, there was a spoiled king's daughter who got tired of ivory tower life. That's all she had known—books, dance, and song. She found her moment and escaped. The reward for this was getting lost, wholly lost in a big city.

She decided to throw herself into lostness and not be half-lost. That way, she'd never be sure which half of her was right.

"Fortunately for this princess, an old woman befriended her. This crone was so thin, the princess could easily picture her pelvis riding on top of her leg bones, the knobs of her spine like pebbles on a string, stretching up into her skull. She took the royal to a hot, humid underground chamber. The girl was soaked in her own sweat the moment she walked through the door.

"The peasant said, 'You, my child, must learn to earn your keep.'

"The girl was now not only wholly lost, but fully frightened. She had no useful life skills.

"The hag understood. 'As you can plainly see, this underground room is a kitchen. And we all know what kitchens are for, don't we?'

"No, in fact, she didn't know. Food had always appeared on set tables. She looked into the dark corners of the room, filled with cut logs. No tables, no place settings. Only an ax, propped beside logs. She skittered her eyes to the room's middle, where a blazing fire burned under a covered pot.

"She answered, 'Uh, food grows here?'

"The elder replied, 'Kitchens are places of transformation, child. Raw stuff, from farms, is brought here. It's chopped, sliced, diced, grated, rolled, and dumped in the pot. The pot's put on that fire. Food transforms if it stays in the fire. It suffers into something that can feed others.'

"The girl didn't like the sound of this, not at all. However, she kept her eyes off the covered kettle, as if to make it go away. The lid of this blackened iron cauldron chattered from whatever was boiling inside.

"The elder said, 'Girl, three things are needed. Chop this wood. Feed the fire. Don't look in the pot.'

"The royal picked up an ax and walked to the woodpile.

"The hag said, 'Ax overhead, two-handed grip, swing straight down, knees bent. This way, you stay grounded and don't cut yourself. I'll return later and tell you what's next.'"

I filed my nails and sighed. I nodded pleasantly, but only so Jesus' words would have a place to rest when they hit the air. I didn't get the whole parable thing. Or maybe I did but didn't want its scorch.

Grandpa leaned in, interested.

"The girl chopped wood until her hands were blistered and raw. She fed the fire. Food appeared through a side door on a tin plate that was left on the floor. It was enough to feed her. Time passed.

"The hag finally returned. The huge pile of firewood was all gone. The kettle was still covered, still boiled.

"The elder said, 'you've done well. Sweep up the sawdust and put it in that bag. That's your pay. Bye.'

"*What?* The princess, now with callused hands, felt angry enough to squeeze the hag's throat till her scrawny neck bones broke. But instead, she controlled her temper and bagged the sawdust. She carried the burlap sack up, and up, out into the light of day where ordinary people lived. Her mind, so wedded to quiet, became quickly confused by the clamor of people, the push and pull of their greed and need.

"She trudged out of her father's capital city, took a dirt lane. She came to a farm where a lonely man weeded a field of turnips. She sat under a shady willow on the border of his property, a quiet place where she could observe this humble man from a distance.

"After a while, she fell asleep, her bag for a pillow. When she woke up, she stood and lifted her pillow. It had become way too heavy to carry any further. She decided to ditch the sawdust. When she opened her bag, she saw that the sawdust had all turned to flakes of gold. A long, 'ohhhh' came out of her mouth, three long notes of wonder made from one sound. She picked up her bag, turned to face the farmer, and took her next step."

Grandpa was silent, chewing on his white, droopy mustache.

Jesus said, "We've all been given fires to tend, secret mysteries that bubble under the chattering lids of palsied hands or dancing feet." Jesus looked at Grandpa's hands and my fidgety feet.

His eyes assailed mine, but without doing violence. Even so, my discomfort deepened, seeping down, past my skin.

Jesus shifted his gaze to Grandpa. "Do you wish to nourish others with your legacy? My Emperor, don't leave, live. Good character is pure gold. Anything else is fool's gold."

Grandpa replied, "Nice fairy tale. Hard work, delay of gratification, that's the stuff of alchemy. Got it. Might apply to Claudia, certainly not me."

He made a whirling, upward motion with his right hand. "You, you deal in metaphor, mystery, Jesus. All very windy. But I'm a practical, down to earth person. I don't go for wild tales of bubbling pots, bags of sawdust twinkling into gold."

Grandpa's tone sounded like something he'd found in a rusted cage. "Science, technology, engineering, math—they're the ticket. They stem the tide of superstition in *my empire*."

If I'd been Jesus, I'd have become defensive. Instead, he said, "Some uncover mystery quickly. Others, like you, have got a lot in your pot— and you've kept it covered for years." The golden flecks in his amber eyes sparkled. His smile was enough to make a man like Grandpa forget he was dying.

Despite this, Grandpa parried. "Perhaps, seer. Most politicians twitter, not to voice truth, but create it. Whoever's in power gets to dish up truth from their bubbling pot, slop it in the common man's bowl. The unthinking snuffle along and chow down."

Jesus turned from power to death. "Mystery cants along behind such power-slop, led by Death, on a short leash."

Grandpa snorted. "Indeed, Death *is* in the pot, seer. For example, a few miles back I couriered a command for Postie's body to delivered to his mother—on her exile isle. He should be ripe by the time he arrives. My soldiers will strip the island of any food, leave his body naked on the rocks for the ravens. Food for thought—for my lovely daughter, Julia. And if my little *Cleopatra* wants a quicker exit, she has her adders."

I mused, looking at Grandpa gnaw his mustache. Watched his hands shake. He didn't like clouds to blow unless he told them which way to go, and now his hands went their own way, without asking for permission. He was losing his grip, for sure. And Julia! Starving to death was perfect! Balanced out her gluttony, that sex pot.

Jesus looked at me kindly, "And such were *you*, always onstage in your ivory tower while running from life's fire. But you, you are being redeemed for Father's purposes."

I smiled sweetly, my best effort at a hot, redemptive smile.

The outskirts of grandpa's villa emerged out of the haze. Grandpa's complex of white-washed villas, trimmed in sky blue, overlooked Nola.

I'd wandered through his orchards as a child and gotten lost more than once in his two-acre labyrinth. Today, though, I could barely see those tall hedgerows. Mostly what I could see was the vog itself, even as I inhaled its sulfur stench.

A mile later, when we pulled into the two-story courtyard, Grandma awaited us. She wore a flowing, purple gown that rippled in the breeze. Her silvery-gold hair, done in a bun on top of her head, glistened when she turned. Livia was lovely and kind. Augusta, on the other hand, was cool and calculating. Both lived inside the same body. *What had happened to a simple life with just one cuddly, warm grandma?*

One of these two personas had arranged a welcome party for her husband—an orchestra and a bunch of old friends. She'd positioned the orchestra players in the courtyard and on the balconies. As we came through the gates, they broke into one of grandpa's favorite tunes. The music sounded like a hyped-up funeral march, planned by someone with an eye toward her son's career advancement.

We suffered all the introductions. Blah, blah, blah. So happy to see you. After, Jesus went to his bedroom for a nap. He didn't seem to want company, so I wandered off alone, trying to find the kitchen. I suspected it was below ground somewhere.

69

JESUS

I'd bathed and napped in a guest cottage down the knoll from Augustus' main villa. The marble tub was emperor-sized and filled with hot, eucalyptus-scented water. I soaked. Afterward, ironed Egyptian cotton sheets cooled and soothed my sprained joints, ripped skin, and gathering bruises. I didn't know till later that this was the only time I would enjoy this water, these sheets.

I woke up refreshed but still achy. A new suit of clothes had been laid out for me, complete with leather sandals, just my size. I hobbled up the path and into the main villa. Claudia sat in the main entryway under a portrait of her grandfather, reading a leather-bound tome. She was extraordinarily lovely, hair done up in an elegant roll and shining like water flowing over sandstone.

She looked up and moved across the space between us to steady me on her arm. She acted the role of tour guide. "Grandpa's apartment in Rome is very ordinary. First Citizen is careful to avoid envy from the other citizens. But here, far away from the power center, he allows himself a bit of splendor."

I said, "Huh. Not wanting another's life. Sounds graceful."

She said, "In that case, Rome's had a run on grace—beginning seven hundred fifty years ago with its founders, Romulus and Remus."

We entered a massive hallway in the main villa, one with twenty-foot ceilings, lots of crown molding, and a ton of flowers.

"Don't you just love the fresh jasmine, orchids, hibiscus, African violets, and bromeliads? And these Persian carpets, packed with gold, scarlet, and royal blue colors. Those colors dance my eyes." I smiled into those blue eyes happy enough to make a peeled onion cry.

A thin man sat beside a very unusual water clock in the main entry. His bald dome fringed tufts of wiry, white hair. The water clock, shaped like a nymph, had been disemboweled. Piles of elaborate levers, wire springs, and tip-weights had been scattered across the floor.

Claudia hugged her old friend. "How sad, Chronos! Grandpa's favorite clock breaks during his 77th birthday party!" He smiled at her briefly and kept working.

She said to me, "Chronos designed Grandpa's clock. He named the nymph Kairos and gave it to his emperor twenty-seven years ago, on Grandpa's 50th birthday. He was hired full-time, ever since, to tinker with time—this and all the other clocks on the estate.

"As a child, I sat for hours, watching Kairos unwind and transform. As water drains from her reservoir each day, the *puer* grows into a *senex*—a cherub into a wrinkly old woman. And then, at midnight, old becomes young again. Mysterious. I never did figure out how that worked."

We left Chronos fussing with Kairos.[40]

The hallway led to a large library, walls lined with scrolls and books on three sides, floor to ceiling. Oaken ladders on wheels leaned against silver railings anchored in the top shelves. On the fourth wall, on either side of a massive fireplace, the Roman god of fire, Vulcan, bent toward the Greek god of volcanos, Hephaestus. Together they bowed toward each other, outstretched arms holding the granite mantel between them.

A log fire on andirons crackled quietly, background music for an ensemble tucked in the far corner. The trio consisted of harpist, lyrist, and soprano soloist. They plied the air with melodies of love gained and love lost. The singer's slender arms folded and unfolded, as though calling the errant home.

Claudia took me in her arms, and we danced a few slow dances, gently. She soothed, we swirled, shush-shushed our feet and bodies together in front of the fireplace, the only people in the library apart from the musicians. Music poured over us, healing bruised parts of my body and soul.

The musicians took a break. We left the library to wander in the garden, hand in hand. We meandered by a pair of giant tortoises with stout candles stuck to their backs—light traveling at the speed of turtle.

A growling male lion had been staked out in the corner of the garden. He strained against four silken, stretched cords that were attached to spikes driven deep in the ground, inches from an unblemished, white lamb—also staked out. The lamb faced away from his predator, shivering. Lion and lamb lay with one another, but by another's choice.

The night could not have gotten any weirder. If a host of seraphim had flowed through the hedgerows singing a praise chorus, I'd have considered it business as usual.

Claudia said, "Please no parables about truth for our party-goers—like in Herod's palace. I need a calm night. Way too much excitement lately."

The words had barely left her mouth when Augustus tore himself away from a clutch of senators across the garden. He strode our way, stopping abruptly to pick up a scrap of trash. I asked Windy, *Is it because he's emperor that he detailed his estate, emperor because he attended to detail, or a detail-distracted emperor?* Windy was silent, leaving me to grow my own judgment.

Augustus approached us, lips pressed white and tight, forehead wrinkled, trash pinched between his fingers. "Come with me." He dropped the trash in a servant's hand on the way in the door. We strode past Chronos cursing Kairos.

After a few more turns, deeper into Augustus' home, we came on a panel of stained-glass windows, ornate as a fairy tale. Eerie, blue-black Vesuvius glowered white vog-drizzle in the background. Backlit candlelight flickered behind the volcano's dome, making an explosion seem imminent. A small boy sat cross-legged in the foreground, gazing at the volcano, eyes all affright. This interior window, an invitation to wonder, was fastened shut with a golden padlock.

Augustus took a sharp left turn down a circular flight of stone steps. We walked down the hollowed steps stained by ground weep, one floor down, and then another.

Claudia asked, "Kitchen down here that I don't know about, Grandpa?"

Augustus looked over his shoulder at her. He said, "I'm taking you to a place full of fire, covered containers, and uncertain outcomes. Decide for yourself if there's food enough for thought."

We followed him down the torch-lit hallway into this sub-basement. He abruptly stopped at a broad oak door, and Claudia almost ran into him.

The door was different than the others down there—iron strips reinforced it top to bottom and side to side. He squinted at his crowded keyring, found the right skeleton key, and slid the oiled bolt open, silent as you please.

He stood aside for us to pass. An eerie, flickering expanse of candles crowded the grotto's floor. Their light mixed with shadows in the corners and on the stone ceiling, slick with soot—a waving sea of burning light.

He said, "We're below my childhood bedroom. The biggest dream of my life happened up there." He pointed overhead.

Now I knew why he'd wanted me to come to Nola.

70

WINDY

Augustus surveyed the grotto. He spoke now with a weakened voice, without bluster. "In my dream, seer, a gaunt figure dressed in black took me from my mother's parlor. His teeth, needle spikes, dripped blood. Fire burned from each of his eye sockets. His fingers, like iron pincers, clamped my elbow. He led me into a vast room.

"That room, like this one, was crowded with candles—fat and thin, tall and short, simple, ornate. Some burned brightly, others guttered. Some burst into flame, and others winked out, even as we gazed at them. There was a fierce, ordered beauty it to all."

Claudia gawked at the ocean of fire before her. Sweat dribbled down her brow like she was in a furnace—or hot kitchen. She squeezed Jesus' hand so tight he thought it would pop off at his wrist.

She whispered in his ear, "I've never known this was here, all these years."

Augustus' hands trembled violently. He clasped them together and said, "The Figure's voice was like a whiplash with metal bits in it. When he spoke, I checked to see if my skin had been flayed.

He said, 'You think you're in charge of life and death? Ha! That's my job, not yours. Those who interfere are given a special punishment. Do you know what yours might be, boy?'

"I soiled my britches. My knees knocked together. I wanted my mother, the only safe person in my world."

Claudia whispered to Jesus, "Doesn't he get it? Mothers are as safe as tarantulas."

Augustus kept speaking, "The Figure said, 'Play by my rules, and you get to burn. Break them and be banished into outer darkness. Choose your path.'

Claudia said, "Any other options, Grandpa?"

The Emperor pressed on. "The Figure said, 'Guess which candle is yours, boy. Go ahead, pick.'

"I couldn't pick. Didn't know which was my candle. I closed my eyes and waited, waited. I'm still waiting."

Jesus pried his eyes off the Emperor's face and found himself gazing at an ivory candle. This tubby candle sat beside a closed urn in a chest-high niche.

Augustus, distracted, followed Jesus' eyes. "Some of my father's ashes are there. A bone or two I had to pick with him." His grim smile didn't lie, but it did tuck truth's edges way down deep.

Claudia said, "Grandpa, I thought your father's body was in Rome."

Augustus walked over to the urn, removed the lid, and tucked the vase under his left elbow. He tipped it toward his trembling right hand, poured out a little ash and bits of bone.

"Yes, Claudia, your great-grandfather *is* in Rome—except these few handfuls. Before he was entombed, I went to the crematoria, looked at the post-burn slab. My father's life had burned down to almost nothing. I scooped a cupful of ash, dumped that into this urn. I had him where I wanted him."

Claudia groaned, perhaps with the weight of what had been left unsaid. She tightened her arm's grip around Jesus' waist.

Augustus turned to Son again, "Enough of *him*. Seer, speak to me of *my* dream!" As if he could command a secret cache of clairvoyance from Jesus. Son linked arms with Augustus on his left, Claudia on his right. Father and I held him. The Eternal led the Son of Man who led Emperor and princess.

Together we watched a blazing candle abruptly gutter into darkness. Father spoke, and my wind gentled from Jesus' mouth. "Emperor, there's always enough dark not to believe."

After some moments of silence, Son turned sideways, under my impelling. Grandfather and granddaughter swiveled on our hinge. There in front of us was a humble flame flickering bright from a wickless puddle.

"And, Sire, there is always enough light if you wish to believe."

Augustus drew closer and searched Jesus' eyes, a few inches away. "Help. Me. Believe." Each spoken word rested alone, like the tone a velvet-covered hammer makes when it hits a copper bar dangling from a wire.

Jesus said, "Logic sifts ash, gains terror."

Augustus murmured, "My father had no interest in mystery."

I kept breathing my words from Jesus' mouth. "All truth is Father's truth—what is mysterious *and* what you can count. Counting candles on a grotto's floor doesn't count for much. Soul mysteries count very much indeed."

Claudia unlinked arms with Son and moved into a shadow on the other side of her grandfather. Jesus looked at her half-lit face. "Faith weighs the evidence, counts the cost, and jumps into storms."

Son swiveled his face to Augustus. "Better to drown in a deep sea than suffocate with your nose in a cup of ash."

Augustus replied, "Speak plainly, seer."

Son picked up a lavender candle, stout, blazing, serene. Held it between the emperor and himself. Looked in Augustus' eyes over the flame.

"Six centuries ago an emperor not unlike you, Nebuchadnezzar of the Babylonians, stood in one of the world's great wonders, his hanging gardens, and admired all *he* had done.

"My Father struck him mad for seven seasons of time.[41] This emperor crawled through the forests and ate grass. His fingernails twisted into talons. His uncut, newly whitened hair tangled in knots around his waist. And for what purpose?"

Augustus shook his head.

"Humility, a deep sea indeed, schooled and saved *that* emperor."

Augustus asked, "So what of Nebuchadnezzar's pain should become mine?"

"Right-sizing yourself, Sire. You're a minor magistrate given one inch of ground to rule for one second of time."

Augustus made a roulade of his eyes, shouting silently at Son, in layers.

"Father put you here for your one second of time to love others, not control them, Emperor."

Augustus replied, "I *can* control many things. It's my job. I say, for example, 'Starve Julia,' and my daughter starves."

Jesus answered, "One of our Jewish kings, David, said to God, 'Keep me from stupid sins, from thinking I can take over your work.'[42] *Father's work is life and death, not yours. He is the Figure in your dream. Father prods you down the path of surrender,* now."

"Seer," Augustus said, "Surrender to what?"

"Not what, Whom. Father. He's in control of you and your destiny."

Augustus' eyes flared, defiant. "*No!* I'm in control of ending my time, not him. For instance, if a man were on fire, would you fault him if he was handed a sword and fell on it?"

Jesus said, "Only if my Father handed him the sword, Sire. God has been known to walk in the fire with his people.[43.] On the other hand, if you reject Love, the prophet promises that you will burn.[44] Emperor, I am God's Love. Accept me."

Augustus' knees trembled. He jerked downward.

Claudia held him up. "Don't hurt yourself, grandpa."

Jesus shot her a sharp glance, *let him fall. He'll not be hurt by this fall.*

Augustus replied, "I played my part well, this role of emperor that was given to me. I came to Rome when it was clay. I leave it in marble. And I've always thought it best to leave before the party's over—leave while they're still applauding."

The door slid smoothly open on slippery hinges. Augusta stood in the entry, clapping. She said, "How touching, Tavius. Your favorite line. Come back to my party now, dear. It's almost over. Everyone wants to applaud your reign."

She held a plate of her specialty figs, taken from the orchards that surrounded the villa. Jesus had noted that all of her fruit trees were bordered by white oleander and nightshade hedges. He imagined them out there now, nightshade and fig flirting in the vog, one shiny, wet leaf sliding into the other, pushing into their hedge beds like lovers. *What fruit would come of this commerce between poison and produce?*

On this night, only Augusta knew what she had taken from her kitchen. The colors of her hair, piled on top of her head, caught candles' shimmering and reflected shades of gold folding into silver. She maneuvered over to her husband. Her diamond necklace clinked, light bouncing off the sharp facets. She lanced a kiss on his cheek, a loudish peck, and rebounded into her own splendor.

Velvet tones hid something harsher, "Augustus, you wander in this gloomy basement with your weird collection of candles that will all go out, sooner or later. I can always find you here or in the labyrinth when you go missing."

Augustus gazed at her through glazed eyes, mute.

"Your guests look for you and your seer as well, wanting to siphon off some of his small value. But before you go, my dear, refresh."

She held out the plate of figs. Sampling her wares didn't appear to be optional.

71

LEAH

We'd finished lunch. I said, "Mary, how do you ever manage here in Rome?"

John, lying on a sofa, jumped in, "She prays all the time, Leah, that's how. Small woman; big prayers. She's become her prayers."

Mary had changed. Life had boiled her down to a strong, nourishing broth. Now she didn't seem to harbor as much worry. My baby drooled happily on her hand, stuck his fingers in her mouth. She cooed back at him.

Mary angled a comment past John and James to me, "You and Rabbus arrived right on time. So like God. Jesus isn't here now, but his Spirit is. And our prayers release the power he needs now."

James said, "All this talk about super-duper Jesus bores the poo out of me, Ma. I want to ditch school and take Sofia with me on that shady river walk. She could listen as I recite Torah."

Mary rolled her eyes, "Nice try. Back to school, but after we pray."

I said, "Sofia is a lovely girl. After school could the two of you show me that river walk?"

Mother Mary said, "Sure, go with Leah after school, James. She'll keep a sharp eye on you two lovebirds."

I said, "I've felt the power of prayer. Especially when Tiberius died."

Mary raised her eyebrows.

I bore down on my memory of that time. "Life gushed through me, not from me. Spirit power wouldn't have been released without your prayers."

John piped up. "Hey, don't leave me out. Jesus and I *both* prayed for you. And speaking of him, I think we should all join him in Nola. Face it. He's the central piece of our story."

Mary's face grew sober, "Yes, that's true, but it's also true that *our* stories count. History is only a collection of people's stories; that's all." She paused, thought a moment. "Besides, Father and Windy were in Nola long before Jesus arrived, and they'll be there long after he leaves. Wait. As it is, you're not strong enough to carry the weight of God's destiny for you, John. That happens only with patient prayer."

James eyed his mother, taking all this in.

John asked, "Can we pray on the roof? Not enough air here."

We all trooped up to the roof garden, and each of us prayed in our own way. John stalked to the edge of Mary's garden on legs tough and thick as ironwood, resolve strong enough to kick down the walls of tradition. Kind, green eyes softened his anger. He got on his knees and pulled weeds with his left hand while jabbing his right index finger heavenward like he was firing arrows. I imagined each jab rapping on heaven's gates.

James prayed rapid-fire, standing and bending up and down from the waist in a fast, spirited cadence. I sat in a chair and nursed Gabe, feeding prayers to God, and being fed in turn.

At first, Mary leaned on the balcony's edge, one foot tucked behind her, looking like a forward-leaning flamingo in her light pink singlet and white hajib. Then she began to pace, walking with Father like Enoch, angling toward heaven, maybe with a grave by-pass chit in her pocket, for all I knew.[45]

I took Gabe to his father, who stood in a corner, eyeing the street. A country shepherd with his ragged flock passed by six stories beneath us, on the way to market, sheep baa-ing loudly.

After ten minutes or so, we gathered in a circle. She finished by praying aloud, "Thank you, Father. Strengthen my sons, please. James, in his journey of shuckling scriptures from head to feet—and don't pass by his heart, please, Father. John, son of my heart, grow pity and patience in his piety. And for your *Taleh Elohim*, your Lamb, our Son, night-walk him as he struggles with lions in dark and misty places. Show up and show off your glory, my heavenly Husband."

72

JESUS

Augusta gave off a tight smile and passed the plate. We took her offering. Augustus closed his eyes, lifted his well-sauced fig with a palsied hand, and squashed the fig on his chin. Took aim again, scored. He smacked his lips and groaned with pleasure.

Claudia certainly looked uncertain. She squeezed her eyes shut and bolted her fig down, like a woman with no taste buds running through a house on fire.

I ate mine in bits, slowly. Immediately, I understood why this was Augustus' favorite food. The ripe fig, dipped in Augusta's secret sauce, dripped with the taste of pomegranate, raspberry, crushed basil, peppermint—and who knew what else? The flavors kept changing from the tip of my tongue to the sides and back.

I asked the Empress if she wanted the one remaining fig. Her tongue, sharp as a pruning shear, clipped off her retort, "No, thank you."

I ate the last one. "Exquisite, Madam Empress."

Augusta tossed off my gratitude. "I don't give a fig for anything but the Fates."[46]

She looked down at Tavius. "And some of their threaded spools are shorter than others. Yes, my darling?"

Augustus appeared to have gone deaf to her meaning. He had knelt in front of his father's niche and now returned the ashes to their home. He stared at a guttering candle, fig juice dripping off his chin.

Augusta led her husband up the stairs by the hand, like a lamb to the altar. Claudia and I followed, leaving this Room of Candles behind. We two couples climbed up and up into outer life, arriving apart-together in the garden. The orchestra had relocated among the carefully tended ornamentals, backed up to the labyrinth's seven-foot-tall hedges. The strings, accented by woodwinds, played sweet tunes that mingled with vog-creep.

The evening's sky above was so heavy with stars that the net of night overflowed. Glittering ingots of white, blue, and yellow-red filled the moonless sky. Tortoise-backed candles and staked out torches lit the garden. Augusta wandered away to work the crowd.

Windy intoned, *the Empress harbors much unresolved grief—all those past losses! She refuses not only my influence, but necessary suffering. Now she's become insufferable. But her conspiracy with silence has not kept her from suffering, only changed its shape. She flows toward power as naturally as a river flows to the sea.*

Augusta had closed her ears to Windy's words or influence long ago. Now she mingled with all the tinkling, jeweled chinwags that clinked as they walked and talked.

Augustus had cordoned off the two-acre maze of close-trimmed hedgerows with "No Admission" signs and red tape. Guards circulated, eyes watchful for false moves, hidden daggers.

Augustus had led us to the maze's entry. We stood there in the shadows, red tape blowing in the breeze behind us, just beyond where the hungry lion strained toward the lamb, stretching his cords. Claudia looked at him, shivered, and tucked herself further between Augustus and me.

Augustus turned his head to me and muttered, "You like my little touch, like what I read in your prophets, during my long nights when I can't sleep, the passage about lion lying with lamb? I ordered that pair in, especially for you, Jew—and maybe for me."

Windy's finger strummed a shiver into my spine. I looked left at Augustus. His face had grown grimmer, longer than I thought was possible in one human.

Claudia said, "Grandpa, you're checked out. Where's the man I remember, the life of the party? Your admirers probably wonder, *where's the funeral?*"

Augustus said, "Soon it will be mine, and what a funeral it will be. It's the way of the world, darling—the strong man comes, rousting the doddering old fool off his throne."

I said, "I see a more fitting image for you, Emperor—your life rising through a blade of grass like a drop of water, quivering, and bursting into eternal morning."

Augustus stood on the edge of the crowd, surveyed his old friends, guards, and the musicians. "Bah! Eternity isn't a scale I can fathom. My life is a chip of wood, lost in the river's rapids at flood time."

He motioned to the crowd around us. "It takes a long time to make old friends. But soon they will scatter, as do leaves in autumn, leaving only a faint memory trace behind. Even now, while I wasn't looking, they've turned into black and white cardboard cutouts."

The Death Demon reflected from his face. Satan had joined the garden party, playing hide 'n seek in the maze behind me, quirking malicious grins through the hedgerow when I turned to look.

Claudia held onto my arm, tight. "You suddenly feel spooky, like me?"

I squeezed a 'yes' into her arm. "You winnow your inner circle, Sire—perimeter players first, then others, till you remain alone in the dark, with God and Satan both calling, 'Choose me.'"

Augustus turned us toward the mouth of the labyrinth. I reached around Claudia and lightly touched his arm. "And the cardboard-cutout stuff? In years to come my followers will do that to me. Plaster me on their church walls, complete with halo, strip me of humanity, and in so doing, distance themselves from the Holy."

Windy whispered, *Your words were wasted, Son. Be quiet. Listen to the sound of a man right-sizing himself.*

The sound of the orchestra dimmed. We moved past the "No Admission" signs into the labyrinth's mystery. Suddenly the Emperor stopped, dropped Claudia's hand, and turned to face me. "Seer, if you're divine, find the center of my maze without making a wrong move. Then I'll believe you can lead me into being more than a compost pile, crawling with worms."

Claudia snatched a pitched torch from a stake. The ground stake had been designed as an upward bound, writhing snake. She lifted up the snake and Augustus' eyes followed it.[47]

She said, "You've told me yourself, grandpa, that no one's ever found the center of your maze without help. Even you, the designer, need a map to make it to the middle. Aren't you being unreasonable, particularly since it's dark?"

"No more unreasonable than this one who claims to be the only guide to eternal life. If he's indeed a God-man, this is child's play. Surely his Father can step our steps to maze center—and then from there to…."

I held her arm tighter. We took a step forward.

73

WINDY

I hovered over, within, before and behind Son. I took him by the hand and guided him along his path.[48] The plain thing was the main thing. The main thing, the plain thing. He kept his body in step with me.

Claudia, in the middle, stayed half-step behind him, and Augustus stayed in step with her. Claudia's outside torch dimmed. Son's inside light brightened.

She said, "Grandpa, I want you to live. I *need* you to live. Father and brother died. Poisonous women surround me. You remain. Please, Grandpa, *want* to live." Her right hand was slick with sweat in the silvery vog. She'd dropped the cloak of cleverness, the easy lie. She'd upgraded from showing skin to showing spirit, and Son admired her naked grit— this one who would gladly have him as husband.

Son continued dark-walking, step by step, his faith extending no further than the next breath I gave him. Satan's presence, palpable, swirled behind and around them.

Augustus leaned on Claudia's arm, bent over, a paper kite in a gale. He said, after three more turns, a right, and two lefts, "I've been caught in the draught. Nightshades surround me. I trust only you two with my life." Claudia's torch guttered, on the brink of oblivion.

Son said, "Sire, though younger than you, I am your older brother. I represent Father on earth. I'm his exact image in human flesh. He is carefully guiding you home through me. Bow your knee to Him and live eternally."

Satan pirouetted in the nightshades. His face looked like he'd frozen a belly laugh in place. He acted like they were his dance partners, and he was *so* amused at the trick he'd played on them. His voice schmoozed, like oil off a press, *very slick, Junior, getting that old windbag to fall down and worship you. Ain't nutin' funnier than real life, huh, bubba?*

Son moved through his mist and wiped off a felt layer of grime. He asked Claudia, "Did you hear his voice?"

She said, "Who's voice? All I felt were prickles and like I wanted to throw up."

Son caught up with Augustus' voice. He said, "Could you repeat whatever you just said? I'm sorry. I missed it."

The Emperor said, "You said for me to bow my knee. Do you know how humiliating it is to ask an immigrant teenager, and my granddaughter, to get these shaking sticks home after dark?"

"Point taken, Sire. You're almost there. Your succession, secure."

Augustus waivered. "Get to the point, seer. I know you have something else to say to me."

"Succession is not legacy, Sire. Legacy is not what you leave *to people*, but what you leave *in people*—fear or courage, love or law, kindness or cruelty. You've yet to decide your legacy."

They rounded a corner. Satan slid through the silvered vog, backlit with a dark light he carried inside himself. *Stench of sulfur fingered through the air.* Blood dripped off his lips.

Son said, *Lucifer, leave. His soul's course is not for you to decide.*

Satan threw out a net of viscous, smothering dark before he jumped back of a hedge. The trio's feet moved through mulch that felt syrupy, like ankle-deep treacle.

Claudia whimpered. Augustus vomited. Son held his companions tight, strode left, straight, then right. "Sire, we all leave our essence behind in our legacy. If fear fills you, you can't leave love behind. That's like trying to come back from somewhere you've never been. Your legacy hangs in this sticky darkness."

Claudia's torch fizzled. Darkness ruled. Blackness snuck into any open hole. They bumped up to the next hedge, stopped. Son waited for my next command, one he couldn't hear. I conspired with his muscles and bones, directing his choices.

He turned right, pressed into this darkness, thick as the ninth Egyptian plague.[49] As they came around the last bend, Augustus' false face finally fell, melted wax in a furnace. Heavy eyebrows drooped toward his nose. He wept, allowing himself to heal what he could now finally feel—his father's failed blessing, a hollowed marriage never hallowed, failures in love to himself and others—it all flowed out in tiny trickles of right-sized grief.

Three chairs had been set in a semi-circle between two low-lit torches. A marble table rested in front of the chairs. Two jeweled platters sat on this table. One fig rested on each platter, each drenched in a different sauce—the one on the left looked and smelled familiar. The fig on the right looked and smelled different. Its fumes almost knocked Son out.

Satan, dressed in black as a maître 'de, stood with a white linen napkin on his forearm. He bowed, as if ready to decant a fine bottle of wine. He'd set life and death before the Emperor.

They sat, Augustus, in the center; Claudia, to his left. Son sat at his right hand. Augustus didn't hesitate. Before he had barely reached the seat beneath him, before he could change his mind, he slammed the right fig, unerringly, in his mouth. Chomped down hard, swallowed. The poisoned fig went straight down.

Horror flashed across Claudia's face. "Grandpa, what have you done to you, to me?"

Augustus smiled sadly. "It is as planned," he said softly. "All was arranged—my time, done."

He turned to Son, took his hand, rested his forefinger in Son's palm where Postie had driven his dagger, and felt the scar.[50] "Jesus, you led me straight to the heart of my creation, perfectly. I now believe. Tell Tiberius, in Claudia's presence, to pardon Julia. Ordered choice, with a hint of kindness—my legacy."

Claudia sobbed, threw her arms around him, and clung on. Augustus' voice weakened into a whisper, each breath a bit shallower than the one before.

"Tiberius was the only one who didn't want my job. Now he's got it. Beware the Dowager Mother. Tiberius and I have long been under her soured spell."

A convulsion of pain throttled him. He recovered, momentarily, spoke in a whisper loud enough for Claudia and Son to hear. "I will greet your Father face-to-face, Jesus. He is Emperor of this frail and foolish old man, who only now, only now, begins to love. Good-bye, granddaughter. You've always been my favorite, so beautiful. Stay close, stay close, to Jesus."

Augustus doubled over when these words had been spoken and fell on his knees at Son's feet. Claudia too kneeled beside him, holding tight. When he stopped breathing, his head rested on Jesus' lap.

Son saw Augustus' spirit spritely rise. The Emperor held a blazing, blue candle in one hand and his crown in the other. He'd extended both as offerings to whomever he might first meet. In no time at all, he found heaven's back door. We always keep this door, a narrow needle's eye, open. It always will be kept open for wanderers who've lost their way.[51]

This bent and lonely man lowered himself to crawl on his hands and knees through this back door, the one with a brushstroke of Son's blood always fresh on doorposts and lintel.

Father waited inside the door. He rose and stretched his arms out to this suicidal son. Augustus fell on his knees to worship. Father held him while he cried, wiped away his tears. Son's mouth dropped open in gratitude to his loving Father.

The new Dowager Mother, Augusta, stepped out of the dark, moved through Satan's shadow, just beyond where the torchlight ended. She came forward, iced Son down with her kiss, turned the night frigid, and slipped the untainted fig in her mouth. She turned to the blackness behind her. "Guards, behold the man! Arrest my husband's assassin and his conspirator."

Rough hands chained both Claudia and Son hand and foot, dragged them straight through the slashed hedge rows furthest from the housing compound. Two oxcarts awaited, each facing different roads. Son was loaded onto one cart. Claudia was dragged to the other. Augusta stood by, arms crossed over her chest, overseeing their departure.

Claudia did not go quietly. She grabbed the bars of her oxcart prison and used them as a bully pulpit. She pointed her finger at the stiff matriarch, ten paces away. "Grandma, *you* killed grandpa, not us. You did it for Tiberius—no, for *you*. Will you also kill us and claim we *too* committed suicide?"

Augusta, inscrutable, held her arm up and pointed. A guard trussed Claudia, hand and foot, within the covered cart. The oxcart driver clucked a command and clipped the ox with the tip of his whip. Her cart moved east, toward the Apennine mountain range.

Claudia cried aloud, "Jesus, Jesus, pray for me."

Son called back, "Claudia, I love you. Take me with you, in your heart."

Augusta turned and entered the maze again, passing straight through Satan, even as he passed through her, lingering long enough to leave his essence.

A whip snapped. His cart lurched north toward Rome, the same way he had come, into the not-knowing of night, and the start of a whole new day.

End of Book Two

DISCUSSION QUESTIONS

1. Jesus is between the ages of 18-23 in *Parable*. He experiences what all folks go through in this period of life—leaving home for a grand adventure in the big world, the choice to partner up or stay single, how to finish off his formal education and choose an occupation.

2. The thin border between the visible and invisible is a continuing theme. Visions and dreams are presented as a major gateway to God. For example, Windy comments, "Dreams became physical, in the normal way of life, visible coming out of the invisible." Discuss a time in your life where a dream, vision, or daydream provided a significant turning point for you.

3. Jesus chose in-house Instructors, Windy and Father, as well as human mentors. He hitch-hiked on Claudia's love of theatre to learn more about parables as well. Psyche's journey into maturity was a four-act parable. Bathenia's story and snippets of life back in Palestine, all wove practical layers of truth into and through the parable of *Psyche*. Talk about one or two of the movies or plays you've loved the best, and what they taught you about life, how they shaped the person you are now. And what part of Psyche's journey most spoke to you at age and stage of life where you are now?

4. Satan and God, angels and demons, heaven and hell—all of them were a very real part of Jesus' way of looking at the world. How do you see the role of "spirits" and spiritual conflict in your day to day world?

5. Crispus is a parable within himself. Light and dark vie, in mortal combat. He quotes scripture, views himself as a "man of sorrows," a freedom fighter, and drop-kicks self-justifications into Thursday of next week. Ferret down a bit. Have a conversation between the darkest and lightest parts of you. Use your smart phone's voice memo, or jot the conversation down in the notes section of any device. You might

even want to draw or sculpt these parts of you. Use any method to get them both up where you can see, hear, or feel their presence inside you.

6. Slow is also a parable for the divided self. She's an object lesson parable in how to make friends with disparate parts of the self. Think of any Jekyll and Hyde part-selves within you that need to learn how to get along better. Give them names. Get out a journal. Have them write letters to each other, back and forth. Perhaps begin with hate mail and then see where that takes you.

7. The princess in the subterranean kitchen and Claudia, below ground at her grandfather's villa in Nola, are parallel parables. What's cooking in your pot, what wood are you chopping, what kettles are chattering in your basement?

Preview of Book Three

Jesus' Silent Years, Journey

1

MARY

Jesus finished last. He brought up the end of Caesar Augustus' funeral parade. Thousands of Imperial troops had already passed. Senators, statesmen, royalty of all kinds had followed the golden casket and golden carriages. The parade had gone for miles on this hot August day.

All the while I stood beneath our sixth-floor apartment on the corner, waiting for Jesus. Waiting was so hard in this heat, but the corner fountain, fed by an aqueduct, helped. It splashed happily in the bowl beneath and James filled our drinking jugs time and again. Justice, Jude, and Miriam played with other children, but Deborah mostly wanted to be held.

And also, there was cousin Elizabeth's son, John. I'd more or less adopted this earnest, eccentric, lovable nephew since Elizabeth and her husband, Zechariah, had died. He paced in circles, sweat popping out on his forehead. "Aunt Mary, I have to find Jesus! I have to prepare his path. *That's my* job. How can I do that at a standstill?"

"Why waste precious, preparation time with movement, John? There's more going on between heaven and earth than either of us will ever know. Stand still, like warriors have done through all Israel's history, waiting for God to work on their behalf. Surround him with prayer, like a fortress wall."

He wasn't good at this whole "still-thing." Instead, he hmphed, sighed, took Deborah from my arms and raced around the fountain, dunking her time and again, to her delight. He would scream, "I baptize you, child, in your big brother's name!" She'd flop around, not having a clue what he meant, other than he loved her.

Now, finally, in the heat of the afternoon, here Jesus came. He clanked along barefoot, clad only in a loin cloth and chains. He was the rag-tag tail end of all that pomp and circumstance. Half-trot, right leg trailing, behind the last beast of burden. Covered in the dust of all who had gone before him.

I told John, "Please. Don't go to him now. Let me. You keep the other children here."

He must have seen my desperation. Yes, now was the time for action, but not his action. I knew, certain as the Son, certain as the air in my lungs, this was for me to do.

I raced across the street, pushed past the guards. "Have mercy. I'm his mother. I beg you, let me give him water."

One guard looked at Jesus, saw he was dragging. On his last leg. Took pity and let me pass. I knelt in front of Son and lifted a two-liter jug of cool water. He stood before me, hands on knees, panting. Under the layers of grime, a long scar ran down both his right arm and right leg—long, angry welts. Thin, black thread held his skin together.

So many questions, so many hugs. But now, none. The only thing the guard allowed was a drink from my gourd. Jesus tipped the jug back and drained it. After he drank, he fell to his knees briefly, head bowed. When he looked up, tears had streaked their way through the mud on his face.

He said, "Mother, Father's will has fallen upon me. It is his pleasure for me to be brought low. It will also be his pleasure to raise me up, in due time."

The guard prodded him with the sharp end of his spear, "No more talk. Move!"

Jesus rose, half-trotted and was half-pulled by the pack mule in front of him. I longed to run after him, rescue him from such pain.

A stronger voice, one I knew well, the voice of my Heavenly Husband, rose in my heart. *Don't rescue him from his destiny. He's in my care. Your place is apart, in a quiet space. Cover your head. Be with me. Pray for him.*

Jesus didn't look back.

I didn't know then what I know now. That very night, after John had gone for a run in the hills, Rome's troops came for us in this fancy apartment Augustus had provided. They didn't knock. Instead, they knocked down the door, trashed the furniture, shredded the children's toys, and threw it all out through the windows to the ground below. We were herded down the steps, all six floors, to the street where a wagon waited. Between the door and the wagon, we crunched glass—broken windows, wine glasses, crystal ware, shattered windows. I remember it now with tears still in my eyes, this night of broken glass. We rattled down to the port on side roads, twenty miles or so, and were on the next ship back to Israel.

I wouldn't see Jesus again for almost a decade.

2

AUGUSTA

I sat in my gold-plated carriage at the very front of Tavius' funeral parade. Rome's next two emperors, blood of my blood, sat beside me. The Fates had smiled on me. Tiberius and Caligula, dear boys, both loved privilege and hated responsibility—a perfect marriage of my competence and their potential.

I patted Tibbie's hand and reminisced. My, my. Fifty-two years of marriage to Augustus. We had started out with a bang. Love at first sight. He divorced his wife. I divorced my husband. We hopped into bed. Perhaps not in that order.

When did it start to fizzle? I suspect it was when Augustus left me more and more alone. Out there roaming the empire, glory-mongering, and bedding his consorts. My spies had dossiers on all of those trollops, one in every port across the empire. That wouldn't have been so bad. All those women were out there. He always came home.

But here's the thing. When he came home, he didn't ask about me. Forgot me, he did. All he wanted were the financials, complicity in his conspiracy theories, and endless adoration. And yes, a blind eye to his affairs.

One more item. He loved his figs. The ones I had brought up from his orchards in Nola. So, as usual, I fell into line. I cooked up a consummate marriage of blind eye, conspiracy, and figs. Let it stew for years. Over time I added a few special ingredients—hemlock, adder venom, bitters, and a bit of nightshade extract.

One glorious night, we'd invited a whole batch of those generals and senators, the *current* conspiracy cabal, to a gala dinner. After dinner, they all trolloped into the drawing room. Smoked cigars, drank brandy, oh'd and ah'd at Tavius' stories of conquest. Noses all becoming quite brown.

I waltzed in, flirty as you please, and served dessert on a platinum platter. Tavius went on about my special fig sauce with its secret recipe. One general in particular, a hobbied, gourmet chef, was curious. I fed him my most salacious smile. Told him the exact amounts of vanilla, maple syrup, and lemon bitters. Mentioned how important it was to marinate in a cool cellar. I might have forgotten a few ingredients. But I did stress how important it was to let everything simmer for some time. And, of course, froth well before serving.

He and our other guests gobbled down those delicious figs. Everyone frothed well, right before we carried them out, feet first, to the crematory. A very efficient evening.

That was years ago, a favorite memory. Long before Tavius' shaking sticks and fuzzy recall took him over some edge. At the end, on his birthday ten days ago, he pled, "Help me. Help me cross over. I'm tired. I've seen it all, done it all, and want no more. I want to go home. Home to Nola, have a fig or two, and be done with it."

I obliged. There was a bit of drama in his maze at the end, but once he'd flopped over, I felt *so* relieved. And the delight of it all? I rid myself of that bastard granddaughter *and* the Jew. Tavius liked both of them entirely too much. Thus, the rope-a-dope, wrapped around lots of plausible deniability.

Truth was, I never could stand Tavius' daughter, Livena—the bastard daughter of an early dip in some Greek honeypot. Livena, dear girl, went bonkers after her son, Claud, died. Devolved into a true nutcase. But Claud's twin sister, Claudia, remained a threat.

Tavius had come home from roaming abroad a time too many asking for Claudia before he asked for me. I'd be in the executive suite, poring over my ledgers, plotting the next disinformation campaign, and they'd be tittering in the library. She'd sit on his lap, play with his beard, whisper local gossip in his ear. Conniving, wee bitch.

I confronted him. He'd argued back, "Everything always comes back to you!"

I replied, "Quite. And I have the very great advantage of having *me* on my side."

After I helped Tavius trot off to paradise, my guards trussed the Jew and the bastard granddaughter like hogs to market. Jew in the Dungeon,

Claudia in exile. Which island was it? Oh yes, Trimerus, the one where I'd smacked that other hot-pants granddaughter.

Right, here's the thing. I wanted her to realize the error of her ways. Tangle her nighties into a proper worry-wad. Not know which day would be her last. A delicious recipe for revenge, best served cold after a lovely, long simmer.

I roused myself from these pleasant memories. Caligula stroked Tiberius's arm, imbibed from his flask, and chattered on inanely. Boy this, girl that—a real omnivore. Unfortunately, he'd never learned to read properly. Got his letters all tangled up and ended up twittering endlessly about intrigues and bodies between the sheets.

Just then, Cal looked over his shoulder and waved at his sisters. Agrippina, Drusilla, and Livilla all sat straight and pretty in their carriage. Quite proper.

Cal said, "They're good entertainment, Uncle. When I have an urge, in they lather. Agrippina's *so* frisky, compared to Dru and Liv. Only one problem with her—she's less than adoring. Just yesterday she went on, 'Cal, Uncle Tibbie will dump you soon. He's so erudite, compared to you.'

"I disagreed and told her I was *totally* erudite. She said, 'you don't even know what that means.' I replied that if I *did* know, I'd certainly be that too."

Tibbie tipped his head, amused. "She reply?"

"She agreed that was hard to out-argue and changed subjects. 'Cal, your wig just slipped over your ear. You look like an unmade bed.' An unmade bed she's willing to crawl into, mind you. But tell me, how does one get a yapping mouth like hers to shut up?"

We approached Palatine Hill. A clutch of senators awaited us. I prodded my progeny. "Sit up and stop your chatter, boys. Rome is watching. Mind your manners and hide that flask. Mustn't let them see you both drunk. And when we pass by those senators, remember the magic phrase, '*Memento mori.*' It's the law for emperors at state funerals. And, a good reminder—life is so brief."

I lifted my veil and glared at Tibbie. *Why are you so obtuse? Have you lost all discretion? Act your age. After all, you are in your fifties, and he's a pimply-faced teen.*

Tibbie stared back at me. *That child always could outstare a corpse.* He signaled the driver and our carriage creaked to a halt just short of where those cloying senators simpered. Son and grandson quit the carriage, surrounded by guards.

Tiberius' next words wounded me. "Mother. Read up on sows, the ones who eat their young. Might be instructive."

He nodded at the senators. "I no longer have to abide you or your soporific echo chambers. Further, I deserve relaxation at the bath house with a certain young thing." His voice positively hissed, "I do find it so *very* challenging to steam you off me, Mother! Your presence lingers, like a cloud of wee beasties over tainted meat, gone off long ago."

He certainly did know how to hurt his loving mother. Such poisonous talk, and after all my years of training him in political culinaries. I'd return to my cookbooks. Revise my recipes.

ENDNOTES

[1]Genesis 3:15, *And I will put enmity between you and the woman, and between your offspring and hers; he will crush your head, and you will strike his heel—NIV*

[2] These letters spell "word" in Hebrew.

[3] Hebrews 11:3, *By faith, we see the world called into existence by God's word, what we see created by what we don't see—MSG*

[4] Psalm 91:5: *Fear nothing—not wild wolves in the night, not flying arrows in the day—MSG*

[5] Psalm 24:7: *Lift up your heads, O you gates! And be lifted up, you everlasting doors! And the King of glory shall come in —NKJV*

[6] Jude 1:24: *Now unto him that is able to keep you from falling, and to present you faultless before the presence of his glory with exceeding joy, to him be glory—KJV*

[7] *Last night as I was sleeping, I dreamt—marvelous error!—that a spring was breaking out in my heart. I said: Along which secret aqueduct, oh water, are you coming to me, water of a new life that I have never drunk?* https://allpoetry.com/Last-Night-As-I-was-sleeping. Antonio Machado.

[8] Stone sellers in the Roman Empire waxed over their flaws and polished the stone. Thus, the expression, *caveat emptor* (let the buyer beware). Further, the word "sincere" means "without wax."

[9] Esther 4:16, *Go, gather together all the Jews that are present in Shushan, and fast ye for me, and neither eat nor drink three days, night or day: I also and my maidens will fast likewise; and so will I go in unto the king, which is not according to the law: and if I perish, I perish.—KJV*

[10] Isaiah 53:3, *He is despised and rejected of men; a man of sorrows, and acquainted with grief: and we hid as it were our faces from him; he was despised, and we esteemed him not—KJV*

[11] Matthew 13:34: *All these things Jesus spoke to the multitude in parables; and without a parable He did not speak to them—NKJV*

[12] 1 Samuel 25:18–25 details the story of Abigail soothing David's homicidal rage.

[13] Job 12:7-15, *Put your ear to the earth—learn the basics. Listen—the fish in the ocean will tell you their stories. Isn't it clear that they all know and agree that God is sovereign, that he holds all things in his hand—Every living soul, yes, every breathing creature? —MSG*

[14] Deuteronomy 29:29: *The secret things belong to the Lord our God, but the things revealed belong to us and to our children forever —NIV*

[15] Micah 6:8: *He has shown you, O man, what is good; and what does the Lord require of you but to do justly, to love mercy, and to walk humbly with your God? —NKJV*

[16] Titus 1:4-5, *Dear Titus, legitimate son in the faith… I left you in charge in Crete so you could complete what I left half-done—MSG*

[17] Matthew 18:2-5, *Jesus called over a child, whom he stood in the middle of the room, and said, "I'm telling you, once and for all, that unless you return to square one and start over like children, you're not even going to get a look at the kingdom, let alone get in. Whoever becomes simple and elemental again, like this child, will rank high in God's kingdom—MSG*

[18] Acts 16:14, *One woman, Lydia, was from Thyatira and a dealer in expensive textiles, known to be a God-fearing woman.*

[19] Cassius Dio, *Roman History* LVII.16

[20] Psalm 34:6, *Those who look to him are radiant; their faces are never covered with shame."—NIV*

[21] In Roman armies of this era, a *decanus* led a *contubia* of ten legionnaires; a *turma* was a unit of up to thirty cavalry and their horsemen; a century was a unit of 100 legionnaires.

[22] John 10:16, *And other sheep I have which are not of this fold; them also I must bring, and they will hear My voice; and there will be one flock and one shepherd—NKJV*

[23] Matthew 6:6, *"Here's what I want you to do: Find a quiet, secluded place so you won't be tempted to role-play before God. Just be there as simply and honestly as you can manage. The focus will shift from you to God, and you will begin to sense his grace—MSG*

[24] Hebrews 5:8, *Though he were a Son, yet learned he obedience by the things which he suffered—KJV*

[25] 2 Thessalonians 3:5, *May the Lord direct your hearts into God's love and the perseverance which the Messiah gives.* —*CJB*

[26] Psalm 121:1, *"I will lift up mine eyes unto the hills, from whence cometh my help? —KJV*

[27] This echoes Julius Caesar, Augustus' adopted father. His final words to Brutus, a trusted friend who betrayed him, "Et tu, Brut?"

[28] I Sam 17:38-39, *Then Saul dressed David in his own military clothes. He put a coat of armor on him. He put a bronze helmet on his head.* [39] *David put on Saul's sword over his clothes. He walked around for a while in all that armor because he wasn't used to it. I can't go out there in all this armor," he said to Saul. "I'm not used to it." So he took it off*—*NIRV*

[29] John 17:1-2, *Display the bright splendor of your Son, so the Son in turn may show your bright splendor.*

[30] Proverbs 27:4, *Wrath is cruel, and anger outrageous, but who is able to stand before envy? —KJV*

[31] Job 19:26–27: *"And after my skin has been destroyed, yet in my flesh I will see God; I myself will see him with my own eyes—I, and not another—NIV*

[32] Hosea 1:6, *Gomer conceived again and gave birth to a daughter. Then the Lord said to Hosea, "Call her Lo-Ruhamah, which means "not loved"—NIV*

[33] For this story, see I Samuel 14:1-15

[34] 1 Chronicles 10:13–14: *Saul died for his unfaithfulness … because he consulted a medium for guidance … [and] did not inquire of the Lord; therefore, He killed him, and turned the kingdom over to David the son of Jesse*—*NKJV*

[35] Psalm 139:7–8: *Is there any place I can go to avoid your Spirit? To be out of your sight? If I climb to the sky, you're there! If I go underground, you're there*—*MSG*

[36] Psalm 8: 3-4, *I look up at your macro-skies, dark and enormous, your handmade sky-jewelry, moon and stars mounted in their settings. Then I look at my micro-self and wonder, why do you bother with us? Why take a second look our way? —MSG*

[37] Kurzban, Robert (2010). *Why everyone (else) is a hypocrite: Evolution and the modular mind.* Princeton

[38] Jeremiah 35:17, *God-of-the-Angel-Armies, the God of Israel, says, 'I will bring calamity down on the heads of the people—MSG*

[39] Judges 4:21, *Then while he was fast asleep from exhaustion, Jael wife of Heber took a tent peg and hammer, tiptoed toward him, and drove the tent peg through his temple and all the way into the ground. He convulsed and died. —MSG*

[40] The Greeks had two words for time. Chronos referred to sequential or clock time. Kairos symbolizes deep time, inspired time, or an opportune time for action.

[41] Daniel 4:33: *Nebuchadnezzar was driven from human society. He ate grass like a cow, and he was drenched with the dew of heaven. He lived this way until his hair was as long as eagles' feathers and his nails were like birds' claws—NLT*

[42] Psalm 19:13: *Clean the slate, God, so we can start the day fresh! Keep me from stupid sins, from thinking I can take over your work—MSG*

[43] Daniel 3:24–25: *King Nebuchadnezzar jumped up in alarm and said, "Didn't we throw three men, bound hand and foot, into the fire? … But look! I see four men, walking around freely in the fire, completely unharmed—MSG*

[44] Malachi 4:1-3, *All arrogant people…will be burned up like stove wood, burned to a crisp, nothing left but scorched earth and ash, a black day—MSG*

[45] Genesis 5:24: *Enoch walked steadily with God. And then one day he was simply gone: God took him—MSG*

[46] The Roman goddesses of Fate were Nona, Decuma, and Morta. Respectively, they spun, assigned, and cut the thread of each human life.

[47] John 3:14: *And as Moses lifted up the serpent in the wilderness, even so must the Son of man be lifted up—KJV*

[48] John 16:13, *I still have many things to tell you, but you can't handle them now. But when the Friend comes, the Spirit of the Truth, he will take you by the hand and guide you into all the truth there is—MSG*

[49] Exodus 10:21: *God said to Moses: "Stretch your hand to the skies. Let darkness descend on the land of Egypt—a darkness so dark you can touch it."—MSG*

[50] A reference to the doubting disciple, Thomas, who needed to put his hands in Christ's wounds in order to believe. John 20:27

[51] Revelation 21:25: *Heaven's gates will never be shut. —MSG*